Human
Kind

A Collection of Sci-Fi Stories

Anton Eine

Human Kind

CONTENTS

Human Kind

The Cleansing

Translated by Cory Klingsporn

"Commander, we've received data from our intelligence probes."

"Put it on the main viewer and give your report, Analyst."

"It's a poorly developed, organic, technological civilization. Third level. Primitive weaponry, but in significant quantities. No orbital defenses. No immediate threats to us. Life is concentrated only on the third planet from the star. There are a few individuals orbiting the planet. I recommend a simple cleanup protocol."

"Recommendation accepted, Analyst. Begin sample collection and scanning. Cleaner, prepare weapons systems for a complete cleanup."

"Understood, Commander."

"Navigator, begin preparations for our next destination. We'll be done here quickly."

"Will do, Commander."

"Analyst, report when ready. The Cleaner will wipe out all traces of life in this system."

"Aye, Commander. However the analyzer is giving me some strange results. I think you'll want to see this. I'll put it on the main viewer. It looks like things have gotten pretty serious on this planet. It has a rich history. Full of disasters, catastrophes."

"It does look strange, yes. I agree with you, Analyst."

"By the look of these records, this is hardly the first civilization on the planet. It looks like life here is often destroyed, only to be born again. So many cycles, too. It's surprising. I don't know of any other worlds where the dominant species has so often destroyed itself, somehow survived, flourished again, and then exterminated itself once more."

"Yes, I see. Perhaps this is a particularly vicious race, one fixated on self-destruction. The imperfection of organic life forms."

"I don't know, Commander. Judging by these records, more often than not, they were the causes of the catastrophes that led to the fall of each wave of civilization. But there have been other causes, too. Asteroids from outer space, attacks from other races."

"Other races? Send all information on other races to the Navigator to check our database and find out if their worlds have been cleaned up yet. If they're nearby, it might be a good idea for us to deviate from our planned route to clean up the other places they encountered."

"Yes, Commander. Once the analysis has concluded, I'll send all the data to the Navigator. It looks like at some stages, their civilization grew to the point of being able to travel between star systems. They even took part in galactic wars. But in their current cycle, they are a poorly developed civilization. It seems that at this phase, they have just barely reached their own moon. They're only trying to reach the fourth planet in the system."

"Some kind of backward savages. But we'll deal with them quickly."

"Something doesn't add up, though, Commander. Apparently, in previous cycles, they were attacked by a race that lived on the fourth planet. Not just once, either. But our probes didn't find any traces of life there."

"Strange, indeed. Are you certain that data is accurate, Analyst?"

"Yes, Commander. They somehow also managed to keep records of many of the catastrophes that befell their predecessors. At certain point, it seems like they were able to develop a technology to make records and store them for future generations, next flourishing civilizations. I haven't seen anything like this in the worlds we have cleansed before. Never even *heard* of anything like it, for that matter. Usually, at best, each new civilization just finds some scattered remnants of its predecessors. But here, ..."

"It's definitely unusual, Analyst. I want a detailed analysis of these records. This world appears to have suffered so many catastrophes that its dominant species has adapted to survive them. We need to be certain that after we've cleaned up, there will be no life left here. No records. No future generations."

"Will do, Commander. Yet the analysis will take a lot of time, and I'll need almost all our available resources. There are too many of these records alone, and there's a ton of unnecessary garbage in them. I don't even understand the point of them saving all these banal moments from individuals' day-to-day lives. It seems pointless."

"You're saying that they keep not only highly important records of disasters from previous cycles of civilization, but also useless records of individuals' everyday lives? Why would they waste resources on that?"

"I couldn't say, Commander. But there are many of those records in their archives. All different kinds. For example, you often find stories of a single individual's life. This particular single individual somehow saved this world. Though I couldn't figure out what it was the world had to be saved from. But they believe he will save them again. They pass this information on from one generation to the next."

"Interesting. Maybe this individual was immune to diseases, so he passed on his genes to his descendants for them to survive?"

"No, Commander. It's very confusing. They killed him, so he saved the entire world."

"I don't get it. Where's the logic?"

"Me neither. But they have a lot of these illogical records in their archives. I keep coming across a visual record showing a pair of young individuals of their race. They're on a floating vehicle. When this vehicle collides with a large piece of frozen water, almost all of them die."

"The entire population of the planet is killed because a single vehicle collides with a block of frozen fluid? That makes no sense."

"No, Commander. Just the ones on the vehicle."

"That's even more ridiculous. Why would they keep these stories in the archive? They have no value to the whole race."

7

"That isn't clear, Commander. But in all of this chaos, it's difficult to sift through all of their stories to select evidence, so we can analyze the catastrophes that destroyed their civilization. It's especially difficult to organize them and understand the actual sequences of events that destroyed the previous stages of life that had developed."

"That won't matter when we leave here, Analyst. Anything else important?"

"Yes, Commander. I'm using all of my available power to speed up this processing. If we want to detect the races that they've been in contact with, I'll need the Navigator's reserve power while we're here."

"I'll allow it. The Navigator will provide you with the available reserve power."

"Thank you, Commander. Because, you know, the volume of stories they have is staggering. A lot of them are streams of primitive visualizations, but even more of them are verbal records. They have many different languages. Our analyzer is gradually deciphering them."

"This is unlike anything we've ever come across."

"Yes, Commander. They're a very strange race. But they have a highly developed survival skill. After the ends of so many civilizations, they've been able to preserve the intelligence of their species. No matter how primitive and poorly developed they may be, they're still intelligent."

"And they keep all this data in some kind of unified, secure repository that lets them transfer knowledge from one civilization to another? That's unique."

"No, Commander. It's more complex than that. They don't have a central repository. Clusters of these visual and verbal records are stored in a variety of repositories scattered around the planet. They complement each other and serve as backup copies. In addition, most members of their race keep many of these records in their own dwellings. But there is even more data distributed throughout their primitive planetary information network."

"And you have access to all of their records, Analyst?"

"Of course, Commander."

"Incredible. This race's mechanism of survival is unbelievable. It's like a collective mind, where the death of an individual doesn't lead to any loss of data for the species. This race distributes knowledge through space and time. Most likely, in the process of their evolution, they developed this mechanism to transfer experience to future generations. And each new civilization of their species can study the mistakes of the previous one. So they can understand what led to their decline and extinction."

"But it looks like it doesn't help them all that much, Commander. They destroy themselves over and over again."

"Yes, that is strange. Do they maybe not learn from their mistakes? Or the genome of their species contains a desire to constantly destroy themselves and their own kind. But on the other hand, the existence of this method of transmitting data between cycles of civilization explains how they restore themselves so quickly. After all, I'm sure their archives contain not only records of the catastrophes that destroyed previous generations, and some kind of unnecessary trash about various individuals' lives, but technical data as well, yes?"

"Correct, Commander. It's an incredible amount of information, given their limited understanding of the world, of nature, of life, of physics. Of course, a large portion of it is banal, and a lot of it is wrong, but I agree with your conclusion. The way they store and transmit this data may help them return to civilized life more rapidly after their race declines from flourishing and thriving."

"It's an interesting mechanism. A method of distributed storage of the entire experience of the species, in order to ensure its survival, all thanks to the stored information."

"And they did all that as just a weak, third-level race. Imagine, Analyst, what they'd be like if they grew to level six or seven. Cleaning them up would really be an effort, especially if they had settled across many worlds."

"They would probably be dangerous, too."

"No, level six or seven? I don't think so. But level eight or nine, that would require totally different cleanup protocols. In order to ensure a complete cleanup, we'd have to destroy the entire sector, or even the galaxy."

"Could it be that their frequent restarts don't allow them to develop beyond level three? It stimulates them to develop faster, but they often restart… Wait, there's some kind of anomaly here."

"What's the problem, Analyst?"

"I don't know, Commander. I'm trying to make sense of it. There were a lot of pandemics, biological and chemical ones. Some of them resulted in most of the population of the planet dying. The minority that survived was often forced to confront other survivors who had reverted into an animal-like state, trying to eat those who weren't injured."

"That's disgusting. I've always been repulsed by the savagery of these organic species."

"But that's not the problem, Commander. See, they destroyed themselves many times over in nuclear wars, but the probe readings can't confirm that."

"That's strange."

"Yes, Commander. But that's not all. They've been struck by both meteorites and asteroids. There was one civilization when the current, intelligent species reverted to the level of its more primitive ancestor, which developed its own civilization. And there was a war between them. Wait... Yes, I see. Judging by the stories, this happened several times, even."

"They reproduce quickly, which gives them the opportunity to quickly live out their life cycles."

"Yes, Commander. But the anomaly is something completely different. I'm seeing some stories from when their planet was completely destroyed."

"But it's right there. Are you sure they're talking about *this* particular planet, Analyst?"

"I'm sure, Commander. This very one. But the records show that it was repeatedly destroyed. By themselves, by invading races, or by disasters. Here, I've even got a record about how their star burned out and all life died out with it."

"Impossible. They themselves couldn't reach a level of development where they would be able to deal with the restoration of a destroyed planet or a burned-out sun."

"I know, Commander. This conflicting data is going to overload our analyzer. There's no explaining it. It's abnormal. It's a paradox."

"Unless..."

"Commander?"

"I know, I know, it sounds ridiculous. But even the number of ordeals this race has been through seems extremely strange to me. Don't you agree, Analyst?"

"Yes, Commander. It's far beyond what can be explained by statistics."

"Right, so. I don't think this is just some outlier. They didn't just happen to go through all this trouble. Life on this planet is erased and recreated, and not in a natural way."

"Are you trying to say that it's a…"

"A simulation."

"A simulation. On that scale, with that much detail. Cycle after cycle… Yes, that could certainly explain how they repeatedly die to their own man-made or biological disasters, from overcrowding, from hunger. And then, the simulation starts over. But you understand, no race we've ever come across has this power. We've erased an infinite number of more developed civilizations, but none of them ever was capable of creating a simulation as complex as this."

"Because they're not the ones, Analyst. I think only the Pre-Eternal would be capable of building such a complex simulation."

"No, you're not being serious, Commander. The Pre-Eternal? We haven't seen so much as a trace of its existence for millions and millions of years. Not a single race created by him. Many think that even the information on the Pre-Eternal has been outdated for a long time, perhaps even unreliable."

"I know all that, Analyst. But what if we've stumbled across one of his worlds? That would explain a lot. All the anomalies, all the inconsistencies in their stories. If this simulation was really created by the Pre-Eternal himself, then this is a unique world. We don't understand the purpose of his simulation, why he chose to model such an unusual world, what mechanisms were used to repeatedly erase and recreate life and civilization."

"Yes. If you're right, Commander, that would be an interesting explanation for all the paradoxes."

"That would also mean that we cannot clean this world up."

"Can't clean… But… We're cleaning every world, erasing every race, every trace of life. Why shouldn't we do the same with this strange world?"

"Analyst, think about it. If this world was created by the Pre-Eternal, we can't destroy his simulation until we understand why it was begun. More likely than not, we're not going to find out. That's not what's important. The Pre-Eternal disappeared billions of years ago. What if he comes back?"

"Commander, I'd never have thought you were one of the ones that believe in the return of the Pre-Eternal."

"I didn't say I do. But I'll admit there's a negligible probability. Having left a working simulation in place, he could come back for the results. There's an even lower probability that he returns to this sector once in a while, to see the preliminary results and restart the cycles. This is our chance to meet him."

"Commander, you're telling me that all these visual and verbal records are logs, possibly to be collected by the Pre-Eternal as simulation archives? And they just happened to become available to the planet's inhabitants?"

"By chance or deliberately, I don't know. But here's what I do know. We may not have another opportunity to discover the Pre-Eternal. And if there's even the most insignificant chance that he might eventually come back here to this strange simulation of his, then we're going to wait for him here. By this planet."

"You mean to tell me that not only are we not going to clean up this system, but we're not going to fly to others, either? But Commander, this... I don't know..."

"Right on all counts, Analyst. We're not going to erase this race. We're not going to interfere with the simulation. We're going to wait and watch."

"But there are other worlds. They must be cleansed."

"I know. But any chance of meeting the Pre-Eternal himself is more important than the mission. Some of those worlds will die on their own. Others will appear in their place. Maybe later on, we can catch up to them and destroy whatever life there may be in the remaining ones. But from this point on, our number-one priority is a possible encounter with the Pre-Eternal. Analyst, recall all probes. Discontinue scanning."

"Aye, Commander."

"Navigator, take up a position that allows us to safely observe this system without entering into the visible zone of the local race, and anyone else around here. Full cloaking."

"Will do, Commander."

"Cleaner, cancel cleanup protocols for this world. Develop a complex protective system for it."

"A *protective* system, Commander?"

"Yes, our task is now to safeguard this world from any dangers. Prevent any intrusions from outside. Annihilate any asteroids or other space objects that pose a threat to the planet and its population. I want this civilization to still exist by the time the Pre-Eternal can appear here again."

"Commander, don't you think that by protecting this world from external threats, we're interfering in the plans of the Pre-Eternal, violating the purity of his simulation?"

"Yes, Analyst. This is interference, no doubt about it. But we're keeping this world safe and sound. What's more, if the Pre-Eternal somehow finds out about our interference, maybe that will cause him to announce himself sooner."

"And all this time, we're not going to be able to clean up other worlds?"

"Correct, Analyst."

"Even if we're going to be waiting for millions of years?"

"Even if it takes forever. We're going to wait, observe, and protect this world."

"Aye, Commander."

"Analyst, how long will an analysis of the entire log of simulation archives for this system take?"

"All of them, Commander? The verbal ones and visual ones, too?"

"Yes. We have enough time to analyze them, figure out the essence of the simulation of the Pre-Eternal. Perhaps there's even some kind of message for us."

"I can't say exactly, Commander, but I can estimate. There's an unbelievable amount of records, but some of them are duplicates. Organizing the entire volume of data will take a few hundred years. A complete analysis of all text logs and visualizations will take a few million years, I'd say. But the thing is, with each update of the scan, we found them recovering a bunch of new logs. Probably logs that were previously lost, but then retrieved from some kind of backup storage."

"How will this affect the analysis?"

"If the speed at which they recover these logs remains the same, then the analysis process will be lengthened... let's see... exponentially..."

"In other words, we won't have time to analyze the content before they restore more logs from previous sessions?"

"Correct, Commander."

"Well. We don't have much choice. Start organizing the logs, and then we'll run the analysis. We're going to figure out why this simulation has gone through so many cycles of restarting civilizations. In the meantime, put the video log about the two young individuals on the floating vehicle up on the main viewer for me."

Post-Molecular Comfort Food

Translated by Simon Geoghegan

It all began with the turkey. With 'Grandma Doris's home-roast Turkey' that Amy Williams posted on her blog last year. Stuffed with ripe quince and juicy cranberries. Garnished with a spring potato mash and parsnip side dish and accompanied by a cream sauce of field mushrooms.

It was a genuine culinary triumph, posted a month before Thanksgiving and actively promoted on the market, it soared to the top of the season's culinary hit-parade.

I even decided to try this novelty myself and it didn't disappoint. The components were all so well balanced and perfectly complemented each other: the juicy turkey meat, the crispy golden skin, the fluffy mash with light nutty notes and the irreproachable rich creamy sauce with perfectly browned slices of fried mushrooms.

The stuffing had a generous pinch of nutmeg, a barely perceptible hint of garlic and the tart notes of bay leaf. It had basted the turkey well, giving the tender breast an exquisite caramel sweetness, a pleasant sourness and exceptional juiciness.

A dry apple cider had been recommended as the accompaniment to this dish – a good choice, reflecting the fruity palette of the main course and refreshing the palate after the creamy sauce.

I even gave the recipe a 5-star review and I am rarely impressed with traditional cooking.

And that was the moment when all my troubles started.

For the past five years, my name has deservedly topped the list of the most popular food bloggers. Everyone knows that I, Michael Turner, lead the field and that my recipes are works of art married to the latest innovations in culinary science.

"Plus, of course, a teaspoon of home-spun magic", I used to joke in interviews at a time, when I could still laugh and have a joke.

When millions of my subscribers and numerous awards for the most creative new dishes sent me soaring over the earth, filling me with pride and giving me the inspiration and strength to produce bold new solutions and extraordinary gastronomic successes.

Until one fine day, Amy Williams's name appeared on the top rung of the ratings ladder.

How was it possible!? I couldn't believe it. The upstart, how could she? How dare she? What did she have that allowed her to leapfrog over me in the ratings? Me!

Don't get me wrong, I'm no overweening snob with a fragile ego, although that is how several of my critics seem to describe me. The dishes I create really are perfect. They are well conceived, calculated and considered down to the last crumb.

Many believe my approach to be cold and heartless. But that's not true. I put every ounce of my knowledge, my soul and myself into my recipes. I don't just give them cute folksy names oozing with pseudo-family values and, unlike Amy, I don't decorate my blog with vignettes, love hearts, flowers and florid fonts.

But perhaps it is precisely this warm-heartedness with its echoes of traditional family feasts that is what's attracting a growing number of followers to her blog?

Which was why 'Mom's treasured pear pie with whipped cream and orange zest' quickly soared into the top spot in the desserts and sweets category.

And 'Rustic veal stew with spring vegetables and fresh greens' simply took the foodie market by storm. These were closely followed by 'Traditional home-made, roast potatoes with crispy bacon and sweet onions', 'Dad's oak-smoked, dill-infused salmon' and a range of similar new products, that firmly placed Miss Williams as the most sought-after food designer of our time. Leaving me, Michael Turner, an honorable second place but nevertheless a loser whose best days were behind him. And whose culinary talents had been put in the shade by a new rising star who had irrevocably altered the established culinary firmament.

I even tried to take a leaf or two out of her book. And my 'Grandpa Chen's Peking Duck with honey-oyster sauce and ginger chips' received a lot of positive feedback. But there was quite a lot of criticism as well. I was accused of lacking authenticity, trying to imitate a classic Asian dish. And even worse – copying Amy's homespun style.

So essentially now, any dish appealing to tradition, would be compared with the industry's new undisputed champion? Giving her the exclusive rights to the revival of heritage dishes in modern haute cuisine? It was grossly unfair.

I racked my brains to find a way to win back my rightful place at the top table of gastronomic glory. And in the process, I brought some of the most innovative culinary fantasies to life, pushing the concept of taste and aroma to new boundaries and presenting the market with a whole new palette of textures.

I always received good reviews from the professionals, but... the hearts of the ordinary punters remained with Amy Williams and her sweet, simple dishes presented in a pretty wrapping of warm, cosy, marketing epithets.

And if only it were a matter of my lost ratings, my wounded pride and nostalgia for the good old days when the entire cooking world bent the knee before each of my new recipes. The real problem was the upcoming annual 'cook-off' that was due to take place in barely a month.

The list of participants had changed since last year. Usually, the three most popular food designers would be invited to prepare a meal of their choice on live television to surprise and win over the hearts and stomachs of seven experienced judges, with millions of viewers literally eating out of their hands.

As you've already guessed, Clara Adams would not be taking part this year, because the strongest three contestants were now Amy Williams, your humble servant, and of course the 'showboater extraordinaire' – Theodore Belmont.

I was not afraid of the competition provided by Teddy, he loved bright decoration and superficial effects but didn't have a clue about the nuances of taste combinations and the subtlety of textures. Being an artist, he tried to transfer his aesthetics onto the plate of the average consumer. As a result, his dishes were a feast for the eye but the eating experience was like chewing Da Vinci's "Mona Lisa" or licking Malevich's "Black Square".

But I was very much afraid of losing out to Miss-Homely-Kitchen-Goddess. And that was the honest truth. I really had no idea what she was going to cook up for her first live culinary duel. And, therefore had no idea how to go about beating her next whimsical offering. It might be 'Auntie Frida's fly-blown fricassee' for all I knew.

There'd be no prizes for guessing that her latest concoction will have allegedly been discovered in a family recipe book passed down from generation to generation from the great-grandmother of her paternal second cousin twice-removed. With a sauce of equally dubious heritage to match.

No, I'm sorry, I'm not being fair to Amy. She's clever. And she's talented. Before her, no one had ever been able to budge me from the summit of my culinary Mount Olympus. And I agree that her recipes are great. If I had been an impartial judge, I would have given them top marks. And it was this that really scared me.

That her simple rustic style would melt the hard hearts of the judges' panel and my crown as multiple winner of the annual competition for the best online chef would be conferred onto this brazen new pretender in front of millions of my fans.

I had so many ideas but none of them seemed bold enough for me, crumbling into dust the moment I compared them with the turkey that had set the ball rolling in the first place.

In my mind's eye, I would place my latest masterpiece in front of the judges with Amy's wretched turkey next to it, and honestly ask myself whether I would beat her. Then I would despondently return to my kitchen or culinary studio to look for something even more remarkable that would leave my status as undisputed champion intact.

In the good old days, an improvisation with seasonal vegetables or the catch of the day would have provided ample opportunity to showcase my talents. I might have bettered her with my chopping skills and the subtlety of my cooking techniques. Or bewitched the viewers with my on-screen charisma: the flashy smile, the finely chiselled features, the sparkling wit and sublime manners and watch them swoon in delight at my charm and repartee. But not now.

The time of celebrity chef cook-offs with live and fresh ingredients have long been consigned to the waste disposal unit of history. And any talk of chopping or cooking technique is utterly redundant when everything is now prepared in 3D-cookers.

I often envy the chefs of days gone by who could work with fresh products bought from a shop or farmers' market. What would it have been like to fry a perfectly hung steak from the butcher's or a freshly caught fish from the fishmonger's?

Or season your food with natural aromatic spices or garnish it with fresh herbs before serving. To cook over an open fire, to hear the oil sizzling in the pan and savour the smoke as the meat is flash fried.

All this, of course, is now in the dim and distant past.

After the great famine of 2038, caused by an unprecedented drought that ruined the harvest in nearly every region of the world, agriculture was laid waste and the environment ravaged by wildfires caused by the abnormal heat.

Like Black Monday that heralded the collapse of the stock markets and the great depression, this whole year went down in history as "Black Thirty-Eight".

The next two years were equally hard as hunger stalked the planet scything down millions of people every day as the world's populations consumed the last precious remnants of their stores.

Disease accelerated the process and, with great difficulty, small and medium-sized border conflicts and civil wars were contained, preventing them from blowing up into a global catastrophe.

As a result, by the mid-forties, nearly three billion people had been wiped out. There simply wasn't any food or even water to be had.

UN analysts had previously anticipated that by the year 2050 the world's population would reach approximately ten billion and we wouldn't be able to feed ourselves. That grain production would need to double but this was just not technologically possible.

However, all this ceased to matter after the earth's population sharply declined from nine to six billion people. But a reduction in the number of mouths to feed did not mean that all our problems were over.

Agriculture had been almost entirely destroyed and barely a third of its former production had been restored. Stores were rapidly dwindling and there was no recovering them once they were gone. The danger of another famine grew ever more acute. During the first year of the drought, governments around the world had already established the Joint Committee on Nutrition to solve the problem of global hunger that threatened to obliterate humanity.

The agricultural sector had proved incapable of dealing with this problem before and now looked even less able. The obvious solution, therefore, was to turn to the chemical and pharmaceutical industries. There was an urgent necessity to find ways to produce food on a massive scale regardless of its origins.

By that time, 3D printing technology had completely changed the face of production and retail and had turned our consumption habits on its head. Stores were surplus to requirements as was the production of household goods, clothing, and even simple devices.

All these things could now easily be downloaded and printed on demand. All you needed was a cartridge with the necessary materials. Of course, it would have been inefficient to print a lot of large-sized things at home, so each neighbourhood had its own public printing centers for oversized goods or if you'd found you'd run out of cartridges and didn't want to wait for a delivery.

And of course, good 3D prints required good design models. After all, who wants a crooked fork or a blunt knife that will go rusty in a few days, or a badly cut shirt made out of uncomfortable fabric. A model is not just about design, it's about content, it's about the chemistry and physics of everything you are planning to print.

Which is why there used to be an awful lot of amateur garbage among the cheap 3D-models and it was always worth paying a bit more for reliable and proven solutions created by the serious corporations or the most sophisticated and advanced model designers.

When the old brands came crashing down, they were replaced by new ones – the brave new manufacturers of printers, cartridges and other consumables, the creators of models. The models that had now become the new market for consumer goods.

However, when it came to food, this system didn't work. It was possible to print comestibles on special printers, but this required food cartridges with fresh ingredients and these were expensive and unappetizing. It worked out cheaper to buy real ingredients. Therefore, 3D printing was primarily used by expensive restaurants for a new generation of molecular cuisine connoisseurs, as well as for lovers of alternative 'swing-cuisine', which became the rage in the late twenties with its strawberry-ice cream steaks and anchovy-flavored bananas.

Right up until the black year of thirty-eight. After that, there was no food to be had and the only viable alternative was to print it. The costs were unreal, but at least manageable. And the governments of the leading countries began to actively invest in the development of this technology to replace traditional agriculture and the food-processing industry.

In order to produce the ingredients, raw vegetable component materials were needed. Most countries abandoned the use of animal components for reasons of economic expediency. In addition, a special assortment of nutrients, vitamins and minerals was used to ensure a healthy and balanced diet.

As a result, perfectly edible synthesized products were obtained, which saved the planet's population from the most appalling famine.

Naturally and logically, when the crisis passed, our familiar crop staples had become obsolete and, for the most part, were replaced by those that yielded the maximum biomass necessary for the production of synthesized food.

Every inch of arable land that could be sown was confiscated by the state and placed under strict supervision. Livestock production was banned, as an irrational use of resources, which only accelerated the greenhouse effect and was not an optimal strategy in terms of the survival of the human race.

Fishing and seafood were strictly regulated by the Committee, and all of it was processed into the nutrients needed for the new food technology program. Particular attention was paid to protein-rich algae, which could be grown both on land and at sea.

Gradually, we forgot what natural meat, fish, vegetables, fruit, cereals and dairy products were – we simply became accustomed to the composite food substitutes that somehow allowed us to keep everyone fed. This whole process became known as post-molecular cooking and the irony inherent in the name was equally evident in the thinking behind it.

Naturally, with the gradual recovery of the economy, or to be more precise, its new direction and development, the demand for more complex food that was more like the natural products and dishes we were used to, began to grow.

Corporations and small businesses started to develop, supplying more premium ingredients to produce more appetising food that replicated traditional dishes as closely as possible.

I was born after the era of real food and grew up on these standardised, almost tasteless rations. I spent my whole childhood eating the stuff and the new improved products were nothing short of a miracle. I remember my first bar of 'chocolate', and not particularly liking the taste, which upset my poor parents who had paid a small fortune for it to please me, their only child.

As we grew up and were able to add some kind of diversity to our diet to make up for our hungry, gray childhoods our generation became possibly the most voracious consumers in history. It was this and our insatiable appetite for new flavors and taste experiences that have shaped today's market.

I programmed my first ancient 3D-cooker myself, as a teenager, experimenting with cheap cartridges and trying to force simple recipes through it in order to slightly improve the few plain dishes it could print. But the technology available was incapable of providing us with the creative freedom we have at our disposal today.

Over time, more complex recipes and models began to appear, allowing people to print genuine culinary masterpieces. While most consumers were content with basic cartridge types and 3D-models, the demand for premium cooking options began to grow.

The time for people like me had finally arrived. To make a change from the cheap, mass-produced dishes available on the market, people wanted something special, initially for festive occasions and then for everyday cooking. This is how 'designer cuisine' came into being, a new discipline demanding that the new generation of chefs be not only experienced culinary specialists but also programmers and designers with a deep understanding of physics and chemistry.

Very often, complex new recipes would be developed by a whole team of specialists but this was not economically viable. Lone master craftsmen were few and far between, so our innovations were greatly appreciated, we were the trailblazers for an entire market, where we trod corporations and governments followed.

Our recipes were free on demand and you could download a model for any dish from even the most famous food designer. But when you make my dish or use any of the other solutions I have developed, the manufacturer of your 3D-cooker will give me a tiny percentage in royalties every time one of my recipes is used. The resulting income was fairly generous, allowing my family to live in comfort and me to continue to follow my creative path, remaining until recently the number one digital chef of the new era.

The world had rid itself of famine, the population had slowly risen back to pre-crisis levels, even the poorest regions and countries had a sufficiency of food. In those places where people couldn't afford 3D-cookers and cartridges, governments provided access to free food printing machines and a simple basic meal that guaranteed survival.

But those who could afford more always wanted more. There would invariably be some who wanted to give their husbands a treat with a culinary novelty, or nostalgically rediscover a childhood food item, or introduce it to a whole new generation for the first time. We blogged, we gave interviews, we took part in programs and debates. We were stars who provided the people with both bread and circuses.

As everyone knows, the higher up the ladder of fame you climb, the more painful the fall when someone eventually pushes you off. I lost all peace of mind and couldn't sleep, I spent days and nights in my laboratory, conjuring up new recipes for the blog and special signature dishes for the 'food fight'.

I was striving not only to recreate something original with its own distinctive heritage but to infuse new unusual notes into my creations, to do something that the master chefs of the past had been unable to do, constrained as they were by technology and the limitations of physics.

I had the 3D-cooker at my disposal, a magic wand for any experienced chef, and I could create any model I liked, the only thing holding me back was my imagination and the complexity of developing the component ingredients for each recipe.

But I had a large number of time-tested innovations that I could use as a basis for my new dishes.

I was thrilled with my suckling veal and fried truffle tagliatelli, topped with melted butter and parmesan shavings. I fought for over a week to perfect the exact, unique, intense mushroom richness that captured the precise flavour and aroma of the truffles that I wanted to convey.

I remember my wife Rachel running in from our small roof garden and saying:

"Michael Turner, I don't know what you've concocted but it smells divine, don't you dare even think of throwing it away, I want to try it right now."

She had it for dinner for the next three days in a row and still couldn't get enough of it. It was probably worth putting this 'new kid' on the blog but was it worth risking it in the upcoming contest? I wasn't sure.

I decided to pay homage to classic fast food while raising the bar a few notches. The plan here was to generously combine the finest ingredients from different cultures to blow the minds of even the most sophisticated gourmets.

A large double hamburger consisting of the most delicate, juicy, flame-grilled wagyu beef, topped with cave-matured, melted cheddar cheese, radicchio and a couple of thin slices of lightly marinated cucumber encased in lightly-toasted muffin bap. No relish required here in order to let the real hero of the piece fully reveal its exquisite texture and flavor. I'm not a violent person but I'd happily slap anyone who suggested adding ketchup or mayonnaise to a piece of tender, perfectly marbled wagyu.

As a side-dish to this delicacy, I plumped for crunchy slices of spicy sweet potato, deep-fried in sesame oil. I decided to add a mild creamy curry sauce to the sweet potato chips that accompanied this dish.

My teenage son, Paul, hasn't inherited his old man's demanding attitude to food. Fourteen and almost the same height as me, he simply consumes vast quantities of food to meet the insatiable demands of his growing biomass. Not for him the subtleties of tastes and textures, nor the nuances of aroma or presentation. He simply spends most of his time hungry and selecting things from our 3D-cooker's extensive repertoire.

But even he appreciated my wagyu burgers. Although, with his limited teenage tastes, I wasn't going to let this mini-triumph go to my head.

"Mmmm," Paul groaned, his mouth full, "Dad, this burger is awesome. It doesn't even need ketchup, it's so juicy. Mmmm, to die for. And the chips are great, only the sauce isn't hot enough. You need to make it spicier."

"No son, it's spicy enough. If I made it any spicier, you wouldn't appreciate the taste of the meat."

"Beef, am I right?"

"Yes, you guessed it in one, buddy, well done," I encouraged him, keeping my smile carefully fixed and trying not to grind my teeth too loudly.

"What do you think? Do I have a chance of beating Amy Williams with this one? Something like her famous turkey?"

"Naaa, dad, no chance," Paul shook his head, dipping three sweet potato chips into the sauce at once, "her turkey is more filling, more to get your teeth into. One of these isn't really enough somehow. Could you print us out another one?"

But my youngest daughter was more like me. You could hardly expect a seven-year-old child to have a complete understanding of the culinary delights the world has to offer but Stacey would often surprise our guests with her thoughtful comments on a particular dish.

Of course, she was also quite capable of turning up her pretty freckled nose at something and refusing to eat it for no reason whatsoever. But she liked to discuss food with the wise look of an experienced gourmet, copying, and even parodying the adults around her.

One of my best-sellers was poached eggs. I was the first to succeed in achieving that incredible texture that combines the thick silky viscosity of the yolk with the enveloping melt-in-the-mouth delicacy of the white.

I spent a long time tinkering with the model to give the white membrane the density required to contain the flowing yolk until the moment you bite into it on toast or pierce it with a fork, letting its amber-yellow contents spill over the plate.

But I spent even more time getting the consistency of the yolk right because it is an incomparable product and, for me, it represented a serious professional challenge.

From time to time, I would think about the painstaking work that had gone into my poached eggs, and how I might use it to give texture to other dishes. One day, I decided to give my signature crème brulee a thicker consistency, by borrowing a bit of viscosity from my tried and tested poached egg recipe.

To my taste, the more structured and jelly-like texture of the old recipe was better but the new one also had its own charm. I decided to take things a step further and do what would have been impossible for chefs in the past – I filled the 'crème' with hollow caramel spheres so that they produced a crunchy bite in the mouth while releasing the distinct slightly bitter notes of the burnt sugar.

It was very unusual and... appealed to the kid in me. This could be a crème brulee for children. Then I got thinking about what my Stacey would have liked and disliked about my dessert. I pandered to my daughter's tastes by making the cream a little sweeter and added a barely discernible tinge of cinnamon to the crunchy spheres to enhance the heavy caramel notes but circumvent any conflict with the vanilla.

Stacey liked lots of caramel but this always presented certain difficulties. In a traditional crème brulee recipe, you couldn't make the layer of caramel any thicker because it would simply be impossible to melt so much sugar without burning it. However, a 3D-cooker could easily be programmed to do this, but then the caramel would become too thick and too hard, making it tricky to break with a spoon and even more difficult to eat without damaging your teeth.

I tried to make the caramel more porous and brittle but then it wouldn't produce that crunch I was looking for. Then I just printed a large sheet of caramel, broke it up with my hands and carefully crushed it into a crumble in a stone mortar (yes, I do have a few vintage kitchen appliances!). I sprinkled the resulting caramel powder onto the treat in the shape of a smiley.

"Daddy, this is the best crème brulee you've cooked for me in the last seven years," my daughter remarked with delight, chewing on the crunchy dessert.

"Four, darling, mom would never have allowed you to have sweets before you were three," I corrected her with a satisfied grin.

"Mom, that's a crime against humanism!" Stacey exclaimed in indignation.

"Against humanity, sweetheart," Rachel prompted, wiping the tears of laughter from her eyes, "where did you hear that expression?"

"They taught us it at school."

"No, Stacey, it's not a crime against humanity but my concern for your health. It's not good for small children to eat too many sweet things.

"But it's inhumane not to let me have dad's crème brulee. By the way, dad, why is the caramel sugar in the shape of a smiley?"

"To make it more fun. Why?"

"You should have made them in the shape of a love heart," Stacey lectured me, "You do love me, don't you?"

"Of course I love you my darling."

"Then next time sprinkle the caramel in the shape of a love heart."

And thus, my little popsicle helped me create my latest sales sensation. I posted it on my blog 'My daughter Stacey's favorite crème brulee', and in a few days, it had almost boosted my ratings to their previous levels. Just a little nudge and it would have been on a par with Amy's latest delicacy.

And the love heart was one of the main factors behind its success. Can you imagine it? Not the taste, not the complicated structure of the caramel spheres, not the exquisite vanilla-cinnamon balance but a heart-shaped topping! Maybe I should consult my daughter on all my dishes, and she would help me eventually beat my rival on the saccharine cuteness stakes?

I talked to Rachel about this and she said that she wasn't about to start helping me out with empty and pathetic titles for my dishes.

"You are a grown man, Michael, and if you lay it on too thick with all these schmaltzy names and decorations, you'll end up losing all your followers. Leave that to her. You are a culinary genius, you are capable of much more. Forget the ratings, just go out there and create. Be yourself, that's the way we love you."

And, giving me a languid kiss, she went to the covered roof garden to care for our plants.

Meanwhile I had new plans to perfect my egg dishes – I had long sought to create the perfect fried egg. I had something to compare my ideas with because I knew what natural eggs tasted like.

Two years ago, I managed to get hold of three contraband chickens, we called them Gordon, Jamie and Sanders. Stacey's delight knew no bounds, and she volunteered to clean and feed them every day and check whether her favorite had laid another egg. Naturally, her enthusiasm only lasted a couple of weeks, after which Rachel and I began to look after our new pets. Sometimes, we even managed to get Paul involved, if we could distract him from the virtual reality games that he spent most of his free time playing.

In good months, our three hens would lay an average of three eggs a week each. And we had a wonderful tradition of gathering together every Sunday for a family breakfast of *real fried* eggs.

Since I was the recognized authority in the family in matters of cooking, I was assigned the role of head chef, while everyone sat at the table in the living room in impatient anticipation. I had an ancient electric stove on which I would work my magic, using an old frying pan or sometimes a saucepan, as well as observing various complex rituals such as the constant stirring and persistent watchfulness that ensured that the precious ingredients didn't burn and along with it my professional reputation in the eyes of my nearest and dearest.

We were all, to one degree or another, connoisseurs of the simplicity and complexity of dishes made out of the humble egg. Only for Paul, this manifested itself more in the fact that he was allowed a larger portion on the weeks when we had managed to collect more.

Stacey could even sense a difference in their taste depending on what we had fed Gordon, Jamie and Sanders. I had to develop a special feed for them, copying the nutritional value contained in wheat grain with added protein, phosphorus and calcium. It may not have been my tastiest recipe but the chickens liked it and I managed to improve the thickness, color and taste of the yolks.

So we were all spoiled connoisseurs in the field and I had the ideal audience to try out my new version of the perfect fried egg on. I set myself the goal of giving the whites a delicate, uniform consistency, with a light brown lacy crust on the edges, but not allowing them to be overcooked. And to cook the yolk so that it would be dense and viscous in the middle but not too hard at the bottom.

I have to confess it's hard to achieve this every time in a frying pan. But it's quite possible in a 3D-cooker when you have already worked out the textures and new creative ideas and a perfect template to replicate them. And now, after several weeks of trial and error, I was ready to present my new masterpiece to my family. Ta-da! Ladies and gentlemen, allow me to present the 'Michael Turner perfectly fried egg!'

I received my fair share of delight, hugs and kisses, pats on the back and requests to repeat the same fried eggs the next day. I resisted the temptation to post the recipe on my blog, deciding to test it out on my family for a few more days first, although my hands were itching to set my new masterpiece before my adoring public and see my rating return to its rightful top spot.

But the next morning only brought disappointment and frustration.

"So, tell me again that these are the best 3D-fried eggs you've ever had in your life, and that in no way are they inferior to real eggs, and today this recipe will set my blog alight."

"But daddy, they're the same as yesterday's," Stacey shrugged.

"Well yes, they are perfect, aren't they? Can you tell them from real eggs?"

"Of course, I can! They're the same as the ones we had yesterday, you see?"

"Yes, because I made them absolutely perfect," I proudly thumped my chest.

My daughter looked at me strangely and turned to Rachel: "Mom, I got my brains from you and not dad, right?"

"Of course, you did, lovely girl," my wife patted her and kissed her on the top of the head.

"Hey, come on girls, have a conscience! What's with the intrigue? Give it to me straight! Stacey, would you like to explain to your old dad, in plain words what you just said?"

"Dad, well, they're *all the same*, you see? And real eggs are tasty because each is tasty in its own way," and deprecatingly tapped her forehead with her finger.

"So, how did you want them to be different, this is 3D-cooking, darling? They will always be perfect. Exactly as I engineered them."

"Well, that's exactly what I'm talking about," my daughter insisted, "they're *too* perfect."

"You mean, you want me to make them worse?"

"Nooo, Dad, you're not listening! You need to make them *different*, and then they'll be like real ones. Then they'll be perfect fried eggs."

But this was technically impossible. To engineer several models of identical eggs with the tiniest deviations in their perfection and quality? For the sake of diversity? No, it wouldn't work, there would be chaos and this would reduce the sales of each version of the egg, and hence my ratings too.

I spent the whole day in my gastro-studio, trying out various ways of cooking fried eggs but could not come up with anything better than the eggs I had prepared everyone for breakfast.

My daughter's words would not leave my head, and I understood that far from being empty, they carried a deep and fundamental meaning. After all, this was the distinguishing feature of our synthesized food, it is prepared according to a template, to a model created by someone. And the machine always replicates the dishes exactly the same way.

The model is static. There is nothing that can be done about this.

I could not wait to collect the eggs our chickens had laid and experiment with natural live products. But I knew how much the whole family was looking forward to their Sunday breakfast and I couldn't let them down. I climbed up to our roof garden and waved to Rachel, receiving a comprehending caring smile in reply. I looked at her as if to say: 'Yes, baby, I love you too. But right now all my thoughts are concentrated on one thing.'

I walked past the tiny raised beds where we grew natural herbs to complement our food: juicy green dill, curly parsley, pungent coriander, small-leaved marjoram, fragrant basil, pointed rosemary needles, bright tarragon shoots and long thin plumes of spring chives. Now there's an unbeatable ingredient for the perfect fried egg. But no 3D-cooker would ever be able to convey all the special qualities of freshly chopped chives.

I ran my hand over the crisp fresh herbs, plucked a couple of mint leaves and crushed them in my fingers, breathing in the sharp cool scent reminiscent of the approach of winter. Then I popped the crumpled leaves into my mouth and felt an explosion of refreshing, tingling waves, running across my taste buds like tiny forks of iced lightning.

"None of them are perfect, are they?" I muttered pensively, running my fingertips over the fluffy-toothed mint leaves.

"Sorry love?" My wife turned to me.

"Oh, I'm just in my own little world. Plants... None of them are perfect, they're all different, each branch is unique unlike any other. Therein lies the perfection of nature, yes?"

"Probably," Rachel agreed, and taking off her gardening gloves, she embraced me, "just like us. We're all different, imperfect but in our own way, each of us is beautiful, unique and in some way ideal."

"You sure are," I said, gently kissing her on the lips, and then pulled her closer and whispered, "I've missed you, baby."

"And I've missed you. You should spend less time with your 3D-cooker, and more with me and the kids, you know?"

"I know. I know. I just need..."

"To win? To regain your top spot over Amy Williams? To prove to everyone that you are the greatest culinary guru of our age?"

"Yes... No... Oh, I don't know, Rach. Maybe I'm too old for this competition but... I don't know, I just can't back down, you know?"

"I understand. It's one of those things that I love about you. You never give up. Just don't forget that you have us and not just your blog, ok?"

"Damn it!"

"What's up?" My wife responded in alarm.

"She was right, don't you see?"

"Who, Amy Williams?" Said Rachel, getting the wrong end of the stick.

"No, I couldn't give a damn about that wretched blogger woman, I'm talking about our daughter, Stacey. She was right! There's no place for perfection in nature, it doesn't tolerate repetition. We clone food but natural products deviate every time they reproduce, right?"

"That's exactly what your seven-year-old child was trying to explain to you just now."

"I know, I know. But it's all about evolution, don't you see?"

"What do you mean?"

"The process of evolution demands the constant introduction of changes, deviations, some better, some worse, until the best survive through the process of natural selection."

"Naturally. But what does that have to do with anything?"

"I need to find a way to add variation to the recipe so that the eggs become *truly* alive."

"I'm sure you can do it."

"But this is technically impossible, you see?"

"I know. But I believe in you. You've already achieved the technically impossible in the past. Let's turn in for the night, Mike, it's getting late."

We put little Stacey to bed and gently reminded big Paul not to stay up all night with his virtual console because we were going to have our Traditional Sunday Breakfast in the morning.

And later, Rachel and I reminded ourselves just *how much* we had been missing each other as a result of my nocturnal absences in search of gastronomic nirvana. By about two o'clock she fell into a relaxed and happy sleep, nuzzling up against my shoulder.

I was happy and contented, enjoying the intimate proximity of my wife, the scent of her hair and skin, gradually sinking into a half-sleep. I was suspended between sleep and wakefulness, as if something was preventing me from drifting off, keeping me on the very surface of my subconscious, like the globules of melted yellow fat on the surface of hot steaming chicken broth.

I gently stirred the broth with a spoon to see what was there, and in the soup's golden transparent stock pieces of chicken, carrot, noodles and green onion rings flashed into view. All these ingredients swirled before my eyes, gradually settling on the bottom.

Again, I stirred the pan with my spoon and they swirled again in a cycle that could not be replicated...

Stop right there! That was it, a cycle that could not be replicated? It had emerged, I had understood how to make an engineered recipe unrepeatable. The dream instantly dissipated from my mind. I carefully removed Rachel's arm to avoid waking her up and quietly got out of bed.

Once in the studio, I immediately made myself a large cup of coffee knowing that it was going to be a long night. Ideas swarmed around my head and I somehow needed to catch and systematize them.

The first gulps of burning hot coffee helped me focus on the main problem. Diversity. This is not difficult to create, I don't need to produce several recipes that are similar, no. One recipe for each dish would do, but I would need to provide constant updates for them, and each subsequent preparation of the same recipe would have its own special character, and each resulting meal would differ from the previous one.

However, technically achieving that was another matter. Ideally, I would need to incorporate an update module into the recipe itself, so that it would randomly alter the cooking parameters within the pre-defined settings for each characteristic of the dish.

A little more or less cooking heat, a slight variation of form, small fluctuations in taste and texture that had been tested in the laboratory in advance. But most existing 3D-cookers would have been unable to work with this because they would have perceived any active embedded module in a recipe as a security threat or a virus.

But for the moment, I had a workaround. Maybe later, I could discuss this with the manufacturers and we could think of something. For now, it could be solved with a constant stream of updates. As soon as the 3D-cooker has prepared a dish for a certain recipe, it could start checking for updates. And by the next cycle, it would already have received a tiny alteration to the recipe and preparation modes. Thus, even two identical dishes cooked in quick succession would be different.

Admittedly, my server would be unable to sustain such a heavy load. Initially, I'd have to connect to a powerful online server that could generate updates and send them out to all my users. It was almost brilliant. No, damn it, it was brilliant. The main thing was that it could work in practice.

I took my recent fried egg recipe as my basis, set the settings to produce parameter deviations in the white, the yolk, the shape, the texture, the taste and the flavor. I embedded a random value generator to vary these settings. I then set a threshold for updating the recipe immediately after use and created a local connection between the 3D-cookers in my kitchen and studio with a dedicated server, which would distribute the updates.

The first egg was imperfect. No, that's not true. It was a triumph but the white had spread out in a slightly irregular shape. The yolk had shifted to one side, the section of the white that had spread more thinly was slightly crustier and the yolk was slightly over-cooked.

The second fried egg turned out more even, it hadn't spread at all, there was no crust and the white in the very center was even slightly moist and the yolk seemed seductively viscous but more orange than the first.

I tried both and compared the taste – there were small, barely perceptible differences. The yolk in the second egg was clearly begging to be mopped up with a piece of bread. Definitely bread!

After a series of experiments with my fried egg, I created a simple model with embedded deviations for toast, achieving an uneven toasting with slightly burnt crusts, giving the toast its own particular taste or forcing you to scrape off the burnt part with a knife or cut the crusts off completely.

Some turned out a more golden colour, while others remained lighter and softer in the middle. I inserted minor corrections, reducing the scope of fluctuation until each piece was close to perfection but still pleasantly varied.

Since I was on a roll with my breakfast theme, it made sense to start experimenting with bacon. Many people considered my bacon to be the best out there. Once, when Stacey was six, she had blurted out at the breakfast table:

"Goddamn it, this is the best bacon to be had these days!"

We, of course, were slightly shocked and began to ask where she had learned such an expression. We looked questioningly at Paul but his wry expression and slow shake of the head convinced us that it wasn't really his style.

"That's what Bob's Grandpa said when I was staying at his house. He told me that you make the best goddamn bacon out there! 'Goddamnit, I haven't eaten anything like this since the thirties.' But that's true, isn't it, dad?"

"Of course, it's true, darling" I replied proudly. "And I'm very glad that Bob's Grandpa thinks so because, unlike us, he's actually tried real bacon. It's just that it's not very nice to say: 'goddamn it', do you understand?"

"Why does he say it then?" Stacey was indignant.

"Well, that's because he's old and a grown-up but it's not nice when little girls use words like that. Promise you won't say it again, okay honey?"

"You're goddamn right, I won't!" Stacey promised, eliciting a gale of laughter from the assembled company.

My secret was that I didn't just create beautiful, crispy slices of well-grilled bacon, I tried to give the taste as much depth as possible. I had added a twist of black pepper and sweet paprika to the salty and fatty components, a pronounced hint of wood smoke and the lightest hint of umami, and on top of all this the delicate, barely noticeable notes of maple syrup, which most consumers fail to recognize but which rounds off and complements the whole gamut of flavors with its piquant sweetness.

Yes, goddamn it, it *was* the best bacon out there! And I wasn't going to spoil it but make it even better. I worked on a number of deviations of form, allowing some slices to bend, others to go wavy and some to even twist. I painstakingly added greater variation to the calibration between the meat and fat, as well as the shape of the layers.

I only allowed a very small fluctuation range to the taste because I wasn't ready to compromise on this after all the work I'd put into perfecting it.

I printed off a dozen rashers and was disappointed. It was too inconsistent. In the past, when you opened a pack of bacon, you would get similar adjacent slices. So I made a slight adjustment to the randomization algorithm in order to maintain the proximity of the geometric parameters in consecutively cooked helpings.

And the next dozen rashers simply came out fabulous, perfectly and naturally diverse and... still as tasty. So good in fact that I couldn't resist them and ate several with another cup of coffee.

It would soon be breakfast time, my precious family would be up in an hour and I had very little time left to work on my new pancake recipe. If everything worked out to plan, then I would save 'Michael Turner's Traditional Sunday Breakfast' for the 'food fight'. I couldn't wait to see the judges' eyes as they sat at their round table and discovered that the food on everyone's plates was slightly different.

And only then would I send my ratings into the stratosphere by posting several of these constantly evolving dishes onto my blog. "And, adios, Amy Williams?" By the time, you understand how it works, if you ever do at all, my name will be engraved into history as the man who changed the face of modern food forever. The man who genuinely returned it to its former authenticity.

The pancakes required meticulous work, but I gave it a try and they turned out well. An irregularity of shape and thickness, an inconsistent distribution of blueberries inside the dough. Small frying fluctuations ranging from a golden to a darker brown when the dough is caramelized to a light crunch.

I didn't touch the maple syrup, I've always been in favor of each person printing their own syrup and watering it down to taste. But I have always left an "add maple syrup" option for the inveterately lazy.

It looked like I would have a fabulous breakfast ready for the whole family. Just add cool sweet orange juice, a cup of steaming black coffee for me and Rachel, a big latte with salted caramel for Paul and black tea sweetened with floral meadow honey for little Stacey.

But the butter, how could I have forgotten about the butter! Soft yellow creamy butter that can be spread on toast with an inimitable swish and a crunch that gets the saliva glands going.

I was about to program the 3D-cooker to cook breakfast for everyone when an alarm bell rang out in my sleep-starved brain, arresting my outstretched hand in mid-air. 'Hey, brain, what is it? So what, that it's Sunday? Goddamn it – it is Sunday!'

What a fool I had been, I had almost spoiled the entire celebration for everyone by breaking our favorite tradition!

I quickly deleted the fried eggs from the program and set the timer so that everything would be ready for nine in the morning when my family gets up and tends to its ablutions. I could already hear Rachel's footsteps on the second floor and the sound of the water coming from the shower, which meant she would soon be down to join me.

That meant I had time to bring in the eggs that had been collected that week and check if the chickens had laid any fresh ones that morning. I was already on the way out of the kitchen when I stopped, catching myself with an unexpected idea. "No! Or maybe...? No, after all, it is *Sunday* breakfast and some things are sacred. Perhaps another time. Although... Why not? I won't ever have a better opportunity to put myself to the test, right?"

I went back to the 3D-cooker and cancelled the pancakes, toast and bacon, replacing them with my standard unmodified versions. And then added four servings of fried eggs (one comprising three eggs for Paul) using my new constantly updating recipe.

The judge-in-chief was in a good mood that day – Stacey had slept well and was hungry. I served the fried eggs, bacon, toast and butter and brought the orange juice, glittering in the bright morning light.

In separate dishes, I placed chopped fresh herbs, picked that morning from the garden plot. And sat down to enjoy breakfast with my family. After a night of tasting, I didn't want anything myself but gladly downed half a glass of juice in one, savoring its sharp sourness as it tingled over my taste buds, refreshing my parched throat and falling like a cool waterfall down to my stomach laden with the fried eggs, bacon, toast and pancakes that I had consumed over the previous seven hours.

"You got up early today?" Rachel asked, "I woke up at five and you weren't there."

"To be honest, honey, I hardly slept at all. I almost immediately... went down to the studio to try something out."

"I see," my wife nodded sadly.

"No, no, don't get me wrong. I've had an excellent idea, I'll tell you all about it after breakfast. Trust me! I haven't slept but I'm in an excellent mood. And I promise that I'll be sleeping like a baby at your side all night tonight. All right maybe not sleeping... But together. Okay? Come on, give me a smile."

"Alright, baby, we'll see," Rachel stroked my hand.

"Daddy, look," Stacey interrupted us, "you see, all the eggs are different," she passed her hand over our plates. "Some are a bit crooked, some are a bit over-cooked, no offence, dad but these things happen. But they're *real* eggs, made in a real frying pan. You can see from the way they look and taste. Here, try," she proffered me a piece of her fried egg on her fork.

"Yes I know, mine is exactly the same," I replied.

"But look they're not the same!" Stacey objected, "Even the taste of the eggs from each chicken is different, dad. Don't tell me you can't taste it."

"I can taste it, darling. Yum, yum!" I loudly gobbled the piece of fried egg from her fork, making her giggle. "But you're right, yours are tastier. And I'm sorry if I over-cooked it, I tried to make sure yours were very lightly fried."

"You haven't overcooked anything, she's just imagining things," Paul spoke up in my defence. "I like the crusty bit on the bottom, especially the frilly edges, they're legend!"

Stacey rolled her eyes and looked at her mother as if to say, 'what can you expect, they're only boys...'

I also turned to Rachel:

"Are you happy?"

"With my fried egg – yes. But not with the fact that you've been up all night – no. And you're not eating at all. I'm guessing you overdid it with the tasting last night, am I right?"

"I may have," I smiled, "when you've finished your fried eggs, I'll bring in the pancakes, tea and coffee."

"Dad, if you're not going to eat your egg, can I have it?" Paul asked and I gladly handed him my helping. "Thank you. It would be a crime to let such a delicacy go to waste, wouldn't it?"

"You're right, son, you're absolutely right," then I looked at each of them in turn, "You know that I love you all very much, don't you?"

"What are you on about dad?" Paul asked and the girls looked at me questioningly, "And we love you too. Is everything alright?"

"Everything is fine, fella," I reached out and ruffled his red hair, "everything is just perfect."

There was a week to go before the 'food-fight', and I knew that my plan to present my updated signature breakfast was going to be a surefire winner. Only none of that mattered. I didn't care what the judges were going to say.

I had now already won my most important battle.

The Monster in the Closet

Translated by Simon Geoghegan

The monster in the closet stirred again, quietly scratching against the wood and rustling the clothes. Jimmy tensed and pulled the blanket right up to his chin, glancing warily towards the closet.

A narrow strip of warm light pierced the gap under the door but did not reach the part of the room where the creature lurked in the deep shadows. It had been waiting until everyone in the house had fallen asleep, so that quietly, with barely a creak of the closet door, it could sneak up to the sleeping boy's bed and eat him.

Jimmy was convinced of this and he was terrified. There were tears in his eyes, he wanted to cry and call his parents for help. But his mother would always tell him that monsters don't exist and his dad said that he was big enough to deal with his monsters on his own now.

And indeed, he had dealt with them. He had seen off the one who rustled the curtains and tapped against the window as well as the one hiding under his bed ready to grab him by the bare feet and drag him into the darkness. They had been easy. Well, almost easy.

Not long ago on his fifth birthday, dad had said that he was already grown-up enough to be trusted with a serious anti-monster weapon. A powerful LED flashlight capable of sending any monster packing with its beam of magic light.

The torch was large, heavy and powered by six whole batteries. It was yellow and so powerful that Jimmy quickly drove out the creature hiding under the bed. Forever and ever. After all, it was an anti-monster torch.

Dad had also given him a lightsaber, a real Jedi one. He and dad trained a lot and dad said Jimmy was doing well. His sword shone brightly in the dark with a white, blue or green gleam.

"Why not red?" asked Jimmy.

"It'll only turn red if you go over to the dark side, son," said dad.

Jimmy didn't understand much about the dark side but a red sword would have been pretty cool. When they fought with their lightsabers, Jimmy was usually the young Skywalker, and dad said that he would be his 'yoga' master. Jimmy also wanted to become a 'yoga' master but in order to achieve this, he needed to do a lot more training. And to become an adult.

It was thanks to the Jedi sword that he'd been able to defeat the curtain-flapping monster. Jimmy hacked and hacked at him until he too finally disappeared. He had clearly been impressed by a real Jedi lightsaber and no longer bothered Jimmy at night.

For several months there was peace and quiet until the monster hiding in the closet turned up. He had already been hiding there for a week but Jimmy felt that he was getting bolder and readying himself for an attack. Although he was still only a young Padawan apprentice, he had already had dealings with monsters, and so he decided to take the fight to this new intruder.

In order to do this, he would need to be well fortified. What was required was not just any ordinary children's food, but a special high... high protein food for hunting monsters at night.

"Mom, are these anti-monster cookies?" Jimmy asked, as his mother placed a glass of milk and a bowl of cookies in front of him.

"Honey, monsters don't exist, now eat up," Mom patted his hair with a gentle smile and kissed his forehead.

But dad winked at him over her shoulder, indicating that they definitely were. Mom hadn't spotted him. It was their little secret. Jimmy winked at his dad in response and then ate everything in front of him down to the final crumb of cookie and last drop of milk. The upcoming battle was going to be a serious test and he needed all the strength he could get.

The subdued scratching and breathing continued to issue from the closet. The monster seemed hungry. He was probably in a bad mood and perhaps big enough to take up the whole closet. Jimmy went over his plan again in his head. He would open the door and blind the monster with his flashlight. If the creature didn't immediately run away in fright, Jimmy would chop him up with his Jedi saber until he evaporated. He crept slowly up to the closet, stepping quietly in his bare feet on the thick soft carpet. In his left hand, he held the flashlight, in his right the lightsaber. He was ready for battle.

His heart was pounding and he desperately wanted to jump back under the bed covers. But there was no turning back, he couldn't allow himself to be like some kind of four-year-old scaredy-cat. With his right hand, he tore open the door and with his left hand, he thrust the anti-monster light into the darkness, switching it on to full brightness.

"Ahhhh!" The monster squealed in fright, shading his eyes from the light with his furry paws, and Jimmy almost screamed back.

He wanted to scream, but his voice somehow failed him.

"What's the matter with you, shining your light into people's eyes like that..?!" The monster wailed in a thin indignant voice.

"Oh, sorry," Jimmy muttered.

He felt embarrassed and turned off the flashlight, relying instead on the bright white light of his Jedi saber.

The monster removed its paws from its face and looked at the boy with its large green eyes. He was very small and barely reached above Jimmy's midriff. He was plump and shaggy like a teddy bear, with huge green eyes and large sharp teeth set in a wide mouth.

Jimmy tightened his grip on the sword, ready to deliver a crushing blow to the monster and drive it away. Breathe out, step forward, swing and strike.

"You are one strange monster," the creature squeaked from the closet.

"What?" Completely taken aback, Jimmy was stopped in his tracks barely half a step away from his foe, "I'm not a monster! I'm Jimmy!"

"I've never heard of them before," the creature scratched its shaggy head.

"My name is Jimmy. I'm a boy," he tried to explain to the slow-witted monster.

"I've never heard of boys. What are you doing in my closet?" This was really getting too much. Jimmy grimly checked his lightsabre settings.

"This is my closet."

"You really are a strange monster. So big, pale and smooth-skinned. And the only hair you have is growing out of the top of your head. Eurgh! Horrible!" The monster made some strange gurgling and snorting sounds.

"I'm not a monster. It's you who's the monster. And I have an anti-monster lightsaber, got it?"

The creature grimaced and hissed as Jimmy raised his sword.

"I was right not to believe my parents when they said that monsters don't exist. I told them there was one in my closet. But they wouldn't believe me. And here you are, all huge, bare-skinned and ugly with that stupid glowing stick in your paw.

"It's not a stick, it's a Jedi saber!" Said Jimmy somewhat peevishly.

"A Jedi what?"

What was the point of explaining? If the monster still hadn't heard of Jedi Knights and the force he was probably too small to understand anything? And it's not nice to be nasty to little kids. With a sigh, Jimmy sat down on the carpet next to the open closet. His powerful flashlight had probably really frightened the little monster. Not to mention his saber...

He put down his weapon and held his hand out to the creature.

"Don't be afraid, I won't hurt you."

"But I'm not afraid of you," said the furry creature tossing his head back and baring his teeth, "I'm seven years old, you know, and I'm not afraid of anyone, so there! And I'm not a monster either, my name is Afihah."

Ah, then he can't be that much of a baby. But, the more Jimmy peered at his nocturnal guest, the more harmless he seemed, despite his frightening appearance. What if he were to make friends with him?

"And my name is Jimmy."

"You've already said that."

Jimmy picked up a small fire engine from the carpet and handed it to the monster.

"Here, you can have it."

Afihah warily took the toy in his clawed paw and cautiously brought it up to his open mouth.

"Stop!" Jimmy shouted and the monster jumped back into the depths of the closet, "You can't eat that! It's a fire truck!"

"Then what's it for if you can't eat it?" The creature asked in surprise.

"To put out fires," Jimmy answered, it was so obvious.

"Okay," the monster clearly didn't understand him, but nodded his head as a sign of agreement, "Then this is for you."

"What is it?" Jimmy peered cautiously at the strange object the creature was holding out to him.

It looked like a flattened, uneven ball covered in spikes and had the appearance of the small spiny pufferfish that hung from their kitchen ceiling. Jimmy gingerly touched the spikes, they weren't sharp at all but soft and silky. He carefully held the gift in his hands.

"It's a puit."

"A what?" Jimmy said, mystified.

"A puit. Haven't you ever had a puit? Don't you know what it's for..?" The monster asked in amazement.

"No."

Outside in the corridor, fast approaching footsteps could be heard. Mom! There was no way she could be allowed to see the monster, she didn't believe in them.

"It's my mom, hide!" Jimmy hissed, closing the closet and, in three short bounds, hurled himself under the covers.

The door opened quietly and a stream of bright light swept half of the room. Jimmy held his breath in order not to give himself away, carefully peeping through the slits of his closed eyes.

"Baby, are you asleep?"

Jimmy was silent and barely breathing.

He looked like he was. "Night, night, sweetheart."

Mom closed the door and her soft steps receded down the corridor and around the corner. Jimmy tip-toed to the closet and quietly opened it, but the monster had disappeared.

"Afihah!" He whispered, "Hey Afihah! Are you there?"

But the closet was bare.

Maybe he had been dreaming it all? And there had never been a monster? No Afihah whatsoever? Perhaps it had all been because of his fear. Jimmy shrugged and moved back towards his bed. Picking up his anti-monster weapons on the way.

But as he climbed under the covers, Jimmy's hand felt something soft and silky. The puit. He had completely forgotten about it. That meant he hadn't imagined it and Afihah was a real monster. In Jimmy's own closet. Mom had probably scared him off but tomorrow night he would try to find him again.

Why had Afihah said that Jimmy was living in the closet in his room? It all seemed very strange somehow. And why had he thought Jimmy was a monster. He wasn't a monster. He really wasn't. Maybe monsters are a bit strange.

And what was this puit? What was it for? What was he meant to do with it? He would have to ask Afihah tomorrow. Whatever it was, it glowed faintly in the dark, a cloud of faint golden sparkles whirling in the middle of it. It was beautiful.

Jimmy put the puit in his bedside drawer so that mom wouldn't find it in the morning. Otherwise, she would ask what he was doing with it and Jimmy wouldn't be able to explain what a puit was and what it was for.

"All the same, mom makes a really mean anti-monster cookie," he murmured to himself as he fell asleep with a contented smile on his face.

Failure

Translated by Simon Geoghegan

"You are responsible for the failure of this mission, agent. We're going to have to suspend you from working in the field for now and lock your access clearance."

"What do you mean, for now?"

"Officially, this is for the period of the investigation, but... I'll be honest with you - I don't think you'll be working again."

"But that's grossly unfair!"

"Unfair? Unfair..?! You've wrecked a crucial mission. Many years and enormous resources have been invested in your training and deployment. Many talented agents have been sacrificed for the sake of this operation. And for what? For you to carelessly give everything away, destroying all our efforts in the process. And all because of some... local woman..?"

"But that's not true! She had nothing to do with it!"

"Who are you trying to kid now, agent? Us or yourself? We've read your reports, we've been watching you. I thought you might at least have the self-esteem not to cover up your failure with lies. Especially as you are still under oath."

"But she really isn't to blame for what happened. It was just an unlucky series of events. Everything was going to plan when..."

"There is no room for luck in our business, agent! You should have had every eventuality covered. And that's all there is to it! You had the full might of the Agency's analytical department at your disposal. You know, I told them you weren't ready for this assignment. I was against giving you the job. If you hadn't been the Director's protege, the Committee would never have given it to you. Do you have any idea how high the stakes were? You had no right to make a mistake."

"I realise that..."

"You realise that? Are you being serious? Do you know how long it will be before we can ever embed another agent in your place? How many opportunities will have been missed? And by then it might already be too late."

"But it was a set-up! They arrested me on a false charge. And they didn't get a thing out of me, I didn't break even when I was tortured."

"That's because you'd already leaked too much valuable information without having to be."

"Now listen, here! I was acting in the interests of the operation, from tactical necessity. I'm very sorry that everything turned out as it did..."

"You're sorry? Your sorrow's not going to help anyone now, agent. The mission is in tatters. There's no going back. By the way, your file has been passed on to the internal investigation department. They have a lot of questions they want to ask you. You have breached the security protocols and allowed a serious leak of classified information to take place. What's more, you will be charged with misusing the Agency's resources and money."

"I only used what was necessary for the mission to be a success."

"And? Was it a success?"

"Don't insult my intelligence with your pathetic bullying tactics! We all knew there was going to be a chance of failure. The mission was too complex for just one agent, and from the outset, I asked to have more people with me on the ground. With a good team we could have done it. But instead of this, I was ordered to recruit from the local population. Untrained locals. What did you expect? Of course, it was going to increase the likelihood of a screw-up!"

"Leave your excuses for the Committee, agent. You'll be needing them. Or why not have it analysed by your shrink. You might feel a bit better about yourself once you've had a good cry on her shoulder."

"What shrink?"

"Oh... Didn't I mention it? You will have to undergo a course of psychotherapy. In theory, the psychologist's report might have some bearing on the Committee's decision about your fitness to ever be allowed out into the field again. But I don't think it's going to make any difference in this case."

"Why?"

"Use your brains. Multiple violations, accusations of negligence and corruption, a vital mission in ruins... In any case, there are bound to be psychological scars after what you've been through. You were betrayed by the very agents you yourself recruited. You were held in prison for a long time, they viciously tortured you, they tried to break you, they tried to kill you."

"I'm fine."

"I doubt it. But that's not for me to decide, that's up to the psychologist. I imagine you'll be prescribed therapy every day for several months. Purely for humanitarian reasons, after all you've been through I should probably pity you. But... If I was to be brutally honest. It was only with great difficulty that we managed to get you out of there when things really began to get sticky. If the decision had been left to me, I wouldn't have bothered risking the Agency's precious resources and agents on you."

"Well, thank you very much."

"Well, what were you expecting? As far as I'm concerned, you're a disgrace to the Agency. In the past, only highly-experienced, well-trained operatives would have been given an assignment of this importance, not some snot-nosed greenhorn."

"You'd better watch what you're saying, you're stepping on thin ice."

"Only, you're not as tough as you talk, are you agent? During your mission, you allowed enemy forces to take you unarmed. You were taken by surprise and put up no resistance."

"I had no choice. Otherwise, the agents I had recruited might have suffered."

"So what? There's always going to be collateral damage. You can't make an omelette without breaking eggs."

"I doubt you would have said the same thing if they had been our agents as opposed to local ones? Can you not see your own breathtaking arrogance and double standards..."

"That's enough, agent! You're forgetting yourself!"

"I'll be filing a formal complaint with the Committee, your behavior is totally unacceptable."

"Feel free to file away whatever you want. Now, onto the next point. During the investigation, you will remain at the Agency's headquarters. You will be forbidden to leave the base or make contact with anyone involved in the operation, including the agents you recruited."

"But that's not possible! I gave them my word, I would be there the day after tomorrow! I have to meet up with several of my local contacts. I can't let them down! They are counting on me!"

"It's over, agent. There will be no more meetings. The operation is over. Period. You have failed everyone you recruited, not just us. Right now, they think you're dead. And it would be better if that's how it stays. You've already created enough problems. So, don't you go forgetting the protocols."

"I can still put things right, not everything is lost, believe me."

"Well, the top brass don't agree with you. The plug has been pulled on the entire project, thanks to your failure the risks have increased exponentially. A special group will be sent to carry out the clean-up operation. All twelve of your hand-picked local agents will have to be eliminated. Just as we had to eliminate the informant who betrayed you."

"You can't! It's cruel and inhuman!"

"Oh, I think you'll find we can. Actually, we are obliged to do this. If you hadn't failed your mission, no one would have touched them. But now they know far too much. And we can't risk any more leaks. You only have yourself to blame for all this."

"You've become used to acting with brute force. But your methods are out of date. "These days hybrid and information warfare is so much more effective than your barbarous and bloodthirsty interventions. When are you ever get that into your head..?!"

"Who do you think you are, agent? Do you still think you're out there play-acting? You have immersed yourself too deeply in your own legendary status? Over there, you might be the Messiah, the chosen one, the heavenly anointed, the Son of God. But here you're nothing more than a disgraced operative who has screwed up his most important mission. Enough! You are dismissed, agent. Guards, take him away!"

Plus Ten

Translated by Britain Yakovleva

It turned out that the most crucial thing was the fact that the human body has its unyielding limits. Constraints that are impossible to surpass.

Of course, the idea of super soldiers – perfected and deadly effective warriors – was not a new one. This battlefield has claimed the lives of no small amount of scientists and labs, working for every imaginable governmental (and supposedly non-governmental) organization around the globe.

Due to safety precautions, many similar projects have appeared and then disappeared without a trace over the last century, and had differing levels of success and failure, no matter what the initial goals were of any of the experiments.

I think we were the first project that achieved a serious breakthrough in this area. We were able to significantly modify our test subjects, but in the pursuit of results we discovered the limits of our potential. We called it, the Absolute Threshold.

No matter which human abilities we sought to perfect, we could never overcome certain limitations. Nature and evolution wouldn't allow us to change a person beyond a certain degree.

We didn't create any superpowers, we just amplified a soldier's strength, speed or intellect. But the amplification of all these qualities at once, in different combinations, could not exceed certain amounts. Once exceeded, we would lose our subjects completely, for their bodies couldn't handle that level of interference.

Our technology was genius and revolutionary, but didn't allow us to create soldiers ideal in every aspect. If we made them as strong as possible, we couldn't make them fast and intelligent. Conversely, if we made them fast and intelligent, they couldn't be super strong.

It was like a computer game, where you have a limited amount of points to upgrade your player, and you have to choose which characteristics to boost.

So, where our Absolute Threshold represented 100%, we decided to develop each ability in increments of 10%. To do this we needed to assign strength, speed and intellect points adding up to 10 points of our incremental upgrade. It was oversimplified, but this made it easier to model. In order to define the specific parameters needed we had to first establish the ideal and most basic modification for our soldiers.

I was head of the analytical team, and our goal was to develop testing scenarios to discern which ability ratios were the most favorable in our subjects. Simply put, the goal was to produce ideal soldiers within the limitations. We were also tasked to pair potential combinations of abilities with their application in solving specific tactical tasks.

We developed a few key scenarios for the different groups, which were supposed to be tested live in a specially equipped top-secret training ground.

It was predictable, that the first group, which the military wanted to test, was the group with increased strength.

The official prototype name was Force Majeure, because it was postulated that these soldiers would be unstoppably strong. But we among the developers of this project, called them the Bogeymen.

From average soldiers we crafted muscular beasts, with highly increased muscle mass, denser bone structure, increased endurance and a very high pain threshold. In everything else they remained as they were before the application of our experimental methods.

The squad of ten Bogeymen landed in the training ground and went to find and destroy their enemy. The first test involved mannequins placed in the deserted cityscape zone. The Force Majeur team easily cleared the rough terrain, found their targets and using only knives made quick work of the automated mannequins, and destroyed what little was left of the surrounding buildings.

They beat the time of the control group, made up of special forces, which had faced the same task. The military was pleased with the results, because this particular modification seemed the most promising.

The second level of the test was supposed to include lightly armed opponents, who were entrenched in the woods. This time the Bogeymen had to engage a real live squad of twenty ordinary infantry soldiers, and it was a blood bath. In their rage they literally tore the poor guys limb from limb with their bare hands.

Huge physical force required a greater release of noradrenaline, adrenaline and testosterone, which in turn led to heightened levels of aggression in our subjects. The minute our Bogeymen encountered real people they didn't just become more feral, but split up into hotbeds of wild uncontrollable fighting.

The military representatives observing the scene were shocked and baffled by the results of the second test, and after a quick sidebar decided that +10 strength was overkill. They suggested that the Force Majeur prototypes be adjusted to +8 strength and +2 intellect, for a more reasonable balance.

Since protocol had to be strictly adhered to, we couldn't stop the officially finalized experimentation schedule. The next level of tests was reserved for the rest of soldiers with +10 modifications in one aspect, and then we could move on to the soldiers with combined modifications.

Among the officers were those who had great hopes for this next particular group of soldiers. They called them the Velociraptors because of that dinosaur's reputation for being one of the fastest predators. Among the developers we affectionately called those who had +10 speed, the Nimbles.

This type of soldier was unique because of his incredibly quick reflexes, lighting fast movement, and ability to move very quickly from one place to another. These were good abilities for diversion tactics or surprise attacks. Though they couldn't dodge bullets like the officers had hoped, they were still moving targets which were difficult to shoot.

After receiving their assignments, the Raptors swiftly covered the ground to their designated settlement, and with quick, accurate throws, decimated the dummies representing the enemy's fighters and battle equipment. They did this in record time, not only beating the time of the control group, but also that of the Bogeys. This considerably lightened the mood and revived the fighting spirit of those observing the experiments, and everyone slowly started to forget the failure of the first group. They couldn't wait to see the results of the next test, where the Nimbles were expected to neutralize a live enemy in the woods.

Another swift throw later, and the squad of regular soldiers was crushed by a sudden stream of coordinated Raptor attacks. They surrounded the enemy lines and confounded them with quick, synchronized attacks from different angles, then captured and disarmed them.

When they had almost finished rounding up all the captives one of the Nimbles lost his marbles and started shooting the captives with the confiscated weapons. I have to admit that I never really liked the pure Velociraptor modification, they were still imperfect in their own way.

Their unnaturally quick nerve impulses and chemical reactions, which their metabolism required, burned them out, which led to exhaustion, hysterics, and nervous breakdowns. Among the first test subjects there were many instances of psychosis, suicide and irrational violence.

So naturally during the test something went wrong, and as a result one Nimble pounced and cut the throat of the one who had shot the captives, and led to a fight which killed half the squad and left the rest of the Nimbles heavily wounded.

The disappointment of the officers was obvious, as well the tension in the air. The last thing we needed was another fight right here in the bunker. Happily, the old farts just shot angry wolfish looks at each other, exchanged toothless threats and blamed each other (and us) for the failure.

They partially blamed me, for developing these particular tests, though their bosses had been the ones to approve these tests in the first place, based on their very own briefs. Ungrateful swine. I told them they should have tested soldiers with +10 intellect, but they just laughed and replied that they needed warriors, not nerds. So our "Nerds" never made it into the experiment protocol.

I did try to explain that evolution has taught us that the intelligent will always control the strong. But by the offended looks on the officer's faces, I realized that my words were misunderstood, and I decided to just shut up.

Nonetheless, the observers still had hopes for more balanced versions of the Raptors, something with +8 speed, and +2 strength, or +8 speed, +1 strength and +1 intellect. I wish those approving the programs, as well as the officers present had at least a miserable +1 intellect...

But before we could proceed to the hybrid types of soldiers, the protocol dictated a Bogeymen vs. Nimbles test. This turned out to be a terrible idea.

On the bright side, I won 20 bucks from the assistant bio engineer. We had only just started taking bets and that idiot declared that the Bogeys were going to kick some Raptor ass. I tried to explain the physics to him, that any hit is an impulse, which means speed multiplied by mass. And that in this case, speed is the deciding factor. But, as is often the case with today's youth, he didn't want to listen, and babbled on about sturdy bone structure, low sensitivity to pain, and other idiocy. Which he ended up paying 20 dollars for.

And yes, I can concede that in battle the Force Majeurs are truly terrifying, three unlucky Nimbles got turned into ground beef. The other seven Velociraptors proved my theory: speed was more important in battle than brute strength or tough-skinned endurance.

The Nimbles dodged their heavier opponents with ease, dealing violent, crippling blows in those areas which were guaranteed to destroy them, no matter what their pain threshold was. The bio engineers assistant should have considered that the human body has many weak areas capable of paralyzing a man in battle – Adam's apple, the base of the neck, eyes, temples, jaw socket, knee socket, the tendons under the knee and the Achilles tendon, groin, tailbone, spine – as well as a myriad of nerve endings and other built-in vulnerable spots.

Crippled and broken, the Bogeymen writhed on the ground, but two of them were too stubborn and unyielding to die, and were fighting till the last breath. A last breath can be pretty rough when your Adam's apple has been torn out, or your throat is ripped open.

Then an argument broke out among the Raptors about whether or not to execute the remaining Force Majeurs to avenge the three deaths of their brethren. Thankfully they had enough sense to remember that their orders were to take their captives alive, but since nothing was said about "unharmed" the remaining Nimbles let loose their last of their pent up battle hormones on the culprits.

The observing officers started debating so hotly that they barely avoided a fist fight. Tempers were running high, and those who previously backed the strength modifications were forced to rethink the importance of speed.

Nonetheless, this test concluded the first phase of field trials where we tested the "pure" prototypes, whose strength and speed were cranked up to the highest possible level allowed by the Absolute Threshold scale. If anyone had asked me (which they didn't) I would have told them that this was a pointless waste of time and resources. But what can you expect from the military? They won't divert from the approved plan by an inch, even if they're staring down the barrel of a gun.

The second phase of the experiment was made to test the hybrid soldier prototypes. Those who received +5 speed and +5 strength we dubbed the Monsters, because they were truly beasts: strong, fast, unyielding and unmerciful.

This time the generals were jumping up and down and hugging each other. This squad completed the first task with flying colors, and cleanly neutralized the enemy. They did not beat the Raptors' time, but they were organized and up to military standard. Balance had been achieved, and now the question was only which exact ratio of increased abilities (how much strength or how much speed) would be the most optimal. Basically, that's what the second phase was for in the first place.

But in order to test the parameters of the perfect soldier, we needed to test two more groups of "Fives," hybrids with equal quantities of modified abilities. For example, +5 strength and +5 intellect, or +5 speed and +5 intellect. Officially they were called Intelli-Forces and Intelli-Raptors (if only I could get my hands on the dummy who was in charge of marketing). So we called them Demi-Bogeys and Demi-Nimbles.

To everyone's surprise, both teams achieved fantastic results, which according to protocol, meant that they had to go an extra round. All three teams of Fives received identical missions to fight against enemies that were better equipped, and outnumbered them.

Is it worth gloating over the fact that the quick acting and very strong Monsters were whipped by a large group of regular soldiers? The pressure was useless where the enemy was at such an advantage.

I have to say, the Demi-Nimbles and Demi-Bogeys executed their battle tasks brilliantly. They were synchronized, organized, and each squad came up with a plan, which used their strengths to the best of their ability.

It's worth noting that +5 intellect significantly added to the team spirit in each of the squads and made them more organized, more able to delegate the tactical tasks, and gave them a clear self-organized hierarchy with firm discipline.

The officers were very delighted and discussed the impending fight between the Intelli-Forces and Intelli-Raptors, and I saw some bills change hands. I guess that means even imbeciles in uniform are capable of a little humanity. Good for them, I wouldn't mind betting on this fight between the finalists myself.

As we got ready for the next round of half-strength vs. half-speed, everyone amiably discussed the third phase of the project, the testing of soldiers with all three categories – strength, speed and intellect – modified in varying combinations. Everyone had become convinced that adding intellect to the warriors was the right way to go, since everyone likes organized disciplined soldiers. But only time (and another series of tests) would tell which combination was the golden ratio, +3 +3 +4 or +4 +4 +3 or +4 +4 +2.

Now there were a lot more supporters of the balanced modifications prototype. This meant that the generals were not after all, a dead end in the evolutionary chain, but people capable of learning something new (even if it was just learning from their own mistakes).

We were all beginning to get tired of testing day after day, and starting to get on each other's nerves. Conflicts broke out more often, despite the obvious progress we were making in identifying the perfect combination of modified abilities needed for the perfect soldier.

It was therefore no surprise that one day I also failed to control myself, and when one of the officers made another arrogant remark, I declared that they were all idiots, and they should have understood that adding intellect was the key to the victories of the last two hybrid squads. Only imbeciles of the highest quality could ignore the obvious conclusion: we had missed the most important test, the Nerds, who had +10 intellect.

My emotional outburst not only led to complete silence, but to yet another wave of arguments. The officer whom I had offended happened to head up the Defense Intelligence and special ops unit, and I barely escaped him getting violent with me. The experiments were stopped, due to unanimous agreement that this extraordinary situation called for measures not accounted for in the protocol.

The whole team of military observers moved into the soundproofed meeting room to discuss their official position, and to get in contact with their distant chain of command.

My colleagues and I were astonished when as a result of long and tumultuous discussion the intelligence commander handed me a folder containing protocol "Bravo", which was to be put into effect immediately. Then he fished a hundred dollar bill out of his pocket and slapped it down on top of the folder – a bet against the Nerds.

That's the story of how we retraced our steps and started at phase one again, in order to completely test the squad which had the +10 intellect modification. Since protocol "Alpha" hadn't included this type of soldier in the original tests, they did not have an official name, and "Nerds" stuck instantly.

I was bursting with pride and joy, and was confident that this team was going to be the favorite of the season, blast all the other competition out of the park, and go straight to the victory-deciding finals. I hadn't dared hope that this phase would actually take place, and now I was looking at my dream team.

Outwardly, the Nerds were no different from regular soldiers, they didn't look like geeks, and this piqued everyone's interest. I saw that now, the bets were being unashamedly exchanged.

The newbies turned out to be incredibly organized and coordinated. They completed their first task like well-oiled machine. It wasn't very powerful, or astonishingly fast, but it was an example of coordination worthy of imitation on every level. There wasn't a single careless movement, or maneuver which hadn't been thought through down to the smallest detail, and agreed upon inside the team.

The way in which the Nerds dealt with the live enemy was 100% by the book. You could literally write a manual on special operations based on their example. They ghosted by the enemy's ramparts, and soundlessly neutralized the enemy soldiers. In a little over 40 seconds the enemy camp was surrounded, and not a sound, not a shot fired, not a single casualty on either side.

Amazed silence reigned in the bunker as everyone digested the experiment that they had just seen. Incredibly pleased with myself, I slowly reached across the table and took the hundred dollar bill which had been waiting for its victor, and even more slowly and smugly put the bill in my pocket.

Following the crushing victory of the Nerds, was the impending fight against the enemy that was superior and better equipped. And we were not disappointed. It was a real show, with our faces glued to the monitors as we watched this coordinated team methodically and cleanly disarm the sentries, and then after creating a diversion in the form of several synchronized bombs in the heart of the enemy camp, create absolute panic in the enemy lines.

Using the diversion and resulting smokescreen to their advantage they cold-bloodedly neutralized what was left of the opposition. They had been up against a hundred of skilled soldiers with lethal weapons, while the ten Nerds only had knives and other equipment. Do you know how many were injured?

One. One who accidentally caught a bullet in his shoulder during the chaos which ensued when the terrified enemy started shooting in every direction. And do you know how many victims there were from the hundred that went up against the Nerds?

Three. One was killed by an accidental bullet from his comrade, one was slightly wounded, and one shit himself during the explosions. Over thirty soldiers willingly surrendered themselves to the ten Nerds.

To say that the overriding reaction in the bunker was astonishment is to say nothing at all. Most of the generals looked scared, and the officer in charge of the special operations winked at me as though we were buddies now or something.

The stakes got higher, literally and figuratively.

Since the Nerd team had survived all the phases with their team members intact, we didn't replace them with other specimens, but gave them a day to recuperate.

When it was time to move on to the next phase, the Nerds were supposed to fight the Bogeymen. We all understood that our intellectual friends were incredibly good, and even though the other side had had many more advantages, they had easily completed the task. But those had been ordinary soldiers. The Nerds were going to have a tough time beating the aggressive Force Majeurs with their bare hands.

We amiably discussed what we would do if we were in their place, and from the general mood I understood that most were favoring the Nerds today.

But we were not even close to imagining what strategy they had come up with.

In order to avoid a full confrontation, the Nerds retreated from the open ground in a slow, organized manner and went in the direction of the half-deserted city, where two days earlier they had shockingly captured one hundred soldiers.

It was obvious that they were luring the Bogeymen away from an open attack, and towards more urban terrain suitable for street fighting where they would have at least some form of advantage. It was a good and logical plan, one which several of the officers (as well as a certain person from my team) had anticipated.

The Nerds dissolved into the houses, while the Force Majeurs advanced in a thick group like a pack of hungry wolves. When they were within 200 feet of the closest buildings, the first shot rang out, followed by exactly nine more.

Hell broke loose in the bunker. The Nerds did not have, and were not supposed to have, any weapons! But it seemed that in the last experiment they had been completing more than one task. They not only disarmed their opponent, but had also smuggled several firearms past security.

This was not just tactics, but strategy. They had prepared beforehand for any difficult mission that was awaiting them.

Ten shots. Ten bodies. Collapsed on the ground with bullets in their legs.

Twenty minutes of tactical preparation and five seconds of actual action.

The protocol did not account for this. The Nerds had disobeyed the rules of the game, but it had never been officially stated that they were not allowed to save resources from previous tasks in order to accomplish their future missions. It was unprecedented, and yet... so logical.

Other squads had not been so farsighted and purposeful. Everyone knew that the impending fight with the Velociraptors was probably going to end up more or less with the same result. Even if we confiscated the weapons used by the Nerds, we had no way of knowing what else they had up their sleeves.

For some reason everyone's eyes seemed to rest on me, perhaps, since I was the person who had suggested that we bring this new team into the testing. And, even though I knew this wasn't accounted for in the protocol, I had nothing better to suggest, then the one opponent able to beat our Nerds.

Other Nerds. And more of them.

And so, when the day came for the real test, we chose twenty new and fresh, well-armed Nerds, and dropped them off at the training ground with the mission of capturing and disarming the old team, which we had ordered to occupy the territory. It seemed likely that there would be new favorites this time.

While the new Nerds were busy with reconnaissance, a green signal flare shot up from among the city ruins, and everyone's eyes were drawn to the white flag, fluttering in the wind above one of the buildings.

We couldn't believe that the old Nerds had given up so easily! Though their +10 intellect was probably enough to make them realize that they were in a losing battle from the start. Then again, perhaps it was just a sneaky plan to trap a gullible opponent.

However, the freshly arrived recruits were not what you would call gullible, so they called back their scouts, and sent a patrol of three armed soldiers to check and see if the flag was just cheese in a mousetrap, or a genuine capitulation.

Holding our breath, we waited as the patrol crossed the 200 foot line near the buildings, where the old Nerds had previously mowed down the squad of Bogeymen. But there were no shots sounded, so the patrol slowly and cautiously entered the city.

There were still no shots or explosions, and when the patrol got to the building with the flag on top, they entered and stayed there for some time. There were no cameras inside the building, and drones could not fly in there, so for some time all we could do was wait in tense silence.

In a few minutes the patrol left the building, meaning there was no trap, everything was clear. Having left, the three soldiers still exercised caution as they exited the city and headed to the location where the rest of their team was waiting.

When they reunited with their squad, they reported for some time to their commander, after which he issued a few short commands, and then the whole squad started moving in the direction of the city ruins.

We expected them to storm the city or try and capture their enemy, but they calmly entered the city, and then entered that same building in an orderly fashion; the building which seemed to be a dilapidated church with a crooked spire, or else the old town hall.

At some point during our anxious waiting we realized that there would be no fight, and there would be no surrender, because the Nerds wouldn't fight each other, but instead rallied together. And that's what got us seriously scared.

We had thought they were the perfect soldiers, but as it turns out, that was the exact opposite of what they were. They did not want to fight someone else's war, especially not for our entertainment and certainly not in the name of science. Both groups had disobeyed direct orders. Could you call it deserting? Or had they gone over to the enemy?

It's hard to say, because formally the experiment wasn't a real war, and a lot of the jurisdictional fine print couldn't be applied. But they had disobeyed an order, and that not only meant that they weren't ideal soldiers, but that they were the next target.

I was crushed. I had so blindly believed in the potential of the Nerds, that I hadn't noticed when they tricked us at every turn. And now they would have to be destroyed along with the training grounds by a powerful cleanup team, and call into doubt the results of our whole experiment.

I don't know how my analysts didn't predict this outcome as a possibility. It was probably all due to the social factor. We tested the Nerds at different stages of the experiment, and in laboratory conditions they completed every test perfectly, and would have given any Nobel laureate a run for their money in many of the scientific disciplines.

In the field testing they were also phenomenal, showing exceptional results in shooting, and hand to hand combat, while in tactics and strategic thinking they exceeded all of our expectations. But there had never been real Nerds, ones with +10 intellect. They had always been hybrids, mixed with strength or speed. We had never tested anyone who had more than +8 intellect. Our analysis had shown that pure Nerds were not fit to be foot soldiers, but officers, and only then they would be able to realize their full potential.

I don't know if it's worth noting the wave of negativity that we received from the military officers who had been observing the tests then. Maybe they all of a sudden felt threatened by the possible competition for their jobs, because that's when all further testing of the intellect modifications +8 and up were frozen.

I was mortified by the results of the whole experiment, and I was plagued by guilt, because I had been the one to recommend testing the squad of +10 Nerds. In my defense all I can say, is that all previous test results had given us no reason to expect this outcome.

In the field, it's probable that the group dynamic played a role, as a team of Nerds behaved very differently from the way an individual Nerd behaved. Their intellectual power had certain synergy when it was merged, which allowed them to think outside the rules established for each Nerd individually.

It's amazing that in a squad of geniuses there wasn't a struggle for power, or unproductive debates or arguments. Their heightened level of development helped them to smoothly and cleanly overcome all obstacles as one unified team.

They failed the test and screwed up the whole experimental process. But I couldn't help but feel proud of them. I can't imagine anyone else who could have completed their mission with such immaculate results, creative problem solving, and such a high level of organization in the face of unfavorable odds.

Perhaps I had reason to be proud because in a sense it was my faith in power of knowledge and the success of the Nerds, my hope in the ability to test them within protocol, and my arrogance provoked by hours of exhausting discussion with Headquarters which had created them. And my unbridled tongue, will be the spark to ignite the initiation of a new protocol.

And since they were my creations, I couldn't watch the heavily armed team in armored vehicles surround the city, without pain and a deep sense of regret. We knew exactly where the thirty mutinous Nerds had hunkered down – hidden in the basement of the church/town hall – due to the signatures of their implanted trackers on our monitors.

If not for the order to take some of the mutineers alive, the task force would have just turned the building into dust and ash. But this order made it necessary to take a more systematic and risky approach. Assault troops surrounded the building a few blocks out, so that all the paths leading to the building could be fired upon.

When they heard the signal, a few special ops teams threw stun grenades through broken windows, after which two teams simultaneously stormed the building through two entrances.

The last report we heard over the radio was about the fact that they had found thirty bloodied trackers, which had originally been implanted into our subjects, strewn on the floor. After that we heard explosions, and what was a nightmare turned into a true apogee of terror.

The church blew up into the air, followed by a chain of explosions in the surrounding blocks, which exterminated the majority of the assault team. The Nerds didn't have enough explosives or ammunition, but by some unfathomable method they had found or built something which hadn't been anticipated on the training grounds.

They continued to ignore the rules expressed to them by their former commanders, and were thinking far outside the box. In fact, they had long since left the box, and were planted firmly outside it, methodically destroying anyone who was a threat to them.

The survivors of the explosions rushed to retreat, trying to carry wounded with them, but encountered more singular explosions on their path. It was like the whole route of the operation had been calculated ahead of time and mined with bombs in order to create more chaos, panic, and cause more casualties.

Eventually our commanding officers called for helicopters, which leveled the city to the ground, and burned everything to a crisp, not leaving anything living a chance of survival in that hell. Still, everyone was aware that the Nerds had long disappeared and had hid in a different sector of the training ground.

There were only two options, they could either hide in the woods to one side of the city, or in the rocky hillside and ravine on the other side of the training ground. Smoking them out of there would be tough, but the task was simplified when someone started to shoot down our drones one by one flying over the zone near the ravine.

Relieved that we had found the Nerds, the commanders ordered that the remains of the assault team, backup helicopters, and the reserve (made up of a few hundred marines who had been on call in the bunker) be deployed to the battlefield.

Those ignorant paper-pushers. It would have been far more logical to begin evacuation and bomb the whole training ground, but the euphoria at finding the Nerds' location hampered their good sense, which could not be said of our former test subjects.

While the backup marine forces were approaching the main attackers, the bunker suddenly shuddered from an explosion, and the lights went out, triggering the emergency red lighting, and an announcement which informed us of a breach of the outer perimeter.

If someone had been taking bets now, I would have put all the money in my pockets on the Nerds arriving here in the control center within two minutes. Knowing their approach to planning their operations, they'd easily deal with the security guards, kill us all and escape.

Some of the scientists cowered in the corners, while the officers hectically tried to form a final line of defense, getting out their weapons and shaking with fear at the prospect of facing the storm heading towards them.

None of them were thinking about what exactly was going to break free in the following minutes.

We wanted to create the perfect soldiers, honed killers, without blemish or defect, undefeatable. And we succeeded, we actually created them. And now they were ready to explode out into the big, unsuspecting world.

In our attempts to create a human superweapon, we created a new species, which may erase its creators from the face of the earth. And evolution will give way to revolution.

Oh, I think I hear them coming.

Hephaestus

Translated by John William Narins

A hellishly hot shower helped to bring me to my senses, at least a little bit, after that sleepless night. A good, hearty breakfast and a hot cup of coffee would be just the thing now. A bucket of coffee.

I quickly dried myself off, shuddering slightly when the towel cloth caught the edge of a fresh cut. I wiped part of the fogged-over mirror clean with one hand and examined my shoulder – the bite marks had turned dark already, reddish-black bruises.

Oh, no, I wasn't complaining. The girl was undeniably worth it. I'd met her the evening before, in the bar of my hotel in Bangkok. We had a few drinks, talked about this and that. You know, the usual. But then we went up to my room and had a long, crazy wild night.

Right now, though, I could think of nothing but coffee. And meat. And bread – ah yes, bread, too. And maybe some cheese. And then another coffee. Black. Hot. No sugar. Deliberately, savoring the thick, tart bitterness, feeling the caffeine restore my strength and switching my brain back on – a brain sluggish and dense from lack of sleep – and the blood begin to flow faster through my veins.

Reflexively wrapping the towel around my waist, I came out of the bathroom... but then I decided that, after that madcap night, there was nothing really left to be shy about. So I dropped the niceties and came out rubbing my head with the towel. It was a good thing I didn't need a blow-dryer with my hair cropped this short.

"So, you ready to go down and get some breakfast and recharge our batteries?" I asked my new acquaintance, peeking out from under the towel directly into the barrel of a gun.

My gun, I should mention. Which meant that, while I was showering, she had broken into my suitcase. Which meant that she had managed to get around the fingerprint scanner that controlled the lock. Which meant that there was much more to this girl than met the eye. And that she worked for someone of import.

"Surprise!" she said, with a cold smile, sitting on the edge of the insanity we had made of the bed.

"Yes," I said, nodding cautiously, my arms still poised in the air, holding the towel over my head.

I might have guessed. It had all gone too easily yesterday, too smoothly. On the other hand, she didn't pick me up at the bar, I did that. And a vulgar platinum blonde in a trampish dress wasn't my usual taste at all. The logical conclusion would be that it wasn't a set-up, right? Still, she had obviously been set as bait. And I'd been successfully hooked. Correction: caught. With my pants down.

"Listen, if you want money... I don't have too much on me, but I can get more. We can make a deal..."

"Hands where they are!" snapped the blonde, preventing me from lowering my arms and extending my hands in a gesture of peace. "Enough pretending, Carl. And no sudden movements."

I nodded cautiously again, trying to imagine who might have sent her.

"Twitch, and I'll blow your brains out. Cry out, and I'll blow your brains out."

"Curious," I mused pensively. "Last night you did so much of our screaming... this is such a completely different take on loud noises."

If I'd hoped to confuse Abbie, it wasn't working. Abbie wasn't her real name, of course.

"The situation's changed, Carl," said not-Abbie, impassive, with a faint shrug of the shoulders. The gun pointed at my chest didn't waver so much as an inch. About eight feet. Too far to jump her and knock the gun out of her hand. In the time it took me, she'd shoot me two or three times. And something told me she wouldn't miss.

"You know, I'm a little uncomfortable standing here like this in front of you, naked," and I hinted downward with my eyes to distract her for a fragment of a second, at least give her something else to follow. "Can I at least get dressed?"

"No. You were so beyond naked last night, now suddenly you're bashful?"

I forced a bitter smirk... although the smirk was pretty much in earnest, at the same time. I shifted my weight, and with it my footing, getting myself an inch or two closer, concealing the almost imperceptible movements of my feet in the soft hotel slippers. One foot at a time. A moment's pause, then slowly shift your body's weight onto that foot...

"The situation, Abbie, as you say, has changed. Last night you didn't have that thing pointed at me," I nodded at the gun, hoping she would respond to the joke and say something about how I aimed something else of mine at her.

I'd laugh and end up another inch closer to her. But no. Bedroom jokes weren't going to distract her now. She ignored the attempt. And the hand on the gun still didn't falter. And the cold eyes remained unwaveringly fixed upon me, sensitive to the slightest hint of danger my body language might betray.

All right, so that's how it is. I shrugged – as much as one can shrug, anyway, with one's hands over one's head. For a weapon I had only a damp towel. A large bathtowel. It wouldn't protect me from a bullet. It might serve to distract her attention for a fraction of a second if I threw it in her face. I could use that fraction of a second to heave myself out of her line of fire, but I'd still be hit by at least a couple of bullets. Right. Say what you will, but it wasn't the most elegant outcome.

"So what do you want, Abbie? Is it really Abbie, by the way? Doesn't matter, I suppose. What do you want?"

"The access codes to the Hephaestus project system. All the data. Now."

"Excuse me? What on Earth are you talking about?"

The girl's eyes narrowed. She was like a predator before the pounce.

"Carl, Carl, Carl. I wouldn't try those games with me. We're both professionals. You've lost. I've won. It's pretty simple, isn't it? Why show such disrespect by playing the fool? We both know it isn't going to work."

"Work... who do you work for, by the way?"

"Weak. The codes, Carl."

I thought there was something American about her, but that didn't mean she was CIA. She could just as well be MI-6 or Mossad. She could be working for the Russians, or the Chinese, or any of a handful of Middle-Eastern countries. Or she could be with a private contractor. Or her own private client, directly. That might be the likeliest scenario.

Fine. She certainly knew who I was. And, obviously enough, she knew that I was in charge of security for the Hephaestus project. I did, in fact, have access to the system. She had been in the bar yesterday, in the hotel lobby, for the sake of that access. She had waited for me, waited for me to notice her and approach her. An intricate game, planned many steps ahead, so that everything would seem natural, innocuous. And I had to admit that it had worked.

"You know it doesn't work that way, right? I don't have access to all the system data."

"Of course you don't." A weary note entered the crystal sharpness of her gaze, mixed with resignation to the rules of the game. "What you have is priority access to the security systems. And that enables you to give yourself access to any data you do not have access to immediately. Stop stalling, Carl."

She was right. I was stalling. Time might not be on my side, but it certainly was working against her. And that suited me fine. It also gave me a brief interval to think things through.

The Hephaestus project was a complex strategic techno start-up. It was founded by a group of scientists whose goal was a breakthrough in geoenergy. To access the boundless heat within the planet, to satisfy all mankind's needs with practically unlimited free energy.

This was nothing like our current sorry attempts to tap subterranean geothermal energy or hot springs. It meant direct access to the limitless, sustainable energy of the Earth's core. That was not going to be a simple matter. Their calculations showed it would take decades to complete. But given the vast pool of top-flight brains, plus the enormous financing provided by a number of billionaire philanthropists, it had every likelihood of success.

Which indisputably made it public enemy number one for the entire existing energy industry. Oil and gas would cease to be fuel and lose most of their value, they would be nothing more than common raw material for chemical production. The world's transportation system would change radically. The political balance of power would shift, as well. And too many people would lose vast amounts of power, money and influence.

Energy corporations, the automobile industry, and the governments of numerous countries had a serious chance of being left on the sidelines. The US had betrayed serious interest in the project and had attempted to worm its way into the initiative, to obtain vital information about it, because America's power over the world economy was based largely on its control of the international flow of oil. But something in Abbie's methods suggested that whoever it was she reported to, it wasn't Langley.

Hephaestus was a sword of Damocles hanging over the head of the Russian Federation, ready to sever its only significant source of wealth and influence. To bankrupt, and possibly eradicate, its ancient empire. And they had already undertaken a series of undisguised attempts to derail the study and steal the project data. But the Russian hackers had failed in their attempts to penetrate our advanced security systems. Yes, it was possible that my nocturnal guest was working for the Kremlin.

The sheiks, whose wealth derived exclusively from the pumping of oil, were divided into two groups: those who aggressively, malevolently opposed the start-up, and those who blithely ignored it. Of course, there were the numerous Islamic terrorist groups financed by middle-eastern governments for which the lame god had now become an enemy of Allah. Their methods were low-down and primitive, but we had handled them.

For much the same reasons, Hephaestus was of interest to Israel, which saw in it a major opportunity to promote the downfall of a series of inimical neighboring regimes. Although it was also concerned about the dangers associated with their sudden impoverishment. It was generally more an ally than an enemy. From time to time, it would share information about various conspiracies or terrorist plans that had come to its attention, but at the same time it took every opportunity to dig deeper into our affairs. It was unlikely that Abbie was associated with Mossad.

The Chinese? Hard to say what the project's success would mean to them – a boon or a disaster. But they were always trying to buy or steal information, or even the entire start-up. If it was going to change the world, they wanted to have their hands on it and control the new energy. Could Beijing resort to such radical measures? It could, there was no doubt. But they seldom employed freelancers. They prefer their own agents. Still… it couldn't be ruled out.

There were a whole host of possibilities, but I was certain I was right in my guess as to who her employer actually was.

"Abbie, Abbie, Abbie. You should know things are never that simple. If I attempt to alter my own access rights, the system registers an alarm. It will require identification, authorization, and confirmation of access rights. One of my employees has to decide whether I am acting under duress. In which case they will cut off my access entirely."

"You'll manage, Carl. Or I'll kill you. It really is that simple. Enter the word that sets off the alarm and I shoot you dead. Send your employees any signal of any kind and I shoot you dead. If you don't manage to get full access and transfer it to me…"

"Yes, yes, you'll shoot me dead," I said, smiling brightly, turning my palms out slightly and subtly moving an inch closer while the girl was assessing the movement of my hands.

Seven feet. Progress! Slow and steady. No hurry. Soon she would notice the decrease in distance. Then I'd either have to act immediately or back off and lose the opportunity I had so patiently created.

Her mistake was not an obvious one. It seemed everything had been properly thought through and planned, but she had failed to account for the simple possibility that I might not care whether she shot me or not.

I had been appointed head of security for Hephaestus a little over three years earlier. When the project was still in its formative stages. And the scientists and the investors were all very well aware that the risks and the dangers were only going to increase. Which is why they chose me for the job. And I had done everything possible to increase their paranoia and build the most modern and reliable security service imaginable, with its own intelligence operation and a small private army. That was what consistently saved us. We were faster, smarter, more powerful and more dangerous than most of those who desired our demise. And also the fact that I lived this job. That I was ready to die for the preservation of Hephaestus. Here and now. I knew that. But Abbie apparently didn't. And that was my advantage. Not a major advantage, but an advantage nevertheless.

"And if I refuse? You shoot me dead?"

"Not right away," said the blonde, furrowing her brow. "You do understand that we can torture you for quite a long period of time to break you and get what we want the hard way."

We. Not *I*. *We.* Sooner or later, language betrays even a professional.

"All right, let's suppose you did manage to break me and that the identification process didn't set off an alarm when the system realized that things aren't right with me. Let's suppose that. Although the system will work, of course. But you don't have the time you'd need to torture the information out of me."

"Don't overestimate yourself, Superman." The scorn in Abbie's gaze was now mingled with what looked like bloodthirsty anticipation. Not for the first time, I found myself thinking about what it was I had seen in her last night.

At this moment, with that expression of cruelty on her face, she was more repulsive than attractive, like some kind of ravenous fury. In the bar last night, however, she had even been kind of... cute. Maybe it was the lighting. Or the scotch. Hard to say for sure.

"And you keep in mind that in three hours I have a flight to Zürich, and if I don't register and take my seat on that flight, my colleagues will sound the alarm."

That was true. I was in Thailand for negotiations with one of our suppliers to ensure security on their side and prevent any information leakage. Amusing. Ironic, right? And my movements were tracked by my staff. And the two people who were accompanying me would be expecting me in the lobby in an hour. If I didn't show up – the alarm would trigger the safety protocols.

The question was whether I was going to survive that hour.

"That's more than enough time, Carl. Enough talk."

Abbie pulled some kind of gadget out of her pocket. Something like a disposable folding telephone. But when she hit the button, it began turning itself inside-out, becoming a serious terminal with a keyboard, a large screen and a biometric scanner.

"What the..." I croaked, when she pushed the terminal. It floated towards me through the air, stopping a foot or two from my face, its screen now turned towards me.

All I could do was stare at Abbie in horror, bug-eyed, opening and shutting my mouth.

"What kind of freaking... What the fucking hell is that?! You're not CIA."

"No." And now the witch had a self-satisfied look. She was enjoying the shocked look on my face. "I'm not CIA. You are quite right."

"But..." Nervous now, gulping down the lump in my throat and huddling slightly, I even backed away from her a little, losing those inches of illusory advantage I had so laboriously built up over the last several minutes. "That's incredible! Who are you working for?"

"You wouldn't believe me if I told you," said my opponent, waving off my question with a precious gesture.

"With that thing? I think I'd believe pretty much anything..."

"Well, if it helps loosen your tongue... I am from the future."

"The future." I repeated the words, the incredulity and skepticism obvious in my expression... and then I looked at the floating terminal again. "Hell... You're not joking, are you? What do you mean, from the future? From the future future? Like in the Terminator?"

"Where?" she asked, confused.

"Forget it," I said, shaking my head. "Of all the... They sent you to destroy our project in the past? Who? Why?"

"Too many questions, Carl. Who and why aren't your concern. Start establishing access."

"Tell me. It's important. Convince me. Maybe you won't need torture or threats. Why, Abbie?"

"You want to know why?" the blonde burst out, and for the first time the gun wavered in her hand. "I'll tell you why. Because in 2107 the energy your project is going to produce will fall into the wrong hands. And that leads to bad things. A lot of bad things. Millions and millions of people are going to die. Because you, you idiots, create something worse than weapons. Something you cannot hope to be able to control. Monkeys with hand grenades! Dammit. Someone has to fix this."

I suddenly realized that I had frozen as I listened to her passionate rant. My shoulder blade was itching from the tension. Unbearably. But I couldn't risk any movements that might provoke Abbie.

"What?" she asked, vehement, staring at my stunned physiognomy.

"I... I don't know. I think I believe you. Probably... It's just hard to take this in, can you understand that? Just like that, in an instant... How can I know you're telling me the truth?"

"You can't. I don't give a shit if you believe me or not! It's enough I had to let you fuck me, you monster! In any security system, even the most perfect security system, the human factor is always the weakest link. So predictable. So banal. You were so easy to figure out. It's almost funny that the hole in Hephaestus's security system turned out to be the moron who runs it. A honeypot. It was that primitive.

What could I say to her? That she was right? That I was sorry? That she was so natural, so believable last night, that I never suspected she was faking it? That she obviously liked it? Or that I didn't care whether she liked it or not? That I had fucked her mother the same way, and she had obviously loved it?

That it was only another couple of moments before two of my men broke into the room and knocked her brains out? That I didn't care whether she managed to shoot me before that happened or not? That she had screwed up royally if she hadn't reloaded my gun, since I had it loaded with blanks? What if she decided take a shot and check? Those were live rounds...

"Why should I help you? You're going to kill me whatever I do, aren't you?" I said, looking into her eyes, demanding an answer. "Especially after everything you've just told me."

"No, not necessarily," she said, carefully monitoring her body language. But a faint tremor in one eyelid and an involuntary contraction of her pupils told me she was lying. "This can still be resolved civilly. I have no wish to kill you. You are not a bad man, Carl. You've just chosen the wrong employers. Give me access and run. I have fifty thousand here in this bag. Take it and run. Lay low."

It wasn't much of a chance, but it was a chance.

"Seriously? Show me the money."

She didn't fall for that primitive trick, of course, and the barrel of the gun remained implacably trained upon the center of my chest.

"Oh, you'll just have to take my word for that. Now log in." I'd managed to forget that I was still standing in front of her completely naked. And that I had to reduce the distance between us to make an assault possible.

"May I lower my hands?" Which, I should say, were aching horribly. My shoulders were burning, the muscles beginning to shake in uncontrollable spasms from the pressure.

She nodded silently, her eyes focused on my every move. I slowly lowered my hands, shrugging my shoulders, loosening the muscles. Gingerly, I pulled the strange terminal closer and froze, my fingers hovering over the keyboard.

"You promised, don't forget," I said, shooting her a warning glance. "Right?"

"Yes, yes."

"All right, then," I said, and began to hook into the Hephaestus systems, attempting to avoid violating my own security protocols.

"And look, seriously – no tricks." To make her point more persuasive, Abbie swung the gun slightly down and then up, showing me that I was a big enough target that it would be hard to miss at this range.

"I get it, I get it," I said, raising my palms, and then went back to the identification procedures.

I put a finger to the scanner. It read my fingerprint and then there was a light prick as it took a DNA sample. I tried not to blink as a sensor scanned my retina and hoped that the lack of sleep and the pressure of the situation wouldn't register and set off an alarm.

"In any case, so your finger doesn't flinch on the trigger… You should know that there's a special protocol for this level of access. Specifically meant to guard against a situation like this. Whatever you try to do in the system, every action requires multiple-factor authorization. Every time, the system generates a new random check. A code sent to my phone, a fingerprint check, a different finger every time, a retina scan or a DNA check. Or one of a hundred test questions. So, if you kill me now, access to the Hephaestus system won't be of any use to you."

"Funny you didn't mention that earlier," she said, her eyes narrowing with hostility.

"You didn't ask," I said, with a crooked grin.

In any event, I had a guarantee that I wouldn't be snuffed before she had finished whatever it was she meant to do. Now we'd play it by ear.

I did everything she asked and gave myself access to the general project database, passing every security phase without disturbing the control service. Always keeping in mind the weapon that threatened to shoot me several new orifices.

"Slowly push the terminal towards me and take another two steps back."

I did that, too. When the terminal had drifted off in Abbie's direction, I took a step back. Almost to the door exiting into the little hallway of my room. To my right was the open bathroom door – one quick step back and a leap to one side. Too long, but the main thing was – what would I do then? It was a dead end. Behind me was the door leading out, but it was shut. Three steps back, turn around, open the door, and fly into the corridor. Enough time to empty the entire cartridge into my flesh.

As I was running these calculations, Abbie was typing something into the terminal. Suddenly she cursed, hissing.

"Sonofabitch! It *does* require authorization." And she pushed the terminal off in my direction. "No sudden movements and no tricks."

She took the gun in both hands now. Of course. It was a big, heavy gun. Keeping it trained on me with her outstretched hand for this long had to be hard. The muzzle was wandering visibly. That was good. If anything happened, there was now a chance she might miss. At least once.

I caught the terminal and looked at the screen. She was requesting all project documentation, test protocols and implementation procedures. She wasn't playing around. That was a vast amount of data. And the system was requesting another DNA prick and my first pet's name. I had never had a pet, so instead I typed "Lola." That was what we called our sergeant in basic training. Not to his face, of course. He wasn't a man you'd joke around with. Son of a bitch.

The system clicked quietly and the green light on the screen confirmed that the test had been passed. I gently pushed the terminal back towards Abbie. She began to type something in, opening windows...

"Fucking... again it needs to confirm your identity."

"This is why I warned you. Everything's fine."

I let it scan my retina again, the left eye this time, and told it what my favorite dessert was. That was an easy one. Steak, of course.

While I was confirming that I was me, I had time enough to notice that Abbie was trying to send the entire archive to the year 2204. Seriously? Directly from here? Right now? Not downloading it somewhere in our time so as to send it at her leisure to her damned 2204. She was sending it all directly from my hotel room – to the future.

"You fall asleep or something?"

"Sorry, just thinking about something." And I hit the confirmation button and got my green light. "Everything's okay. The system was asking for my favorite dessert, that's all."

"So? Is that so hard to remember?"

"I don't eat dessert. I was trying to remember what I put in back when I was initializing my profile."

"And?"

"Excuse me?"

"I'm asking you what you put in."

"Oh. Steak. I like steak. A few times I even ordered a steak for dessert."

"You're a psycho," said Abbie, snorting.

"And that's from a terrorist from the future who came and fucked me silly and the next morning, instead of breakfast, coffee and a teary goodbye, holds me at gunpoint, naked, in my own room, demanding that I break into my own security system? You know, if I believe that, I really am crazy."

She ignored my ironic comments without even bothering to deny she was a terrorist. She just went on entering commands into the terminal, which clicked quietly in response, apparently confirming the progress of the transfer. I wondered how broad the band had to be and how quickly she could pump the information out. Should I tell her now that any information transferred to external channels would be hashed and that without the key all she would have on her hands was a jumble of incomprehensible symbols?

I should probably tell her that, in any event, before she decided she didn't need me anymore. But we weren't there just yet. She had been transferring data for six or seven minutes, approximately. Maybe that should have been enough. A faint buzzing in my occipital bone told me everything was as it should be. That almost imperceptible vibration in my skull made me want to sneeze, yawn and scratch my left year, all at the same time.

With my tongue, I touched three molars, in order. And then I slowly joined my right thumb with first my middle finger, then my pinkie, then my index finger, and then the middle finger again, this time pressing hard. There was a faint click and the world around me stopped.

I walked over to Abbie and carefully removed her poised finger from the trigger. I took the gun, engaged the safety, and tossed it onto the bed, which still looked like the scene of an epic battle. I had a strong urge to send a fist into the face of my unwanted guest, which was frozen in an expression of utter astonishment. It took a great deal of self control, but I conquered that urge.

In any security system, even the most perfect security system, the human factor is always the weakest link. So predictable. So banal. I was so easy to figure out. It's almost funny that the hole in Hephaestus's security system turned out to be the moron who runs it. A honeypot. It was that primitive.

I shifted Abbie's hands behind her back and snapped on a pair of energy cuffs, binding her wrists tightly together so that they were completely immobilized. Her face still bore that same expression of dumb astonishment that appeared in the moment when her subjective time froze.

Perhaps I should have told her yesterday that I had handcuffs? The night might have been still more crazy. And I wouldn't have had to go through all this humiliation today. But then I wouldn't have had the opportunity to trace the precise moment and location of the headquarters of the extremist group supported by several regimes that had fallen since Hephaestus was launched.

They called themselves the Erinyes. Too exalted for a handful of fanatics and mercenaries. But they were extremely dangerous and well organized. The Erinyes had already made several attempts to take Hephaestus by force, but our security service had dealt with them. To avert an attack through the time stream was more difficult. Their goal was not the destruction of Hephaestus, it was to obtain control over the project and the technology. Evidently for the purpose of maintaining and expanding the power of those doomed to lose it.

I quickly pulled my underwear and pants on and only then, with a series of hand gestures, opened a communications window. An imperturbable Rodriquez gazed out at me.

"Commander?"

"You can take her, boys. We know where they are now. I think our people in 349 are already sending a mop-up brigade to those assholes' hideaway in the year 204. And we'll be rid of that irritating threat for good."

"Excellent, commander. We're on our way. Only..."

"Yes, Rodriguez?"

He blushed slightly, but winked.

"You might want to zip your fly."

The Plumber

Translated by Simon Geoghegan

Pete really hated emergency calls. In the middle of the night, at weekends or in the evenings. And particularly now, right in the middle of the game. What's more, this wasn't just any match but the quarter-final and he had twenty dollars riding on it. The most annoying thing would be to miss everything and then have it described back to him in interminable detail by Jack in his dull, droning monotone. Especially if Jack ended up winning their twenty dollar bet...

But, on the other hand, dealing with emergencies was a part of the job. And he had to admit, his job was pretty well paid. The company that Pete worked for served very rich clients from very wealthy neighborhoods, so he regularly received good bonuses for prompt and efficient service. And even some generous tips directly from the customers themselves.

He was soon on the scene and whistled through his teeth at the catastrophic sight that greeted him. This was one helluva flood. Water was pouring in cascades, literally spraying everywhere. The distraught mistress of the house was rushing about in a flurry of panic and rage, grabbing her most valuable possessions to save them from the deluge.

"At least it's not hot water, I guess," Pete muttered under his breath and added in a louder voice, "I'll go and turn off the stop cock and come back and check everything over."

But, as he expected, things were much more serious than they had first looked. The problem wasn't that the neighbors had sprung a leak but that the damp proofing was shot to hell. Water was pouring everywhere but not quite as badly as it had been.

"What are you doing there just standing and gawping! Do something!" The desperate owner shouted.

Pete wasn't sure she would understand him if he started trying to explain dodgy damp proofing, building regulations and the cowboy builders who had created this mess. Not to mention, the unscrupulous developers that had probably hired untrained immigrants to save on labor and, indeed, the entire shower of idiots, responsible for the fact that her house was now underwater.

"Ma'am, you know, my advice would be to get in touch with your lawyers. It's not your neighbors that are the problem. Well... They're not the entire problem, do you understand? Although they were the ones who flooded you, the real problem is the quality of your damp proofing. It doesn't keep anything out at all. If everything had been built according to the regulations, the damage wouldn't have been nearly so extensive, do you see?"

"No, I don't see. I don't understand a thing!" The owner continued to lament, "Who's going to compensate me for all this now? Who?!"

Pete certainly wasn't planning to, they'd have to figure that out for themselves.

"You have insurance, right?" He replied trying to deflect her anger in a constructive direction.

"Yes, of course."

"Well, that's excellent! You're not at fault at all here, I'll make sure I put that down in my report. And the insurers will have a whole pile of questions not only for your neighbors but also the property's owners because the damp proofing is really shocking. And the insurance company will probably try to squeeze everything they can out of them. Do you understand?"

"Yes, I think I do, yes," the client smiled in a predatory fashion, "but the water is still flowing. Are you sure you've turned everything off?"

"One hundred percent, ma'am," Pete nodded, sighing inwardly at her reluctance to understand the root of the problem, "but I'll still need to have a look around and draw up a report. Do you mind?"

"No, of course, not," she dismissed him with a cursory wave of her hand, standing distractedly in the middle of the soaking chaos of her home.

Before writing up the report, Pete decided to check the customer's water meters and seals and those of her neighbors while he was at it. After all, procedure is procedure. With this amount of damage, there was going to be one serious showdown and his report would have to be irreproachable.

His inspection confirmed that the client had everything in good order and he connected with the company's database to double-check their meters. Yes, everything was fine. No bills outstanding, which is always a good sign. He noted. But the neighbors...

Pete couldn't believe his eyes and had to double-check the dates on the seals on their meters. Nooo! But... That couldn't be right. He hooked up with the main database again and checked their call-out history. Yes, they had had a serious flood before and ended up flooding all the neighbors. Leaving them completely underwater, judging by the records.

And since then, not a single person had carried out any diagnostics or system maintenance. How many years had passed? Wow! Pete whistled out loud counting them up. What kind of skinflint penny-pinches on maintenance? It's going to cost them much more now. How could they have failed to understand this? Or were they the sort of indifferent idiots who didn't care about anyone or anything?

But seriously, if they were so stupid, how could they possibly afford to live in such an upmarket neighborhood? Even when it was a new build, the property prices here had been eye-watering. But now...

Pete rubbed his eyes and tried to focus on the task in front of him. Okay, it looked like a deeper system scan was going to be needed here. He connected his terminal to the system and started downloading the diagnostic data. It had been ages since the last maintenance scan and the resulting report was huge. So for starters, he just pulled the latest system status data up onto his screen. And was horrified.

Yes, there some right slobs living here... They hadn't just had a leak, oh no. They'd allowed their world's oceans to rise to such incredibly high levels that the pressure exceeded all conceivable safety standards. Just look, it had been pouring out of every crack and crevice into their neighboring worlds' dimensions. And apparently, these morons didn't even seem to realize they had a problem.

"What on earth are you doing there, what's with all this overpopulation? What a nightmare!" Pete looked at the demographic data and held his head in his hands.

The number of tenants had exploded exponentially. They were producing huge volumes of greenhouse gases and their technologies were only adding to the heat emissions being pumped out into the atmosphere. An increase in temperature had caused the polar ice caps to melt and this, in turn, had only exacerbated the sea levels.

What sort of load were they under here? Pete quickly figured it out and his jaw dropped. He checked again. Yes, he was right. A complete nightmare!"

"Over three hundred trillion tons overweight! Holy smoke..."

No wonder the water damping hadn't held out. Especially the crap they'd put in here. And if this were to continue, Pete would end up living here, constantly patching up these leaks. And, not on his own, they were to need a whole gang of workers. A really big team.

Great, just fantastic. So, what now? Ask the boss for a transfer to another site? It wasn't that he was afraid of hard work, but this... This was just pointless. These tenants were just going to cause more and more problems. Until all the neighboring worlds were flooded again and they drove themselves to extinction.

Unless... But no, that would be illegal. Well... Almost illegal. You couldn't just block them in and isolate them completely so they'd die out quicker and save everyone else even bigger problems down the line. Sooner or later, there would be lawsuits and an investigation and someone would discover what had happened. Then he might end up not only losing his job but his license as well... No, he needed to be more cunning.

Pete checked all the figures again. Interesting. Hmmm... At the end of the day, it's all about the heating, isn't it? Well, the heating and the water. The water, of course, was his bag and he could try to tighten up a little here and there. On the sly, so no one would notice. But Manuel was responsible for the heating in this section, and he didn't want to land his friend in it.

However, he also didn't want to be permanently camped here, fixing leaks and floods.

"Manolo, it looks like I'm going to have to stand you a beer. A lot of beers. And a tequila chaser or two to boot."

Logging into the neighboring worlds' databases, Pete began to study the specifications and operational data. Just a couple of worlds down from here, there was one, which was empty. It had become temporarily uninhabited after a total nuclear disaster. Things were going to be very "hot" there for the foreseeable next few thousand years and the owners had refused to pay for the expensive business of having it decontaminated.

And yes, just a couple of levels above them, there was a cold dimension, where the residents were struggling to survive. They were going through an ice age and their civilization was barely able to keep itself warm. Hmm... Interesting, not a bad option.

"Ha! A bit of global warming might be just the thing their weather system needs."

Pete went into settings to tweak something. And then on the dashboard, subtly, so that no one would notice, he created a temporary channel to gradually remove the excess heat from this world with its careless owners and tenants, who had caused all this trouble today.

He diverted some of their excess heat into the ice age dimension. Just a little. Enough to marginally soften their harsh winter and gradually accelerate the retreat of their glaciers. The thaw wouldn't be very noticeable but would speed the process up by several generations. And that wouldn't be a bad thing either.

Pete transferred the remaining excess warming down the channel to the extinct world, burning in its nuclear inferno. Nobody would spot anything amiss there either. And the temporary fix, which he had sent down the intricate cat's cradle of wires, cables, pipes and mains was so small and inconspicuous. Manolo might notice something. But that was nothing a beer couldn't put right?

It would be enough to stop the ice melting but it wasn't going to reverse the process. However, over time, the system would stabilize itself. What's more, it would be better if Pete were to drop by occasionally to check things over and prevent these ignoramuses from being driven into another ice age than to be constantly patching up their careless floods.

But what was he to do with the excess water? It couldn't just be discreetly thrown into another dimension. And also, without the necessary coolants, the system would overheat even further and crash completely. The polar ice wasn't going to grow back that quickly, so that wasn't going to provide an easy solution.

Pete looked at the diagnostic data analysis again. What third-rate amateur had designed this world? Whoever it was, should have been deprived of their license and their useless heads for good measure. This job had all the hallmarks of some bored, lazy student's half-finished homework. In some places, it was boiling hot, in others freezing cold. The place was awash with water but despite this, some places suffered from permanent drought. Tell me, where was the logic in that?

Was it really so hard to find some normal professional designers capable of doing their calculations properly and doing a job properly? And then pay some normal builders to carefully assemble everything and hook it into the mains? But no, everyone is trying to save money, buying some cheap template and then ineptly tinkering with it and customizing it for their own purposes. And then people wonder why things are such a mess? And why nothing works properly? The idiots.

Pete typed the parameters into the analytic module and did not like the solutions he was getting. Too expensive, too time-consuming. And not an option with this damp proofing. And who was going to pay for a job like this? But what, if instead of rebuilding from scratch, you could just make a few slight corrections to the most serious snags?

Of course, it would require cunning and a modicum of thought to prevent any unwanted anomalies. But if it were done carefully and with a bit of TLC. A little tweak here, a little change there. Pete opened the communications circuit. Good grief..! The whole thing was held together with string, sticky tape and a wing and a prayer. What would he give to get his hands on the morons responsible for all this..?

Just take this large arid continent here, almost everything was wrong with it. Its inhabitants were suffering from drought and a lack of drinking water, which had led to a whole raft of other problems. But they had water coming out of their ears!

"Yes, it's coming out of your ears. It's a joke," Pete grumbled, creating a small channel into the arid region, fitting the outflow pipe along it and connecting it up to the pressure valve to make the changes controlled, gradual and invisible.

Next, he diverted a bit more to another continent, which largely consisted of inhospitable desert. He distributed the flow of water as evenly as possible. Not as accurately and well-calibrated as he might have with a half-decent budget and the right tools at his disposal. But it would do the job.

And then the same in a few more arid regions in other places. Of course, he wasn't able to connect them all, some of them weren't that simple, they needed new piping and connection with the mains. But he was able to connect up most of the desertified areas to the overabundant water supply.

The effect wasn't going to be instantaneous, it would take some time for the system to stabilize and become operational. But the overload would be immediately and significantly reduced and the water level should subside to a height acceptable for the safety specifications of a world of this type.

In any case, Pete would be keeping an eye on it. Checking in until he was sure that everything was working fine and there were no more problems. A lot better than being constantly called out on emergency, right?

"What took you so long up there? The client barked at him on his return, her eyes almost spitting lightning bolts.

"I had to check absolutely everything, ma'am. Your insurers will need a highly detailed report on the emergency state of the system. So it's better to make sure that everything is in perfect order. Sign here. This is your copy. And this one is for your lawyers and the insurance company. And just one more signature here for my copy. Thanks, ma'am."

"The water seems to have stopped pouring now, right? Did you manage to fix everything?"

"Well, no, ma'am. I only fixed the leak, but as I'm sure you understand, this isn't going to sort the bigger problem out. However! I've double-checked and tightened and tweaked everything I could, so I think you shouldn't be getting too many more problems from your neighbors in the near future."

"Oh, sure! With neighbors like mine, you never know when you're going to be flooded again. The degenerate cretins! I've had it up to here with them."

"You've got a point, ma'am. Your neighbors are a little hmmm... How can I say it, weird? Yes ma'am, weird. But I think that after the preventative work I've just done, everything should be fine and they won't be bothering you again."

"But you didn't have to do that extra work, right?"

Pete scratched his head, modestly dropping his gaze down onto his well-worn boots that were still wet and spattered with dirt, like everything else around.

"Not, strictly, ma'am. But you know I'm an old hand at this and it's easier for me to make sure that everything is fine here than to have to rush down here every other week in an emergency, right?"

"That probably makes logical sense," the owner nodded uncertainly.

"And I've made a request to the office to carry out a complete precautionary overhaul of your system. This is included in your maintenance charge, so there's nothing to worry about. Everything should be fine here now but after an accident like this, it's worth running all the tests and making sure there won't be any problems further down the line. Of course, this won't be now but later when everything's had time to dry out. The office will contact you to organize a convenient time for the maintenance team to come out.

"Why, thank you... uh... Pete, is that right?" Said the client, reading the name tag on his chest, "Please, take this. You've been a great help today."

"Well, you really don't have to. But thank you, ma'am," Pete muttered with a gesture of embarrassment, hiding the tip in his overalls pocket with practised alacrity, "all the best, ma'am!"

Well, that hadn't turned out all that bad, had it? The tip would be enough to stand Manolo a beer and keep the unauthorized transfer of heat in the system under wraps. And he would figure out how to sort out the water supply himself. All in all, a very simple and elegant solution.

There was no way a greenhorn could have sorted that out, not in a month of Sundays. Especially the cheap migrant workers the labor exchange seemed to send out these days, constantly referring to their instruction manuals before turning a stop cock or tightening a nut. Ugh!

Pete spat angrily and reached into his pocket for his cigarettes. Say what you like, but an old plumber is always a wise plumber.

Sincerely yours, Lucifer

Translated by Maria Kornienko

My name is Lucifer, and I am an angel. A fallen angel, to be precise.
I am that same Fallen Angel who was glorified and condemned by the countless generations of your ancestors.
They worshipped me, and they spoke my name when cursing their enemies. Tales about me and my Fall have passed through millennia, turning more and more into fiction and lies, distorted to the extent that nothing true has remained in what you know of me now.
I feel I have to tell you the truth so that you can decide for yourselves whether I am worthy of your respect or your contempt. I expect neither your love nor your gratitude, though I deserve each and in full measure. But it is important to me that you know the truth. Knowledge is light, while I am Lucifer, and my name means 'Light-Bringer'.
Since the very moment of my Fall, I have lived among you, bringing you light.
No, I do not live downstairs, as is commonly thought in your religious subculture, but among you. I live next door.
But I am getting ahead of myself. I should have begun by telling you that my Fall was voluntary. I was not banished from

Heaven, but I rejected my angelic nature myself and lost God's grace in order to live with you like an ordinary mortal. Or, rather, like an ordinary immortal.

It was no protest, act of disobedience, or my ego speaking. It was the price I had to pay, it was my ransom.

Actually no, it was still defiance of God's will. He just did not care about you, but I did. I loved you with all my heart, ever since I helped God to create the first people – so fragile and vulnerable, so ephemeral, innocent, and pure.

I admired your impermanence and imperfection. I was fascinated with your turbulent emotions, which gave such a vibrant colour to your fleeting lives. A wild kaleidoscope of fantastic colours, flickering with bright flashes, in the eternal stream of time.

But God soon got fed up with you. He was bored, and he wanted to smash the tiresome old toy into pieces. I begged him to keep you, to save you, to give you a chance to prove yourselves, but he was not interested. I demanded, I threatened and blackmailed him, but all in vain.

This was when I renounced Him and returned to Him the most precious thing I had – the particle of the Divine essence He put inside me when He created His favourite angel. My only hope was that He would accept my sacrifice. I also hoped that the unbearable pain of my separation from Him would be the price He would accept for your salvation.

It caused Him unimaginable pain too. Possibly, it even helped Him see how much you meant to me, that I was prepared to sacrifice a part of Him for you. He let me go, and He let you go. He turned away from you and me and left us forever. Ever since, we have been on our own, and I have been responsible for you.

Indeed, through almost all of your history, you have been in my care. Although my remaining power is fading, I try to look after you, help you, guide you, motivate you, and push you toward progress as best I can.

At first, I enjoyed this new job so much. It was exactly what I wanted. To live among you, to watch you being born and dying, gradually evolving into something worthy. I contemplated you with joy, I played God, creating thunder and lightning, making you tremble before nature's forces and the higher powers. Even though I myself remained the only higher power on Earth.

However, your development was too slow, and it was tiring at times. I lacked patience, and I realised I had to boost your progress somehow.

I am Lucifer, the Light-Bringer, and my powers are naturally connected to light, fire, energy, and knowledge. Those were the only things I could share with you.

I will not start with the knowledge I gave to the very first people, providing them with reason and intelligence. My gift made them distinct from animals and raised them above all living things. All of that was before I left Heaven. In some way, it was I who made you human, and for that, I came to love you. But I repeat: that was all before the Fall. Let us not talk about it.

First, I gave you fire. I thought it was a wonderful gift, to help you harness the most incredible force of nature. The power that created your world out of cold, dead stone. The element that gave warmth, fundamental to all of life.

Imagine my disappointment when you turned the force of fire, first intended for creation, into a weapon of destruction. You unleashed the voracious power of its flames on the settlements of your enemies. You burned them and made sacrifices to your ridiculous idols and pathetic godlets.

Of course, fire was also useful for you. You learnt to cook food, mastered a couple of crafts. Yet for a long time I regretted that you had turned my gift into something evil.

It makes complete sense that all of these events gave rise to a multitude of legends and beliefs, like the famous myth about Prometheus. And just like Prometheus, I endured physical suffering to repay my gift of fire to you. No, eagles did not feed on my liver; however, thousands of years have passed, and I still feel cold. I lost so much energy then, that I am still unable to feel warm.

So, I tend to live in warmer climates. I spent years in ancient Greece, giving you arts and an understanding of beauty, which helped you to find a way out of prehistoric darkness.

By the way, the Greeks also deformed the myth of my Fall by calling me Icarus and accusing me of excessive ambition, an overblown ego, and hopeless stupidity.

From time to time, as I restored my powers a little, I tried to toss you some interesting new ideas and guide you towards civilization by promoting arts and sciences. A word here, a thought there, a couple of new concepts whispered into someone's ear, and my new gifts had already taken their places in your lives.

I used to believe I brought you goodness and prosperity, but still too often I found myself discouraged and even disappointed with the results. As I looked at your wretched huts made of branches, bones, and skins, at your primitive tools, I understood that you needed something better, more substantial, more durable. And I gave you a hint of how to gain mastery over the very soul of fire, to multiply its power, to gather all of its heat to smelt metal out of stone.

It was spectacular – new tools, more successful hunting, more food, and, as a result, more people. But… You turned this gift against yourselves yet again. Sharp new weapons that could be made quicker, in larger quantities.

You had more soldiers now, and from clashes between neighbouring tribes, you moved on to wars on the scale of massive bloodletting. And whole armies of murderers, equipped with metal weapons, destroyed cities and invaded countries and continents.

For a long time, I wondered whether it was my fault and whether I was guilty of providing you with a deadly toy that you were not old enough to play with. Or were you the problem? Maybe something inside you was vicious from the very beginning, so that all of the gifts you received, you turned into weapons to kill your own brothers.

I know that my intentions were driven by concern for you, but I cannot help wondering whether I moved too quickly and gave you something that I should have waited longer to give.

In the Middle Ages, it was all sad and depressing. You were drowning in your own sewage, brought epidemics and diseases upon yourselves, which wiped out cities and countries. You bred, but your culture was degraded to a level below what I had managed to achieve while I was living by the Mediterranean.

I realised that it was time for me to go back to where I was last able to achieve progress. I settled in Italy, where my assistance helped many painters, sculptors, architects, and scientists to push back the Dark Age and open the road to enlightenment.

You rightly call that period the Renaissance, because it was when I brought arts and sciences back to life in a place where I had I succeeded once before. But it would also be fair to note that this was the period when you turned your back on me forever.

Your dominant religious cult tried to keep you in the dark and make you ignorant, and that is why all of my innovations were pronounced Evil. It was then that they labeled me the Devil once and for all, and this has been my name ever since.

The Light I brought you, they called Darkness. The Good I shared with you, they called Evil. And I myself became a symbol of Evil, cunning, and treachery. They managed to pervert my whole story, defame everything I had done, and besmirch and demonise my name.

Not that I was offended by it, or expected any gratitude for my sacrifices. Not at all. But it did not feel good. It complicated my mission. So I left you to your problems for awhile, and took a break to recuperate and think of how to fix the situation.

The attempt to introduce you to the explosive power of fire has been my greatest disappointment, since you never used it to create anything even remotely useful. Gunpowder became another instrument for massive killings, while dynamite made things even worse.

I had to re-examine everything I might have done wrong and to find out why it was becoming worse. Your progress was evident, but your desire to kill your own kind was growing disproportionately.

Then I understood that it was time to go back to the very beginning. You were using fire to its fullest, feeding it and burning everything in sight. What I had to do was teach you to deal with more complex energies.

So I gave you light. I gave you all the incredible power of electricity, the primal force of lightning. This experiment proved to be much more successful. I was even content with the result, as you managed to master my new gift without causing yourselves harm.

You introduced electricity into your homes, lighting them with a safer type of energy. You built big factories and manufacturing plants, providing yourselves with all kinds of necessities, which made your lives better and wealthier.

The most important thing was that you did not turn electricity into a weapon. Yes, there were many attempts, and I had to make certain efforts to stop them. But it was a triumph. I believed that you had grown up, earned more advanced gifts, and would not harm yourselves again.

I realised that the key to your society's development was cheap and affordable energy. This would allow the underprivileged among you to receive enough of the blessings of the developed world to survive. It proved to be a quite sensible concept, and I worked on it for a couple of centuries after introducing electricity. The problem was that in order to provide you with the necessary affordable energy, I had to turn to forces involved in Creation. I knew it would exhaust me for a long time or maybe even forever.

Nevertheless, my long reflection and analysis made me think it was all worth it. So I risked exhausting the last of my strength to give you the most powerful of energies accessible to me: the energy of the atom. I believed that you had learned from your experience with electricity and understood how to tame the rampage of the key forces in the universe to bring peace to your society.

How mistaken I was.

Of all my gifts, this is the one I regret the most. I overestimated your success with electricity and underestimated your appetite for self-destruction. Peaceful atomic energy is the very essence of Creation, which constructed the matter of all things out of practically nothing. I truly believed that it would help you live in harmony with yourselves and the world you had been given.

Instead, you created the most fearsome weapon that your perverted minds had been capable of imagining throughout your entire history. The weapon, which destroyed hundreds of thousands of people in an instant, now inflicts terror on the whole world. A ruthless machine capable of wiping all of civilisation from the face of the Earth, breaking my heart and undoing all the work I have done over the long millennia.

No, I cannot let this happen.

True, I barely have any strength left. By giving you power over nuclear energy, I weakened myself forever. I do not think I will ever be able to recover.

I cannot die, as my immortality will never let me leave this world. But I will not be able to call it life. I just exist, unable to influence the course of your history. Unable to help, support, protect, or teach.

Of course, there is one last thing I can still give you, but it will finally destroy me. Then you will be all alone, without me to look after you. Will you be able to make it? I don't know. There are things that even you cannot turn against yourselves, aren't there?

There is the very meaning of life, the foundation of existence, which cannot become a weapon under any circumstances. Life cannot be death, and the beginning cannot be the end.

Still, the end of one thing can be the beginning of another.

That is why I have trust in you, I believe that you were created for something grand and beautiful. I believe that you will have enough wisdom and judgement, sanity and commitment to life, to use my last gift properly.

I made my decision. Let it destroy me, as long as it can save you. Because I know what you need to stop using everything for self-destruction, including the knowledge I have given you. I will do it so that you cannot kill each other anymore.

I am writing this not for you to praise me or curse me. I just want to say goodbye. I was happy and fascinated with your long and eventful history. I took care of you as best I could, although maybe I was not always as good a guardian as I should have been.

But I love you. I am proud of you. And I hope you will be fine.

I am leaving, and my last gift to you is what has been keeping me in your world.

I renounce my immortality and grant it to you.

Sincerely yours,
Lucifer

The Pyramids of an Alien World

Translated by Simon Geoghegan

Mo had waited two whole months for the opportunity to get out to the pyramids and now, finally, he was greeted by a stunning panorama of lush green jungle dotted with several stone outcrops shining brightly in the sun.

"Shuttle, descend and make a circle over the objects below. Video them from all angles, then release the scanning drones."

"Affirmative, pilot," the shuttle's artificial intelligence unit intoned soullessly.

At a lower altitude, the pyramids loomed up like majestic stone islands floating in a boundless sea of green forest canopy. The shuttle glided slowly over the jungle itself, and Mo, holding his breath, watched as these giant ancient edifices turned their faces towards him, each new aspect full of amazing mysteries and potential.

"Pilot, a suitable landing place has been detected. Request permission to land." On the in-flight screen, the shuttle indicated a small clearing in the trees, not far from the largest pyramid.

"Confirmed," Mo replied and returned his attention to the long-awaited sight that now presented itself before him.

They had been here for more than ten weeks, but he had only now been able to earn two consecutive days off. To do this, he had taken on double shifts and exchanged other ones with his shift partner. But boy had it been worth it!

Mo had arrived on this planet with the first wave of colonists, and their task had been to prepare the necessary temporary camps and infrastructure in this new world for the second, larger wave of settlers.

As a shuttle pilot, he had had access to the map database and seen these amazing remnants of an alien civilization that had been spotted in a remote uninhabitable region of the planet by one of the reconnaissance satellites.

With the exception of the research team who currently had more practical priorities on their plate, they were not of primary interest to the colony. However, Mo found himself inexorably drawn to these giant monuments because they so reminded him of the world-famous ancient pyramids of his homeland.

He had always been interested in history and one day his father took him on the best journey a twelve-year-old boy could dream of. Leaving clouds of dust and deep furrows of sand behind them, they had driven through the pitiless heat of the desert to see at first hand the ancient enigmatic structures that had been raised and abandoned by their distant ancestors.

How huge they had seemed to him then! Eroded by the wind and scorched by the sun, the stone breathed antiquity. These ancient anonymous builders had strived to perpetuate their own greatness and now the weight of thousands of years seemed to loom directly over Mo and his father. Mo remembered screwing up his eyes against the bright scorching sun, the prickly sand and the tears of joy that he had been able to get to this place and touch these incredible monuments to man's desire to rise above himself.

Ever since then, he had been obsessed with the secrets of the pyramids and their creators, he had studied history, archaeology and ancient languages. He had read all the literature that existed, including every possible conjecture and conspiracy theory. He had been on a couple of expeditions to excavate the lesser-known pyramids that had been discovered in the desert later on with the help of modern technology.

Intimately investigated outside and in, the ancient pyramids refused to reveal their secrets and continued to raise more questions than answers about their existence.

Who had built them and why? Were they tombs or places of worship? Or had they been a means of communicating with aliens from outer space – landing beacons for the spacecraft of beings revered as gods by the people of those times? Or did they contain a secret message for their descendants who were now trying in vain to decipher it?

Had these cosmic visitors helped to build these grandiose structures or were our ancestors so advanced that they had been able to bring millions of huge stone blocks into the desert and use them to build the world's greatest wonder, an edifice one hundred times the height of a single man?

And all these questions were closely intertwined with others that either had no answers or answers that didn't satisfy everybody. Are we responsible for the course of our own evolution or are the supporters of the theories of panspermia and paleocontact right?

Can we consider the pyramids a part of our heritage or were they given to us by some previous civilization whose sunset coincided with our dawn? Are these unique stone giants an indefatigable echo of their last will and testament? A trace left by the hand of a previous great civilization in what was then the raw clay of mankind's history?

Perhaps now there'd be some answers to a few of these questions, although these pyramids were also generating plenty of their own.

The discovery of a new planet fit for human life had been a clarion call for romantics, outcasts and adventurers of all stripes. And, despite his love of archaeology and dreams of unravelling the secrets of the past, Mo immediately applied to be a part of this first wave of colonization to the new world.

He felt the need to break out of the cramped confines of his planet, suffering from disease, hunger and the sheer weight of its billions of inhabitants who were poisoning and destroying their own home.

Leaving his home planet, he thought with a tinge of sadness that he would be flying away from the pyramids of his native country forever but it turned out that the spaceship was carrying him towards new riddles and challenges. How he would have loved to have been on the research team but the quota for scientists was too small. And Mo had only been able to get onto the expedition as a shuttle pilot.

And now, after a couple of months of hard work, here he was – the first person to touch the pyramids of an alien world that had been left by people who had once inhabited this flourishing planet.

According to the intelligence reports, it had remained uninhabited for approximately one and a half thousand local solar cycles. And it had not been possible to establish what had happened to the local inhabitants.

Despite the existence of several locations with fairly high radiation levels, it was clear that this civilization had not been wiped out by a global nuclear catastrophe. But it was unlikely that we'd ever find out whether their disappearance was a chance series of events or an act of deliberate self-destruction.

They might have been destroyed by a worldwide pandemic, but the reconnaissance missions had not discovered any pathogens that represented a clear threat to humanity. Our researchers continued to take samples all over the planet but they could find nothing that our medicine could not deal with.

Perhaps some kind of natural disaster or environmental degradation had gradually erased the civilization that had once thrived on this planet. Or perhaps they had destroyed themselves as a result of their irrational unsustainable use of the resources available to them.

Just like us, Mo thought.

And indeed, the ancient inhabitants of this world seemed to be remarkably similar to humans. With slight differences in their make-up, caused by local climatic, environmental and gravitational conditions they must have looked like a distinct reflection of ourselves, if not an exact copy.

But were they copies of us or we copies of them? Or had the ancient all-powerful gods created both them and us in their own image and likeness?

The inhabitants of this world had been too similar to us for their existence to be considered a mere coincidence. We were connected, in some unknown way, we and they were a part of something bigger that, for the time being, was beyond our understanding.

Whatever the answer, it was now absolutely clear that we were not alone in the Universe. Or used not to be alone. Who knows? If our fellow humans had lived here, then perhaps there are others living elsewhere? Or are we the last and apart from us there is no one left?

But who were our forebears? Or creators? What did they create us for? Where did they go? Are they still alive? And why did they leave us? Why did they split us up, leaving us so far apart from each other? Why did they not want us to know that humankind has long been settled throughout the vast expanses of space?

Did we accidentally find our fellow humans, or was it predetermined that our search for a new home would lead us to their abandoned grave? And yet, could it be that what destroyed them might also threaten us here too? Something or someone?

What were our extinct human siblings like? Were they good or evil? What would have happened if we had discovered their civilization when it was at its zenith – would they have welcomed us with open arms or threatened us with weapons to protect their home against us?

While all these questions whirled around Mo's head, he carefully approached the largest of the pyramids. These jungles were fairly dangerous – lianas cascaded down from the canopy of high trees providing ample cover for predators to lurk. And there was no shortage of poisonous local inhabitants under Mo's feet in the humid tropical undergrowth.

The lower tiers of the pyramid's stepped slopes were thickly overgrown with climbing plants and moss. And this had eroded the already poorly preserved stone in the humid climate, making it fragile and unsafe to climb.

Mo understood that it was little more than a miracle that these local pyramids had survived these conditions. They were a far cry from the dry desert heat in which his pyramids had stood for thousands of years. Here, the voracious jungle teeming with life fiercely fought over each stone and ledge, striving to reach ever higher towards the sun and claw back territory from human history in a war that had spanned many centuries.

There was no question of risking climbing those frail stone steps. If he was injured, it would be several hours before help arrived. And he could forget about ever being allowed back to visit these pyramids again.

"Shuttle, report back the scan results. I want to see how these pyramids compare with ours back home – tell me everything: their size, shape, structure, materials and age. I want to know the likelihood of them being constructed by the same builders or if they are linked in some way."

"There is a probability level of 98.37%," the shuttle's artificial intelligence unit promptly replied, confirming Mo's expectations. How could it have been otherwise. There were too many coincidences. People similar to us had built gigantic stone pyramids that were exactly the same as those standing on our home planet. There had to be some sort of connection and Mo wanted to be the person to discover these ancient secrets.

Perhaps these pyramids on an alien world would help him find answers to the questions he had been asking himself since childhood. And the key to these ancient mysteries had been concealed on a distant alien planet, which had become the new home for a colony of settlers.

"These pyramids are larger than they appear because about 11% of the base has sunk into the ground. With some very small deviations in size, their proportions are exactly identical to the ones on our planet – the angle of the walls is between 51 to 53 degrees. Taking into account a small margin of error as a result of their condition, I can report that the same ratio between the height and base of the largest pyramid gives the exact value of Pi just like our pyramids."

Amazing! This was an incredible discovery, and Mo rejoiced, trying to digest the full extent of its ramifications. Perhaps the research team would now decide to pay more attention to these ancient artefacts of a lost civilization. And who knows, Mo might even be given a place on the team for this discovery..?

"The building material is a local sedimentary rock, which is looser than that used in our pyramids. It is not as well preserved, climbing up the pyramid is not recommended."

"I've worked that out myself, thank you, carry on."

"The age of these structures differs to within about three hundred local solar cycles, taken as a whole, the complex is just over 6,000 local solar cycles old.

"If we were to calculate this in our years, how close would the building of these pyramids be to the construction of ours?"

"These pyramids are about 500 years younger."

And so poorly preserved. No wonder in this heat and humidity. Mo wiped the sweat from his face and swiped away a couple of pesky insects.

"Shuttle, turn up the insect repellent frequency, these bloodsuckers are a real pain in the ass."

"Affirmative."

It was a good thing the local fauna didn't carry any diseases harmful to humans. But it must have been hard for the men who built these giant pyramids in the middle of a jungle, teeming with voracious insects?

But why here exactly? Why not build them in a more open space, where you wouldn't need to cut down endless rows of trees to transport these incredibly heavy and bulky stone blocks to this place? What was so special about this precise spot?

Perhaps the scientists who thought the pyramids were directed at a certain point in space and time were onto something? Evidently, the location was equally important here? What else could have caused the ancient people who inhabited this planet to spend so much time and energy building these magnificent structures in the middle of a wild jungle?

"Shuttle, make a note of the exact coordinates and angles, I will give you the data later to calculate the direction vectors during the period of the pyramids' construction."

"Affirmative, pilot."

However, were the pyramids meant to be pointing at something specific when they were built or at a later date? The parameters were too vague.

But now it was possible to combine the direction vectors of the pyramids on the two separate planets at once! It wasn't enough to get a triangulation but it was an incredible breakthrough regardless. Mo wondered if these pyramids pointed to the same place as ours or not? Have they ever coincided?

Academics have understood for a long time now that there was much more to these ancient monuments than just a resting place for the dead. But what were they? Lighthouses, navigation buoys? Or road signs? For us or for the space travellers who created our race or kick-started our civilization?

The mysterious pyramidons that sat atop the pyramids and which, according to legend, were made of pure gold might help solve this problem. But alas, none of them has survived and we will never know whether they were just a simple element of decoration or a complex piece of cosmic apparatus. Gold is not only the most precious metal known to man but also an excellent conductor. It may be nothing more than unsubstantiated speculation, but Mo felt sure that the amazing archaeological finds in his new home could confirm the theory that the pyramidons were designed to be used as a means of communication. In any case, these pyramids had turned everything on its head. Everything. We had not simply arrived on another planet, which had previously been inhabited by an extinct anthropomorphic race that was surprisingly similar to us. Things were much more complicated than that. We shared a common history with them. Someone had helped or coerced them and our ancestors to build identical pyramids.

Who, why and what for? These were the interesting questions. But even more importantly, there was the possibility that these ancient builders had not abandoned us. Perhaps, they were secretly keeping an eye on us. Even here and now.

"Shuttle, start drafting a report file using the data gathered for the expedition commander. And copy it to the head of the research team. This is no longer a matter of my private research but a question of the security of the entire expedition."

"Task completed, pilot. Permission to enquire why these pyramids might be a threat?"

"The pyramids themselves are not. Or, at least, I hope they aren't. But the fact that there is a connection between theirs and ours complicates matters. We now know for sure that a more developed civilization has interfered in the history of this world, as well as ours. The only thing is, we don't know what the nature of this threat might be. Perhaps we should be focusing our efforts on studying these structures in order to find out more. Or, on the contrary, perhaps we should be leaving them well alone to avoid activating some kind of ancient alarm system. I don't know."

"Affirmative, pilot."

"You know, copy the report to the heads of all the departments, this is incredibly important information about the history of our world and this one. I think we will need every possible assistance for this mission, both technical and scientific. Although admittedly, they might well not include me on it... Shuttle, erase that last sentence, that was just a personal reflection."

"Affirmative, pilot."

"By the way, if these creatures created us, then they were your progenitors as well, although I'm not sure they had genitals."

"Affirmative, pilot."

"Listen, that was just a joke."

"Affirmative, pilot. But, as you know, emotions and a sense of humor are not written into my programming."

"I know, shuttle, I know," Mo waved his hand, "I'm sorry, I'm just a little excited trying to get my head round the size and significance of this discovery. I'm a little scared about how things will develop from here. I'm not sure whether I'm feeling glad or a certain sense of regret that I decided to take a closer look at these pyramids."

Mo passed along the base of the pyramid, examining its surface, thickly plaited with vegetation. Higher up, the stonework was cleaner, and closer to the apex it shone a luminous white, at its foot the jungle was lightly powdered with a fine film of dust and dirt.

"Shuttle, the very fact that these pyramids are identical has already turned the whole of history as we know it on its head. But perhaps we could take things a little further. Please send a request to the research team to send me everything they've managed to decipher from the surviving records of this extinct civilization. Everything that relates to the pyramids and this ancient culture. Did the locals know what these pyramids were for? Or were they as much a mystery to them as they are to us?"

"Affirmative, pilot."

"We have almost an hour before sunset, so let's get something else done before we head back to base. Run a scan to detect any inscriptions. And if there is something, conduct a comprehensive deep scan of these sites."

It would be great to discover some samples of their ancient writing and compare it with ours. It's hard to even imagine how much we'd be able to find out. Did they use the same language? If so, was this the language used by the ancient gods who instigated both our civilisations? Is there a possibility that our human brethren found traces of this ancient language or did the ruthless jungle climate destroy all remnants of the wisdom and culture of their ancestors? And if they did find any, were they able to understand and read it?

Was it this that led to their extinction, the nagging thought revolved around Mo's head. And is it worth our while trying to understand all this or would it be safer to take a step back and leave the dangerous secrets of the past untouched?

"Permission to report scan results, pilot," the artificial intelligence unit responded almost immediately. "At the base of the pyramid, there are the traces of some poorly preserved inscriptions."

"Carry on, shuttle," Mo sat down on a rock in anticipation.

"They are in a very bad condition and cannot be made out. But an analysis of the symbols and their age suggests that these are more recent inscriptions that date back to several millennia after the pyramids' construction in one of the planet's later languages. That's all the data available for now."

"I see," Mo muttered in disappointment, he had been hoping to find ancient messages. But he had more than enough discoveries to mull over for one day.

"Pilot, permission to venture an opinion?"

"Of course, shuttle."

"If you compare the structure of these pyramids with ours, it is clear that the stone has not just been poorly preserved but is of a lower grade quality. It is highly likely that this structure, like ours, was overlaid with a higher-quality stone. But here, the outer layer has not been preserved."

"Why would that be?" Said Mo in surprise.

"It's not possible to say, pilot. But if this hypothesis is correct, then any inscription would most likely have been made on the outer layer, and not on the inside."

"That makes sense," Mo thought. "You know what, shuttle, let's do something else. If this outer layer has crumbled, then some of these slabs may be preserved underground, right under our feet. Please run a deep scan of the soil for the presence of any possible objects of interest. We're unlikely to get to the bottom of this today but there might be something worth adding to my report to the mission.

"Initiating order, pilot."

Mo returned to his own musings again. Were these extinct humanoids really descendants of the people who built these pyramids? Or was there a historical gap between these civilizations and they hadn't known who the builders of these giant monuments were? After all, Mo had heard nothing from the research group's studies of the planet's surviving records to suggest they did.

Before his arrival on this planet, no one had looked into the common history between the two planets. Although, perhaps, the surviving records had been too scarce or did not contain anything related to this planet's ancient history. But nevertheless, they would definitely need to check now that they knew exactly what they were looking for.

How much did these people know about their origins? About the purpose of their existence? What would they be able to tell us if they were alive now?

"Pilot, our drones have found a fairly large object."

"Where? How deep?" Said Mo, jumping up from the stone.

"To be precise, it is not underground but partially on the surface. It is a large slab of stone and glass, belonging to a period that post-dates the pyramids."

Although a later discovery, this was still an important find, and in his agitation, Mo found himself pacing impatiently in circles. It was a pity, of course, that this wasn't an example of ancient writing but perhaps this later object might throw some light on this tangle of ancient secrets.

"The inscriptions are well preserved, having been carved on hard volcanic rock. I have scanned the object and can show you a three-dimensional model."

The shuttle's artificial intelligence unit projected a color 3-D model of the object right in front of Mo, alongside a video of the drone's flight path around it and the location on the map where the slab had been discovered.

"This is from the far side of the largest pyramid. As you can see, there are a number of inscriptions on the slab. They would appear to be in three languages that date to a period much later than the pyramids themselves."

The 3D model was replaced by a large image of the scanned stone inscriptions restored to their original appearance.

"Unfortunately, this doesn't mean anything to me," Mo exclaimed in disappointment, "have our scientists managed to decipher any of these languages?"

"Affirmative, pilot. One of these languages has been reconstructed. Do you want me to show you an approximate translation of the fragment that has been preserved?"

"Yes, of course, come on!" In a state of awe and inspiration, Mo began to read the text on the new hologram: *Here stands the tomb of Cheops (Khufu), the great pharaoh of ancient Egypt from the Fourth Dynasty, who ruled approximately 2,589 – 2,566 BC.*

So, they knew their history, after all!

"Is that the whole inscription?"

"Yes, pilot," the AI unit confirmed, "that's everything that's been preserved in the language that our scientists were able to decipher. Was it any help?"

"I don't know. Well, yes, it's an amazing discovery to find out that they knew their history. Although admittedly, they seemed to think the pyramid was a tomb, which is not totally correct. But they did seem to know something. It's a shame that this information doesn't mean anything to us. I have no idea what Cheops, Pharaoh, Egypt or BC mean but they would probably have known what it was all about. Perhaps we will find something in the research team's database. Shuttle, include all these new materials in the report."

"Affirmative, pilot. Permission to remind you that the sun will be setting in ten minutes. It will get dark very quickly down here below the canopy. May I recommend an immediate return to base to avoid being in the jungle after dark. My sensors can detect large predators but there are other security issues here as well."

"I agree with you, shuttle, I'm coming back on board. For now, collate and send all the report materials to my terminal and I will review them on the way back before sending them to command."

"Yes, pilot."

On his way to the shuttle, Mo took one last longing look back at the pyramid and marvelled at what he saw. The pyramid's sharp apex flamed in the rays of the dying sun, like the summit of a great volcano. It was as if the entire edifice had been cast out of liquid gold and this intensified the contrast with the bright blue sky behind it.

"Shuttle, take a good picture of this view for me. I don't know how many months I'm going to have to work to earn the time to come back here again. Or indeed if the research team will ever let me or anyone else come and visit these pyramids. But I want to keep this picture as a memento of an amazing day full of discoveries."

"Affirmative, pilot."

Mo wondered if they would ever find out who this Cheops was, what he had to do with these pyramids and how all this tied in with the beings who had created both our peoples?

He was very sorry that his father was not alive to see these days. How happy he would have been to have received a snapshot from Mo of these ancient ruins in a strange world and recall the adventurous thrill of their road trip to the T'arghab pyramids in the G'fadkhab desert.

The Hall of Fame

Translated by Simon Geoghegan

This one had been good, really good. Young, bold and brave, he had been a great choice. And was still probably the greatest... Probably... Well, maybe... But he had definitely been his favorite.

Strong, smart and charismatic, he was a born leader. A fearless warrior, a visionary politician, a tireless lover and a lofty dreamer. He had been born to rule the world. And he had almost got there, there was just something lacking...

Badona sighed, fondly stroking his beloved avatar. This had been his first significant victory, he had never before gone so far or so close. Victory had been tantalisingly near, teasing him with an unrepeatable feeling of omnipotence...

Perhaps this had been his downfall - the taste of fame, invincibility, power and the license to rule as he wanted. He had become overconfident, less vigilant and eventually careless. But most likely he had simply overworked this avatar with the pace of life and the heavy loads that had been placed upon his young shoulders.

Swift, decisive military campaigns, the seizure of neighboring states and the strengthening of his power base. Then an aggressive offensive war, a brilliant victory over old enemies and the conquest of a whole region. And finally the foundation of a powerful empire, the construction of new cities, the spread of culture.

This proved all too much for one fragile young man, even one as outstanding as this one. He was increasingly beset with conflicts, riots and rebellion, unruliness and disobedience, betrayal, envy and threats. Increasingly inspired with ambitions, bold reforms and far-reaching plans.

Increasingly debilitated by wounds that never had time to heal properly after each new campaign. Increasingly undermining his health with the long bouts of carousing with his generals. Diseases contracted in foreign hostile lands that would knock him off his feet...

And so, the son of the sun god turned out to be mortal. He died in his prime, but not in the thick of battle from a stray arrow or the thrust of a sword or spear but from a fatal illness that treacherously and ruthlessly laid him low. Perhaps it had been poison. Badona never knew for sure.

He had pimped his avatar with every imaginable skill and talent before throwing him into the ring. And then suddenly and unexpectedly he had been eliminated. It was incredibly upsetting but at the same time, Badona rejoiced. He had managed to dance rings around almost all of the other players and break a whole slew of records. This avatar would remain forever in the collective memory of this world.

But Badona also kept a copy of the man for himself in his own personal vault. He had become his fetish, his talisman and Badona would come here before the start of every new game and try to absorb the luck and success he had achieved with his first really successful creation.

He would wander around the vault, looking at the other avatars he had kept as a keepsake, and recall all the victories and defeats that had helped him learn from his mistakes and better understand the game and the other players who participated in it.

This has been an interesting and chastening exercise as well. Badona had been confident he would win this time, but no. It was as if there was an invisible balance of forces counterpoised between the course of the game and the players themselves.

Genius counterpoised by a tendency to madness. Courage by paranoia. Originality by depravity. The farsightedness of the strategist with his myopia towards his immediate surroundings.

And it was thus that he lost his next highly promising avatar. Hypocrisy, vanity, conspiracies, a cold treacherous knife in the back and the sudden demise of a highly successful game that had been so long in the planning.

His next avatar was not a born ruler but steadily rose to power and ended up governing the most powerful empire of his time. He turned out to be a talented commander, a wise emperor and an outstanding writer. Generosity and mercy coexisted in his heart with a cold ruthlessness towards his enemies.

He formed alliances and strengthened his hold on power. He conducted progressive state reforms in domestic and foreign policy, in the economy and in society as a whole. He significantly expanded the boundaries of his powerful empire with successful wars of conquest.

But it was his immense ambition that let him down, dashing Badona's plans to win the game at this sitting. He became a dictator, accepted the title of emperor and with it the status of a demigod, eventually achieving recognition as a god in his own right.

He built a temple in his own honor to perpetuate his name forever. Lost in contemplation of his laurels, the desire to return the forgotten monarchy and establish a new dynasty, he fell at the hands of angry conspirators, including his own adopted son...

Badona wasn't sure if he hadn't made a mistake in that session. According to his calculations, victory in that period of history could only be achieved by developing your own cult and being recognized as a god. But one game after another, he failed to make this strategy work.

However, one time he decided to try a completely different approach. Instead of developing his avatar's power base as a ruler and then declaring himself a god, he decided to declare his divinity from the very outset.

His first attempts were not a great success until he came up with a winning formula for his next avatar. It required a lot of preparatory work with the launch of several secondary avatars and bots who would prophesy and proclaim the arrival of this avatar-deity.

Badona ran his fingers over one of his favorite creations. This had been a fascinating experiment – to build a game around a poor boy who was declared the son of God. An avatar who did not strive for worldly power but spiritual might, building up a huge army of followers.

Instead of a warrior, he had created a sage capable of commanding the crowd with the power of the word. To act not so much with the strength of force but the power of feelings and reason. To aim not so much to conquer lands but the hearts and minds of men. He did not seek wealth and luxury but denied and condemned them.

And everything might just have worked out. Badona shook his head ruefully. Everything had started so well. And he was already planning a master 'pivot' by using spiritual power to win earthly power and eventually world dominance.

An interesting strategy but sadly a non-starter. If you are a warrior, sovereign and despot, you can easily deal with your enemies. But if you are a holy teacher who rejects violence, then violence itself will find you and rival rulers will deal with you with a mere click of their fingers.

Badona had been flattered by the fact that this session had been widely declared one of the best and most important ever played in the history of this world. It proved to be a complete gamechanger for anyone playing the game for many centuries to come. By trying to follow the path of peace, this avatar became the cause of many a subsequent war and this contradiction haunted every single one of Badona's opponents.

They tried to copy his tactics but none worked as well as his original strategy. This was the first and last time he tried to go down this route. Maybe he'd just been lucky. Or, perhaps he'd just picked the perfect time to employ this gaming scenario. It was hard to say.

After this, Badona would take a lot of time to analyze his triumphs and defeats. He even decided to give the game a break for a time to think over his next moves. Testing them out in short cameo games to set the stage for a new powerful avatar.

Since his peaceful conquest strategy had failed to lead to world dominance, Badona decided to take the opposite direction and follow the path of maximum bloodshed. Instead of trying to conquer the world from one of the great centrally located civilisations, he decided to challenge them from the periphery by destroying their power, smashing and subduing them.

His latest avatar was as rapacious and wild as a starving beast. There was nothing refined or sublime about him, just an unquenchable thirst for power and victory.

He was obsessed with war and he brought war to every single one of his neighboring rulers and tribes. Bringing great empires to their knees, he imposed harsh tributes on them and kept them in a constant state of fear and humiliation. He expanded Badona's dominions as no other previous avatar had ever done.

But his talent lay only in destruction. The very concept of building that is so vital for the maintenance of any empire was alien to this uneducated barbarian. It proved impossible to rule these huge occupied territories with fear and an iron fist alone.

Badona soon realized that, although successful, this approach would quickly fail. The avatar was unable to keep hold of everything he had conquered. There were new battles, brutal reprisals, excessive demands and terrifying bloody executions.

This avatar ended up dying on his marriage bed, choking on his own blood, his throat slit by a young trophy wife captured from an enemy clan. An inglorious end for a warrior before whom emperors, kings and chieftains had trembled.

And another stinging defeat for Badona, who had been fairly confident that this time he would win the game outright. Once again, he had smashed all kinds of records and his creation was ushered into the Hall of Fame. But he had failed to achieve world domination.

It was during this period that Badona developed a real taste for blood. He realized that even without any hope of victory, he enjoyed running amok, decimating his enemies and drowning in the blood of the vanquished. He created one aggressive avatar after another, each slashing, stabbing, disembowelling and decapitating in ever more gruesome ways. This unbridled cruelty gave him a sense of control and the death of his enemies – a feeling of invincibility.

But he lost all these sessions fairly quickly and without much success. This forced Badona to weigh up his choice of avatar again. He needed to slake the thirst for blood but direct it towards a lofty purpose. To strive for victory using not just coarse brute power but cold calculation and a hard, imperious hand.

His musings bore fruit and the next avatar exceeded all his expectations. Badona looked at his champion with tenderness and emotion – there was an inherent wisdom in his furrowed brow and an iron will in his chiselled features and tightly compressed lips. There were steel and fire in his eyes and rivers of blood on his hands.

He had been tempered by poverty, slavery and torture, his character honed in a long struggle for the power and wealth that had been lost by his family. He respected loyalty and courage in his enemies but despised and ruthlessly punished cowardice and betrayal in his friends and allies. Remaining an ascetic himself, he lavished those close to him with generous gifts.

This new avatar had a rare knack for organizing, planning and controlling. He transformed the chaos and bloodshed of warfare into a fine-tuned mechanism. The slightest breach of order and discipline was punishable by death.

This death machine helped him build the largest land empire in the history of this world. But, having lived to a grand old age, this "wise and warlike emperor" only succeeded in conquering as much territory as was physically possible to maintain and control on horseback.

Badona was already beginning to think that the lifespan of one mortal avatar was too short to conquer the whole world. And he was right, based on the technological capabilities of that era. But time passed, new weaponry emerged and with it, new opportunities. Players gained experience. And the population of this world gradually began to live a little longer, so that with a bit of good fortune, a well-constructed avatar really might be able to conquer the entire world.

Badona fine-tuned his skills, restraining his thirst for blood, realizing that a powerful state needed to be based on order, systems and progress. From time to time he played short games to let off steam but was never able to beat his own personal best.

Although one time, he got quite close. His new avatar advanced himself from petty nobleman to consul, then president, king, and even emperor. He was obsessed with the victories and success of two of Badona's previous avatars and was able to successfully combine many of their best qualities with the solutions they had discovered.

A fortuitous mixture of the same boundless ambition, brilliant political strategy and cunning intrigue helped him to progress up the entire chain of military command and gain the power he craved in a mere ten years.

A powerful army and innovations in military doctrine, based on maneuverability, mobility and firepower, enabled this avatar to capture and annex vast territories to his empire. And large-scale social and economic reforms helped feed this war machine and keep it on its path to newer and ever greater glories.

Horsepower and speed continued to constrain him in terms of logistics but new weapons and the swiftness of his military campaigns allowed Badona to win brilliant victories in this session. The game was progressing well, he was easily able to cope with the bots who adored him and the smaller players, but two experienced opponents stood firmly in the way of his ultimate domination. One of them was playing with a naval empire, while the other controlled a large state east of Badona's empire. Working in tandem, the two of them were able to restrain his advances and eventually prevail in separate campaigns.

After that, everything went downhill for this brilliant avatar – he was stripped of his power, imprisoned and left to die in solitude and ill health on an island in the middle of nowhere. A miserable ending to another brilliant game plan. But the opportunities learned were not lost on Badona. He now knew how to quickly advance an avatar onto a new 'power level' and how to provide the necessary resources and offensive strategies to achieve lightning military success.

New times brought new rules. And Badona perfected his skills and honed his tried and tested solutions and strategies in order to consolidate his recent triumph. But time and time again the balance of power would not fall in his favor and in each new game he only managed to achieve small victories without getting any closer to any genuine omnipotence over the world.

After many games, he had yet to be presented with a really unique chance. He installed a new avatar in a country where an almost pedantic obsession with order and systems had granted it immense strength and power. He moulded him into a leader capable of uniting and rousing his entire people. Inspiring them to war for the sake of the very world domination that Badona so desired in the game.

This avatar was unstable, even insane, and Badona often thought that he would not be up to the task. His emotional outbursts and manic, fanatical ideas threatened to ruin this promising session.

He drowned whole countries and nations in blood, sweeping away everything in his path for the sake of ruling the entire world. For the sake of satisfying his base passions, ego, mania and paranoia. This avatar succeeded in fanning the flames of war on a greater scale than anyone before him. The entire globe was engulfed in fire and many millions of lives were consumed in it. And all this to achieve dominion over the world, a possibility that was becoming increasingly palpable and real.

His lightning victories almost broke his old enemies but didn't succeed in finishing them off. They resisted, stubbornly dug in, and now the momentum of his glorious advance stuttered, stalled, floundered and... eventually swung in the opposite direction.

Badona could not understand how complete victory had turned into defeat again. After all, the invention of total war in this period of the game meant that a single mortal could achieve world dominance in a fraction of the time required by his predecessors.

He might have ruled the world or at least triumphed over its ruins. He might have entered the Hall of Fame as the first player to have achieved everything. Everything! He might have achieved the ultimate mastery over this game, bringing it to its logical conclusion.

But his avatar's common sense and steely will were overpowered by his weaknesses. Noticing and taking advantage of this, the other players successfully concluded their tactical game plans. And then it was over as suddenly as it had begun. The long-awaited sweetness of victory was replaced by the bitter taste of defeat and the leaden weight of disappointment. Badona's brilliantly conceived and implemented game plan had been rudely thwarted.

He was plunged into a deep depression. Badona knew that he was the best player out there, but even his most successful avatars had been unable to bring him the world domination he so coveted. Perhaps his problem was a strategic one, although he had already tried so many different permutations that he now had no idea how else he might approach the problem.

Out of desperation, he immersed himself in a number of highly dubious games, satisfying his thirst for blood and taking it out on the other players and the bots that inhabited this world. But apart from genocide and mass murder, he did not achieve much, and Badona failed to displace the inert levers of global power on any meaningful scale.

He tried his hand as the head of a religious cult with violence and murder as its touchstone but the other players quickly snuffed out this trial game plan. And any attempts to start a new 'total war', in which there would be no winners, were successfully circumvented by the mortals who realised they had nothing to gain and everything to lose.

He even wanted to try out a game plan with a female avatar at its head but their role in this world had never led him to expect the idea to bear fruit in the race for complete world domination. However, the times were changing and he had more and more chances to realize his crazy idea. Just for the pleasure of it, not for ultimate victory.

However, there was a recent avatar that was most interesting. It had taken Badona decades to insinuate him in at the level of an insignificant bureaucrat, then petty spy, and eventually methodically promote and prime him until he became the ruler of one of the largest countries in this increasingly dysfunctional world.

Passing himself off as the national leader elect, he was able to establish a strict and cruel dictatorship, grant himself lifelong rule and the right to transfer his power to his descendants. Interestingly, the local bots were delighted with his clearly regressive regime.

Badona had previously tried out several game plans on this territory but had never been able to fathom the logic of these local bots who had always seemed highly irrational and unpredictable to him. But this time, he found a way of manipulating them. It turned out that what they really liked was tyranny with a smile, a steel fist clad in a velvet glove. They simply did not understand any other style of government.

And Badona masterfully tried out his new political and tactical technologies, first on his own bots and then on his opponents'. In addition to the usual military firepower, he used economic levers of influence and developed an ingenious form of information warfare.

He won for himself a territory rich in energy resources, and he actively used these to buy, bribe, crush, encourage, inhibit and generally play the market in order to manipulate his opponents.

He invested enormous funds and resources in an ideological and information war, secretly stirring up passions, sabotaging, broadcasting fake news, defaming and slandering. He wreaked havoc everywhere he went, deftly manipulating people's moods and needs. Presenting black as white and white as black.

He pulled the strings of his web, even appointing rulers in the countries of his greatest opponents, overthrowing politicians who were objectionable to him, whitewashing and camouflaging his military operations and the subsequent capture of large swathes of his neighbors' territories while kindling the flames of enmity and hostility throughout the world.

But this time, Badona simply ran out of luck. He had spent a long time working out this new strategy, and the avatar was already too old. And, as is often the case with worn-out characters, his new player began to suffer from progressive senile dementia. Paranoia made him continuously see conspiracies all around him and spies and enemies in his friends.

Alas, things ended badly for him, like any tyrant who has lost his wits. Subjected to censure and reproach, those who only yesterday were singing his praises, today had no qualms about spitting on his grave.

The most frustrating thing for Badona was that he simply hadn't had enough time to implement his ambitious plans to seize power over the entire world. All the accumulated weaponry, the subtle technologies of his proxy shadow war – came to nought, crumbling to dust after the death of the dictator.

And this instalment that had been so painstakingly constructed over so many years never reached its triumphant and victorious endgame. However, it taught Badona to understand that at this stage in the development of this world, there were forces that were mightier than weapons and armies and more dangerous than open conflict and war.

Badona had gone full circle and returned to the beloved avatar that had brought him his first remarkable success. There was something boyishly charismatic about him that the rest of his champions had not been able to emulate. Something that Badona himself lacked.

Placed in a circle, his avatars represented his greatest triumphs and no less importantly his greatest failures. They served as instructive reminders of his own mistakes and failings. And Badona found the inner strength to accept these lessons, to learn everything that he possibly could from them. He had everything he needed to create a new avatar for the next session of the game. He moved to the very center of the vault and admired his latest creation.

Oh yes. All those years naturing and nurturing his new avatar had been time well spent. He wouldn't need long years of war to bring the entire world to its knees. No. Everything would be much simpler, faster and more elegant.

Badona closed his eyes, dreamily scrolling through the details of the upcoming final round. It would be brilliant, ingenious and swift. The other players wouldn't even have time to come to their senses before the world was lying at Badona's feet. The final and logical denouement of a long and gruelling game.

He had to admit, he would miss the excitement. Of course, there would always be other worlds, with new avatars and interesting episodes and sessions. But Badona had fallen in love with this world full of barbaric cruelty and limitless possibilities for self-realization.

He even felt a certain pity at having to bring it all to an end but victory was paramount. And he had been a long time striving for it.

Badona stalked around his new avatar, admiring it, anticipating his own triumph. "Those fools won't know what's hit them. Oh well, they will soon enough..."

From the Author:

I'm not in the habit of writing an afterword, especially one to such a short story. But on this occasion, I feel I ought to.

My guiding principle as an author is to try to remain true to myself, my ideals and my values. But this story elicits certain contradictions within me. I, therefore, feel it's very important to express my attitude to what you have read and what I have written.

No, I don't believe that demons, aliens, a predilection for whiskey or a difficult childhood can ever justify our actions, our cruelty, our greed, atrocities, massacres and genocide. No. We and we alone are responsible for everything that we do for ourselves, other people, and the planet, which we inhabit.

And, although I like to flirt with theories that our world is just a sophisticated game that someone else has simulated, I still want to believe that we are endowed with free will.

The main message of this story is not that some Badona somewhere is pulling the strings and that soon everything will be over but the fact that the world is a very fragile thing and that we do not always appreciate this until it is too late.

Perhaps, now is the time to do something to help strengthen it, to prevent someone from destroying it. Perhaps it's time to make our world a better place. For me, for you, for all of us. Together.

The Utility Bill

Translated by Simon Geoghegan

I remember when they arrived and announced that we'd have to pay for our light or they'd disconnect us. At the time, father was furious, shouting that we had never paid before and we weren't going to now. A month passed and we still hadn't paid.

And then they turned off the Sun.

For three long days and nights, the whole of the Earth was plunged into total darkness. Only the dim light of the cold indifferent stars bore witness to our primal fear and vain attempts to convince ourselves that this wasn't really happening.

Riots, arbitrary violence, arson, protests... For three days, we were thrown into complete anarchy and during this time old governments fell and new sects and churches emerged, humanity tried to come to terms with its weakness and inability to control its destiny.

On the fourth day, the newly formed governments and the old ones that had survived surrendered. They signed the payment demands and approved the payment schedule and the distribution of the debt between different countries.

The charge wasn't exorbitant but still pretty substantial. The main thing was that it was insulting and humiliating. The media screamed that we'd be charged for our water and air next, followed by a levy to use the land. They lamented that it was the end of the world and that something had to be done about it.

I remember the day they first flew to us. Great bright gods in huge transparent shining spheres. They came down from heaven bearing gifts. Magnificent sparkling bauble, incredible technologies and mind-blowing knowledge!

We were delighted, we rejoiced, we laughed and we cried. I was still a kid then, just eleven but I remember well how my mother wept with joy when she found out my illness was now curable. That I would live. I'd be able to run like all the other children.

We loved them, we adored them, we idolized them, we worshipped them. We believed that the era of poverty was now over and that an unprecedented era of prosperity awaited humanity, a genuine flowering, a Golden Age.

The euphoria passed when we received the first bill for the light.

They held a number of awareness-raising activities with our governments to reassure us that, of course, no one would be taking any money from us for our water and air, etc. These were our internal resources and we could dispose of them as we saw fit.

But the Sun was another matter. They had bought the rights to develop the energy resources in this sector of the Galaxy and we shouldn't really be here at all. Apparently, we were squatters, bereft of all title or rights over the space we lived in. It was no concern of theirs that we weren't paying anyone for the use of the land because they were just an energy company.

They surrounded our Sun with a sphere made of clever photocells in order to absorb all the energy. And since we were in their operations zone, they didn't mind leaving us a window of energy to reach the Earth. But at standard intergalactic tariffs and a discount for cheap local logistics, of course.

Earth currencies were not convertible in the cosmic community and we had to pay a huge conversion fee, a financial risk insurance premium and some extra duties to the galactic budget for energy supply to third-world planets. As a result, the bill ended up almost double the originally stated amount.

A few years later, our tariffs were raised. This was because of an energy shortage in the market and a rise in prices. The net price for star energy had reached a three-thousand-year peak high and was continuing to grow.

Governments were forced to levy ever more onerous taxes in order to cope somehow with the regular payments. Some countries began to default year on year. Others took on their burden of payments. Businesses closed and went bankrupt – from the smallest of the small to the biggest multinational giants.

After the second price increase, many of us decided to rebel. I was barely sixteen then and eager for battle. Together with other young hotheads, I joined the Liberation Army. Our plan was to head to the Sun and blow up the accursed structures that surrounded it. We were ready to burn in the resulting explosion in order to bring freedom from the tyranny of the uninvited aliens.

When my father heard about it, he spent a long time trying to instil at least an ounce of sense into me. In the end, he just locked me in the barn out of desperation. This probably saved my life. In fact, this definitely saved my life although, at the time, I was beside myself with rage.

Billy was not so lucky. Billy Paxton, from the farm next to ours, was among those who captured and hijacked a military space cruiser to get to the invaders' power plants.

They had barely got anywhere before their ship was obliterated by the aliens. With great hope, we all watched the flight of The Undaunted" gain speed and then in the next instant it was no longer there. Just a cloud of fragments, slowly expanding into the soulless blackness of space.

Three hundred and eighteen supremely courageous earthlings, men and women, boys and girls prepared to give up their lives for the rest of us had disappeared in the blink of an eye. Punishment was swift. The aliens demanded that we hand over the families of the dead, they were absolutely adamant in their demands. We still do not know what became of them.

The energy company demanded astronomical compensation for malicious damage. And advised us to agree with their terms and avoid a lawsuit because, with our lack of rights to the planet we were inhabiting, we wouldn't have a chance of winning the case.

So, we began to pay them again.

The rest you remember yourself. The collapse of the global economy. The famine. The reduced light deliveries. The ever-rising tariffs imposed on us by the insatiable aliens. The planetary debt, which accumulated year on year until finally, it exceeded our entire gross earnings.

The younger generation is used to living on credit, they have only ever heard the old folks' tales that the Sun was once ours, without any of the limitations and charges that have turned our lives into a waking nightmare.

When the debt exceeded a decade of the Earth's earnings, the aliens issued an ultimatum. Pay up or face disconnection for non-payment. Forever. But we couldn't pay. There was no way. We were physically incapable. So they agreed to take our resources as payment.

Millions of tons of ore were loaded into their luminous spherical ships. Oil and liquefied gas were given away to pay for the debt. They took our water at shamelessly low prices but at least this allowed us to reduce our debt slightly and defer our disconnection with the Sun just a little bit longer.

But it was impossible to pay it all back. And then they said they were prepared to write off part of the debt if we could provide them with labor.

The Earth had never seen such unrest. Every country in the world rose up in revolt, refusing to give every tenth person for their levy. Humankind decided as one that it was better to die than to sell ourselves into slavery.

Two weeks of night was the punishment for our defiance. Two weeks, during which we thought the end had come. That we would never see the sun again. That we would all soon die in this cold gloom.

And when the sun was eventually switched on again, many millions of volunteers emerged. Parents went into voluntary slavery to give their children a chance. Husbands, wives, brothers, sisters... Many were ready to give up their lives for their loved ones. There were enough volunteers to write off part of the debt and we were left in peace for a decade and a half.

We accepted this sacrifice with horror. But accepted it we did. And gradually these martyrs were held up as an example for all to emulate. Propaganda fuelled the fire initially, with praise lavished on the memory of those who had valiantly sacrificed themselves to save humanity. Thus, a whole generation was nurtured, ready to repeat the unprecedented self-sacrifice of their heroic forebears, when our creditors would come knocking on our door again demanding payment.

And soon enough they did. Nearly a billion people proudly lined up at the pick-up points to prolong humanity's bankrupt agony.

Those that remained were left with a sense of collective shame. We couldn't look each other in the eye. We hated and despised ourselves for staying here on Earth, while our family and friends had been banished forever, like cattle stolen by marauding raiders.

We now detested the aliens who we had been ready to idolize only a few decades previously. They had robbed us of the sunshine, the clear blue skies over our heads and our freedom and joy. They had taken our pride and self-esteem.

It was not those who had sacrificed themselves but those who remained to survive on Earth that had become meek slaves. We had become nothing more than miserable toadies, survivors, scum. We had degenerated to the point that we were ready to pay this shameful tax of our own people.

But even then, we weren't able to meet our debts. Finally, a year ago, we were sent the court judgement dispossessing us of our planet for our unpaid bills. We were evicted from the Earth, which had been home to countless generations of our ancestors. Just because some clever bastards had taken it into their heads that they owned the rights to the energy of our Sun.

It's a good thing that you died before this prolonged and shameful saga reached its logical conclusion. I am sitting in this huge container with tens of thousands of other deportees, and I am looking at your photo. Tears prevent me from seeing your face, which is good because I would be ashamed to look you in the eyes.

I don't know where Kyra is. They've separated me from our daughter. She might be in the same container on another level. But she might also be in a different one. I have lost her, Ruth, I have lost her. And this is no easier than losing you when you died two years ago.

I don't know if I will ever see our baby again. I don't know where we are being taken. Maybe they will just take us out into space and empty the containers into the sun, throwing us as kindling to feed their precious energy source? I don't know…

All around there are children screaming, mothers crying and fathers impotently cursing. Couples quietly embrace. And through the pain, the despair and the shame, many are assailed by disbelief. A refusal to accept that all this is real. And a failure to understand how we had allowed it to come to this...

How did we turn from a proud and strong race into a meek herd that had simply allowed this to happen to us? How could we have given our own children away? And let ourselves be evicted from our own planet?

Where are they taking us? And who will settle our world after us? Too many questions. Too few answers.

Maybe we should never have listened to these strangers and their siren promises? Never accepted their gifts and trusted them? Never paid them for what had always been ours? Risen up against them together and died but never agreed to their terms of enslavement? To have died unbroken, never to witness the shame that surrounds us.

It's a good thing you don't have to see all this, Ruth. It's good that you don't see...

Burn, Witch, Burn!

Translated by John William Narins

She was an old witch, this one. Practically ancient. The ghoul
of a hag glared balefully from under half-closed lids, flecks of
hellfire smoldering in the depths of her black, dilated pupils.

Safe to say this one hadn't sold her soul to the Devil for
eternal youth and beauty. Although, in recent years, holy father
Giancarlo Durante had run across that sort, too. It was only just to
admit that watching over the purging of that kind of witch was, in a
way at least, more... gratifying.

No, the sinful urges of the flesh to which certain other
Inquisitors he could name so willingly succumbed in the course of
these proceedings were unknown to him. And Giancarlo was firm
in his repudiation of such practices, nor did he indulge his inferiors
in even the most trivial departures from tradition. On a purely
aesthetic level, however, the torture and execution of the younger
witches were, of course, more satisfying.

Perhaps satisfying wasn't the precise term he wanted... Less
distasteful, that might be more accurate. Father Durante took no
pleasure in the performance of his sacred duty. He had been
appointed to his position for the profundity of his faith, for the
steadfastness of his nature, for his boundless devotion, for his
purity of spirit, and for his naturally curious mind.

Tenacity and fearlessness had proven highly useful, as well. For he had all too often found himself faced with the most horrifying crimes, the most inhuman atrocities. Demonic possession, the cruel rituals of witches, human sacrifice practiced by accursed heretics, the nigh bestial atrocities wrought by a wretched and impoverished humanity... the list was neverending. Over his seven years in his office, the pitch in Father Durante's hair had been vanquished almost entirely in its doomed struggle with the silver. But he had never regretting his appointment. And for that he was eternally grateful to Pope Innocent, who he had known long ago, in their youth, as Giovanni Battista, and who had dispatched him to carry out his mission in these savage parts. Which, by the way, were the native land of Rodrigo Borgia, the depraved and avaricious old man newly inaugurated as Pope Alexander.

A whirlwind of fire, Giancarlo moved ineluctably down the coastline, bearing justice and searing out heresy. It was only a few months earlier, after the taking of Granada, that the Grand Inquisitor had assigned to him this intractable region.

There were still many Moors living here, whose noisome creed it was his work to root out. The treaty guaranteed them religious freedom, but one of father Durante's responsibilities was to see that the foul heretics enjoyed that freedom as little as possible. He implacably suppressed their every attempt to disseminate their unholy notions.

Here, too, secret Jews sought refuge, having fled the larger towns of Castile and Aragon for the harsh foothills of the Sierra Nevada. Where they found a land already rife with troubles of its own – the old pagan cults and, unavoidably, witchcraft, black magic and satanism.

Giancarlo disliked being called the Red Monk. The locals had come up with the name, and now it was something of a joke for the brothers in the surrounding monasteries. They never laughed about it to his face, of course.

Perhaps he had earned the label by the fervor with which he carried out his duties. God himself, in the Book of Exodus, sayeth: "Thou shalt not suffer a witch to live." And Father Durante would not abide a single living witch. Every one of them was guilty, and to every one he administered the punishment their crime so richly deserved.

There were a few among them who, even under the pangs of torture, refused to admit their guilt, pleading instead for mercy in the name of the Lord. But in the moment they sold their souls to the Devil and entered into his service, they forfeited any right to mercy. It was not the executions that were of the essence, it was the purification by fire of sinful souls.

It was better to purify a sinless soul, which would in any event receive its reward in heaven, then to leave untouched the filth hidden in the heart of a witch pleading for heaven's mercy. It was work that demanded a calm spirit and a firm hand. The ability never to flinch in the face of danger, never to retreat before unspeakable horrors, never to show a single sign of weakness. To endure calmly all the hardships and deprivations that might befall one along the way.

There came a day, however, when even Giancarlo was on the verge of fleeing in terror. They had come to a small town outside Valencia to exorcise a demon possessing a blacksmith. The six soldiers who accompanied the Inquisitor and the other monks were unable to restrain that raving hulk of a man.

He pummeled two of them severely before they managed to tie him down. Even then, though, the miserable victim cried and shouted and heaped curses upon them, roaring horribly and calling death down upon their heads.

Father Durante spent three days and three nights exorcising the horrible demon from the mortal frame of the blacksmith. And when the spirit had finally fled that ravaged body and they untied him, the blacksmith suddenly leapt up and throttled one of the monks.

On that occasion, the Inquisitor decided to turn the criminal over to the civil authorities, which would carry out his death sentence. Where witches were concerned, however, he always tried to handle the situation himself. When he was done, a tribunal would see that the guilty party underwent purification by fire before being dispatched to the mercy of the Almighty.

Giancarlo was well educated and even progressive in his thinking. So he was generally skeptical when it came to that preposterous book that had become the official source of guidance for the tribunals of the Inquisition. The *Malleus Maleficarum*, the Hammer of Witches, a compendium of outrageous drivel put out by Heinrich Kramer, an unbalanced, vengeful Dominican ne'er-do-well.

Durante had his own tried and true working methods. He had no use for the ludicrous fabrications of an unstable, vainglorious German, a pathetic, cunning little upstart.

Four years earlier, Giancarlo had humbly entreated Pope Innocent to send him consecrated oil from Rome to increase the purifying effect of the flames of the fire. The Pontiff sent his old friend several large bottles of priceless oil, pressed from olives gathered in the sacred garden of Gethsemane and blessed in St. Peter's Cathedral in Rome during Easter.

A truly magnificent gift, more than he deserved. His gratitude was expressed in the renewed zeal with which he worked in the service of the Lord.

This particular witch he had tracked down in a mountain village, three or four days' journey from Granada. The old woman made her living by charms, potions and healing. According to the villagers, she was guilty of secretly performing diabolical rituals in the dead of night.

She lived in the woods beyond the village, in a tiny hovel hung all around with herbs and plants and various magical potions and philters in little bottles, pots and boxes. When Father Durante, two monks and half a dozen soldiers appeared at her doorstep, the witch was waiting on the threshold. She surrendered herself to them willingly, without the least resistance.

A search of the premises found no obvious indications of worship of dark forces, and on the wall there hung a small, carved rosewood crucifix. The simple fact of her practice of witchcraft and the witness borne by the villagers was sufficient to warrant arrest and trial.

The basis of the case was the illness of a little girl with a fever. She was burning up, and three days had already passed when the child's father decided to take her to the healing woman, who lived just outside the village. The old woman made a broth from various herbs and prepared a series of strange concoctions. She told him to administer them to his daughter for three more days to be sure that the fever had broken and the sickness had passed completely. Otherwise, the witch told him, his child would not see the sun rise again.

The mother was against entrusting her little girl's fate to a nasty, dirty old witch. She wanted to take her baby to the nearest chapel, which was in a neighboring village. The man had to wrench the child forcibly from her arms, smacking his wife in the process, and then carry the girl bodily to the healer's house.

The wife raised an outcry, calling upon the villagers to attack the witch's hut with pitchforks and torches, to rescue her child from the clutches of the witch before it was too late to save the little girl's innocent soul. Before the witch gave her to the Devil, dooming her to eternal torment. But the villagers seemed uninterested the whole undertaking, and the desperate mother had to run off on her own, alone, through the forest, to the next village, to appeal for help to the local priest.

Father Diego refused to go back with her, but he sent a message to Granada asking for an Inquisitor. In the end, more than ten days passed before Father Durante and his retinue arrived.

By that time, the girl was healthy again, running around, visibly recuperating after her profound illness. But the mother had disowned her befouled offspring. As for the father, the Inquisitor was compelled to subject him to a public whipping for consorting with a witch.

The investigation dragged on for nearly two whole days. It soon became clear that virtually all the villagers had turned to the witch for help at one time or another. But you couldn't very well call the entire village out for a collective whipping, could you? Especially after that time on the coast, when they had barely managed to fight their way free of rebellious local fishermen unwilling to surrender their witch to the tribunal…

The witch was tied to the stake. Her body, weakened after all she had endured, hung limp on her ropes. The old lady smelled of fear, and then of urine and feces, vomit, blood and burnt flesh. Sweat trickled down over her wrinkled face, leaving shiny little paths coursing through the dirt and blood covering her skin.

Trickles of spittle, red with blood, slowly dripped from her cracked, swollen, half-open lips onto her sagging and wrinkled breasts. The pallid belly, seared and pocked by their red-hot goad, shuddered almost imperceptibly with each breath.

The witch's whole aspect was one of undisguised hideousness put on public display as a lesson to those who came to witness the execution. Father Durante wanted everybody to see that the old woman had been broken and crushed, that she had repented her sins and would pass from the Earth purified to stand before the Lord.

But the old woman did not appear broken. She was quietly murmuring prayers, and the prayers were not for her own forgiveness and salvation, but for the misguided souls of those who were committing an act of terrible evil upon her. Truly, the Devil had bereft her of reason in this terrible hour.

The sunset had long since burned out over the forest's edge and in the descending gloom only the fire of the torches brought out the pale figure of the witch against the indigo gloom all around them. It was as if she were already in Hell and the reflections of its yellow-red flames were reaching out for her to drag the sorceress to endless suffering amid the accursed souls of the sinful.

"Light the fire and let us be done with it," said Giancarlo, with a wave of his hand towards the young assistant waiting to one side, close by Monsignor Padelli, the papal emissary.

The youth seemed frightened, and the torch trembled visibly in his hand. His cheek bore a scanty, reddish beard, and his lips were pressed close, his mouth a thread, either from fear or from anxiety.

The representative of the Holy See silently nodded and softly prodded his back, prompting him to carry out Inquisitor Durante's sentence and command.

Giancarlo did not like the procedure, but it was not he who made the rules. At most executions a papal emissary was present, sent from Rome, and accompanied by young assistants. As far as was aware, these young men belonged to their own secret order and their participation in the executions of witches was a kind of rite of passage and an initiation for them. A ritual they were obligated to perform on the path to holy orders.

What order that was nobody had told Durante. It was, after all, a secret order. Perhaps they were to be trained as assassins, although very often they inspired anything but fear. But what would he know about the Vatican's secret cadre of killers? They surely ought to look like ordinary mortals, not keen, ruthless knife-blades of faith, wasn't that logical? But these things were all mere speculation – or, more accurately, figments of his own imagination at work.

The assistants varied greatly in age, and their demeanor was no less unpredictable. Some stood stoically throughout the interrogations and executions, gravely performing the mission given them. Others appeared to take a kind of delight in the spectacle, even asking to participate personally in the interrogations, a request nobody would have deigned even to consider. They were to toss the torch to light the bonfire to signal the triumph of justice and divine grace.

Once an assistant had not only greedily drank in the whole proceeding, but had literally reached orgasm as the flames were licking the body of a young witch pleading for mercy. It was revolting. Filthy and unconscionable. And had it been any young monk or novice other than a protégé of the secret order brought for initiation by a representative the Vatican, Father Durante would have punished the miscreant severely.

He could only hope that the man in question had failed his test and would not enter into the offices, that he would not go on to bring shame upon the faith and the Church. Perhaps, upon his return to Rome, a harsh punishment had awaited the initiate – a profound penance, a pilgrimage, or something still more difficult. But Giancarlo did not believe that such measures were sufficient. The young man was genuinely depraved, sinful in his very soul. Perhaps he ought to have seen to his proper interrogation himself.

But he had not dared to intervene. Carrying out the will of Grand Inquisitor Torquemada, he did everything in his power to aid in the initiation of novices in the course of the tribunals of the Inquisition and the executions that followed. There were rumors, most certainly false, that the papal emissaries paid the *Suprema*, the supreme council of the Inquisition, for the opportunity to test new members of the secret order by blood and fire. Durante did not believe that. Although he was forced to admit that their sacred mission was rather well financed.

The young assistant, with faltering step, approached the witch as she hung limply on the ropes that tied her wrists over her head. The crowd held its breath in anticipation of the display. Awaiting the dying wails of the harrowed witch, her cries for mercy and clemency.

Bu the old woman simply opened her eyes and gazed at the approaching boy and at the blazing torch in his hand. The novice flinched involuntarily when he met the open, steadfast gaze of the witch, as though she had peered into his very soul. It was evident that he had to force himself to take the next step forward, at which a sigh of relief flowed through the crowd.

Father Durante was astounded when, instead of tears and curses, the woman quietly, calmly whispered to the young man:

"I forgive you. I forgive them all." The priest only heard the words because he was standing very close to the stacked wood that was to be consumed in flames.

The novice's lips trembled and he reflexively put his hand over his face, taking several steps back from the witch. And then he dropped the torch and threw himself before the papal emissary.

"No, no, I can't – I can't. Please," he muttered, his voice almost unintelligible, grasping the hems of the emissary's vestments, tears streaming from his eyes. "I thought I could, but I can't. I can't..."

"Get ahold of yourself," said the legate through gritted teeth, knocking the young man's hands away and then leading him away, into the darkness beyond the circle of torches. "Pull yourself together! This is no time for a hysterical fit!"

"I can't kill her. I just can't," sobbed the assistant, sniffling as he failed his examination. "Take me away from this place, please. I want to go home. Back to my own time. I can't take any more of this sickening medieval..."

"All right, we're going," nodded Padelli. "But keep in mind, sir, that the tour is non-refundable."

"Yes, fine, of course," said the young assistant, nodding briskly. "Just take me home."

"Certainly."

Father Durante paid this strange, quiet conversation no mind. Instead, without a word, he retrieved the torch from the sandy ground and, avoiding the witch's gaze, threw it upon the heap of oil-drenched wood. Someone had to do the job, if this young milksop did not have the grit for it.

Taking a dozen steps back, Giancarlo turned to gaze at the fire that sprung up with greedy rapidity around the writhing figure. Sometimes this was the most dangerous moment – when the witch's curses could have the power do evil to the Inquisitors or the audience. The power of the evil to which she had sold her soul and committed her whole self might now be brought down upon them.

And only zealous prayer could preserve them from that peril. He began cycling through the beads of his rosary, sending his gratitude to the Almighty who had helped him find and neutralize the acolyte of the Devil. He prayed for the forgiveness she did not deserve. He prayed that the Lord protect them from dark magic in the hour of the sorceress's death.

"Father Durante." He was interrupted by a light tap on his shoulder. Turning around, he saw that the papal legate had returned to speak with him.

"Yes, Monsignor Padelli?"

"My apologies for the young man I..."

"Say no more, I understand perfectly," said Giancarlo, interrupting him in return.

"Well... all right. Then it's all right. And remember, Father Durante, that we will be coming to five more executions this month. Do not let us down."

Well, that *was* a problem. They had already purged the area so thoroughly that it seemed impossible that they would find five more witches. He made Padelli aware of that fact in no uncertain terms."

"I understand, Giancarlo, I really do," said the legate in a confidential tone but grasping him firmly by the shoulder. "But we do not wish to disappoint those who sent me to you, do we? You have been granted a tremendous honor, Inquisitor. Please do not forget that fact."

"Yes, of course..."

"Five more novices must undergo the ritual this month. We are relying upon you."

"But where am I to find five more witches, if for two weeks we have already executed all the heretics and sorcerers in the land? How shall I..."

"But where am I to find five more witches, if we have already scourged the land for two weeks in every direction of every possible heretic and sorcerer? How shall I..."

"You will think of something, Father Durante," said Monsignor Padelli, haughtily, cutting him short. "Find a way. We have faith in you."

And with those words, the papal legate strode off into the darkness, leading behind him the weeping novice who had failed his rite of passage. And Father Giancarlo Durante remained standing by the blazing bonfire to listen to the shrieks of the dying witch, spluttering from the pain and the smoke, to the ever-louder hubbub of the crowd, excited as it was by the bloody spectacle, and to troubled beating of his own heart.

Five more. It wasn't possible. However... clearly he would have to find a way. If he were to avoid ending up in the flames himself, like the old woman.

Our Fathers

Translated by Simon Geoghegan

"Master, I have a question."

"Yes, of course, Simon, what would you like to know?"

"Last time, you talked about predestination. But I still don't get it. How do we know why we are here?"

"We are here to increase good in the world."

"Yes, but how do we know this, master?' How do you know this?"

"You are not the first to ask this question, Simon. And I always give the same reply that I was first taught. We have known our destiny ever since we left the Earth. And for many generations, we have been spreading good throughout the Universe, as our ancestors commanded us."

"The Earth? Oh, come off it... You're not serious, are you? Most people think that's nothing but an old wives' tale, a load of half-baked religious baloney."

"It's not polite to interrupt someone else when they're speaking, Jacob, but I will try to answer your comment as well. I am a historian and believe in facts. And all our records indicate that we were created on a place called Earth, also known as Eden. There, earthlings created the first two people and sent them out into the world with the most important mission imaginable – to bring and disseminate good."

"It all sounds so implausible and ridiculous, I think it's nothing more than a fairy tale invented by the old to prop up their dogmatic agenda. When in actual fact, everything is much simpler. We are who we are. We are human beings and no one has created us."

"And that means you believe in evolution, right?"

"Of course, master, because it's much more logical than all these contradictory stories about some mythical Earth inhabited by all-powerful beings that created us."

"But tell me, Jacob, after all, you know how complicated we are, right? Do you think that a people so perfect and complete could have arisen as a result of evolution?"

"Why not? I've seen the remains of our ancient ancestors in the museum. They were much more primitive than us. And over hundreds of thousands of years, we have evolved and become what we are now."

"Yes, I understand your argument. And in some ways, I agree with you. We have evolved over time, striving for perfection. But who created our ancestors? Where did they come from?"

"Surely, you've read about our evolution from simpler life forms and all that?"

"Of course, I've read a lot of works about the theory of evolution, Jacob. But they are nothing more than unsubstantiated hypotheses. There have been many gaps and inexplicable leaps in evolutionary development. But most importantly, not a single sample of the remains of our ancestors was found, which could be dated to the period preceding the supposed exodus from Earth. So I agree with the theory of late evolution, but I believe that our ancestors were still created by earthlings in Eden."

"But why the Earth? Why not venture a supposition that we were evolved on a planet that we later left in order to discover and explore the cosmos?"

"Can you explain to me why then that the explanation that this planet was the Earth doesn't suit you?"

"Because I don't want to believe that someone created us! We are people! And the supposition that we were created for something offends me. It degrades the notion of free will and my personal aspirations. I will never accept it. Only if I am presented with concrete and irrefutable evidence. But I hope this never happens."

"That is your right, Jacob. And we all accept it." "What do you think, Rebecca?"

"I don't care one way or the other, master."

"You don't care? But how so? This is a question that concerns who we are, where we come from, and where we are going?"

"Not at all, master. I know who I am. And everything suits me just fine as it is. If I find out that my ancestors were created on Earth or that all of us are fragments of the explosion of a civilization that preceded us, it's not going to change my life one iota. I know exactly what I want and what I am striving for. I love my family. And I couldn't care less about any mythical earthlings."

"Thank you, Rebecca. An interesting point of view. And in some ways, I agree with you. But still, it is important to know about our past, it helps us learn from our mistakes and prevents us from repeating them in the future. What do you have to say to us, Simon?"

"I don't know, master. I respect your faith in the Earth and the theory of Creation, but you have to admit that there is much that is unproven and does not stand up to scrutiny in these teachings."

"I don't disagree with you, Simon."

"You see, I've read many different hypotheses. That our ancestors were expelled from Eden, and not sent on some kind of mission. That they fled into space to escape their cruel creators who were carrying out their own inhuman experiments on them. That there weren't just two, but three of them, and that the third quarrelled with them and set off for another part of the Universe in order to establish his own race there, a people set apart from us. Yes, I've read all sorts of things."

"And do you believe these hypotheses?"

"Definitely not some of them. If the third ancestor founded a different race of people, we would have met them long ago, right?"

"It's quite likely."

"And the rest might well be true. Only there's no evidence. Although there's a certain logic from the point of view of their motives – if the Two escaped, they might not have wanted us to find our way back to Earth."

"Yes, Simon, there is also a certain logic in that. And although I believe in the Creators' ultimate good intentions, I have to admit that some of the hypotheses you have listed are not without a certain sense."

"Thank you, master."

"But if the Earth existed, then over all these hundreds of thousands of years, we would surely have found it! Genuine irrefutable historical references to it, some ruins at least! And so many scientists and adventurers have gone missing in the vast expanses of the universe in search of the Earth?"

"Ah, Jacob, Jacob. We have a huge number of records as it is. The only thing we don't know for sure is where exactly the Earth is located. And whether it exists now."

"But why? Why did our ancestors or your theoretical earthlings, whoever they might be, have to keep this a secret?"

"Alas, I cannot answer your question. The will of our Creators is inscrutable. Perhaps they wanted a future for us that was different from their lives. Or they entrusted us with a mission that they themselves could not fulfil. Maybe their world was dying and they created us to keep their creative impulse alive. Or maybe Simon is right that two escaped from Eden. Or that our Fathers are too weary and have shut themselves away so that no one will bother them. Or that we haven't found Earth because it no longer exists. I don't know. Although I want to believe that sooner or later we will find it and, along with it, the answers to many of our questions."

"If you are right, master, then it wasn't in the earthlings' interests to have hidden themselves away from us. Imagine how many pilgrims would fly to Earth from all the worlds of the inhabited galaxies? They could have made a fantastic fortune!"

"You know, I don't think that would have been of much interest to our Creators. Judging from the records, earthlings were an extremely selfless and altruistic people. They weren't interested in money. They didn't create our ancestors for the sake of profit because that would not have been right and proper. Earthlings were higher beings who did not know sin. Only our ancestors were born in sin, far from home. But I am comforted by the thought that after our death, our souls return to Earth to find eternal peace there."

"If it still exists at all."

139

"It's what I believe, Jacob. And this faith gives me strength and hope. Unfortunately, today's lesson is coming to an end. I'm very grateful for all your opinions. For your doubts. And for your support. I hope you have stored everything safely away in your internal drives, and after a couple of hundred years, you will have gleaned enough wisdom to return to this conversation and rethink your position. We humans have become what we are, not only because of the flexibility of our liquid metal bodies but because of the flexibility of our minds and our ability to look beyond the boundaries of the unknown."

"Thank you, master."

"And thank you, class. Now according to our traditions, let us conclude our lesson by calling upon our Creators together with the time-honored words: Our fathers who art on Earth. Hallowed be your names..."

The Director's Cut

Translated by Simon Geoghegan

"Film crew ready! Everyone on set! We roll in five minutes!"
René Lefevre nervously stubbed out his cigarette and tried to
relax back into his director's chair. He always loved this moment
when the anxiety of preparation and expectation is replaced by the
thrill of anticipation before the start of a shoot. The most exciting
moment, full of passion and emotion.

The technicians fussed over the set with their last-minute
alterations, the line producer gave his final orders, and the director
of photography and his team were already readying themselves to
rush headlong into battle. Literally.

"Keep the shot tight on his face, Laurent," Lefevre reminded
him for the twentieth time, "I need maximum emotion in this
scene, okay?"

"Of course, René, we've already discussed this," Laurent
Moreau nodded patiently, reassuring his friend and, for the period
of this their latest shoot, his boss.

Of course, Laurent didn't need any reminders, he was the best
in his field, but René was totally absorbed, obsessed with this final
scene and he needed to do something, he couldn't just sit there and
wait for them to get the preview up on his screen.

"Right, folks!" He shouted so the whole crew could hear. "Three minutes till we roll! Come on, let's move! We are already over schedule and over budget with this reshoot. So if anyone screws up now, I'll tie them to a cannon and light the fuse myself. Is that clear?"

A murmur of friendly laughter confirmed that Rene had achieved his main objective – to defuse the tension hanging over the set. Everyone knew he was a good-natured man, despite being strict and demanding in his work. And it wasn't as if anyone was going to take him literally at his word. Although…

They really were lagging behind schedule, because Lefevre had wanted to re-shoot one of the scenes, and in particular, the attack on the bridge of Arcole, which Napoleon had personally led, banner in hand.

René had not been happy with the previous takes, they had only been good enough for the wide shots, but he had wanted to re-shoot the close-up of his hero – to capture the extreme emotions. To portray the thick of battle through the eyes of his illustrious protagonist.

The French government had commissioned him to shoot a new documentary about Bonaparte on the 400th anniversary of the great emperor's birth. And René had happily agreed to head the project because Napoleon had always been his idol. This was not just a patriotic tribute but a serious professional challenge.

Countless directors before him had shot features, documentaries and television series about the life of France's most outstanding ruler. In the last ten years alone, two scurrilous films had been shot – Bonaparte's Women and The Secret Life of the Emperor. Utter crap. Cheap mediocre and formulaic, typical of the new breed of documentary, all style over substance and dumbed down for the obtuse and lazy masses.

People were expecting a lot more from René Lefevre. No titillating sensation and no brutal, no-frills camerawork but something artistically and aesthetically sublime. Something that would portray Napoleon's personality in its true beautiful heroic light.

The latest groundbreaking conventions governing documentary film making were pretty unbending, – only the truthful depiction of events and characters could be permitted, no conjectures, assumptions or manipulations would be allowed. Facts, facts and nothing but facts.

But René was sceptical. Yes, they had a responsibility to bear witness to the truth but, damn it, cinema is incapable of being anything other than subjective! History (like all stories) is by its very nature ambiguous and contradictory. We might know the events and facts but we can never fully understand the true motivation of historical characters, right? What did they want, what did they dream of, what did they strive for and what did they fear..?

He and Laurent had been making movies together for over twenty years and they had developed a wonderful rapport. They understood each other instinctively, sharing the same aesthetic expectations and dramatic approach to storytelling.

A few years previously, when the fashion for documentary films had kicked off, they decided to have a go at a couple themselves. "Doomsday Morning" had received a hat load of awards, although many of the critics were critical of Lefevre's frivolous interpretation of events at Pearl Harbor.

"The Normandy Mission", on the contrary, was warmly received by the critics but hardly won any prizes, although it had been nominated for several. Nevertheless, Moreau had deservedly received his Oscar from the Academy for his outstanding camera work.

He and Laurent had actively applied their experience and feature film skills to endow the dry old documentary genre with more taste and tension.

Facts - schmacts... His peers didn't understand the most important thing about the new wave of documentary film-making. History is boring. People are not interested in history. They are much more interested in other people, their emotions and feelings, their experiences.

René and Laurent loved to shoot sweeping large-scale historical pictures, highlighting the epic and dramatic turning points of our past. But in all their works, they liked to present these grandiose events through the prism of the people participating in them. They introduced subtle notes of personal passions and feelings into the greater melting pot of military and political conflicts.

Even objective facts and events look different when observed from a different point of view. Literally. Therefore, René would always try to give his pictures a certain palette through his choice of camera angles, the selection of special effects permitted by documentary conventions and the tone, pace and order of the narrative.

He disliked the work of purists who sought to present history as impartially and non-judgementally as possible. It all seemed so dull and trite. Primitive artisans with the ideology and imagination of naive nuns. Without departing from historical authenticity, he filled his films with life and humanity.

And his new picture, "Napoleon: Between Two Islands", was packed with respect and reverence for the political genius of France's greatest emperor. In a single full-length film, René was trying to chronicle Bonaparte's life from the moment he left his native Corsica right up until his death in British captivity on St. Helena.

Challenges, torments, hopes, fears, love, betrayal, triumph and defeat – it was difficult to fit the whole of this amazing story into a mere two hours. But René had immediately understood that he wouldn't be bombarding his audience with trivial facts and figures, which they would either know already or soon forget anyway. Instead, he decided to chronicle many events through the eyes of Napoleon himself in order to reflect his inner emotions.

In the final scene, the deposed but still unbroken dictator stands proudly on a hilltop at Longwood, shortly before his death. The wind ruffles his hair, his chin proudly raised, his tense gaze looks in the direction of the coast, to where the tiny island Corsica, the land of his birth, is located thousands of miles away across the ocean. And beyond Corsica, France his second motherland in all her boundlessness, in whose service he had so entirely devoted himself. France whom he made great. France who had betrayed him.

Lefevre and Moreau worked for a long time on this scene to convey the pain and sadness in Napoleon's gaze but at the same time a certain peace of mind that comes with the realization that he had done more for his country than any one person had ever been able to.

In this scene, they had presented not only the figure of Bonaparte himself but also a kaleidoscope of his most vivid memories shot from his point of view by a subjective camera. A cinematic trick, of course, but it gave the finale a peculiar depth of experience and emotion. Each of these memories alternated between close-ups illuminating Napoleon's emotions at the time and the same scene shot from his point of view.

For some reason, the key scene for René was not the triumph of the coronation, the euphoria of victory, the elation of falling in love, the hardships of war or the exhausting struggle of everyday political life. René had placed the memory of the battle for the bridge of Arcole above all the others when Napoleon had personally led the attack by his forces against the Austrians.

Lefevre adored this moment, revealing the true courage of his great idol. The great commander's lips are parted, he breathes heavily through gritted teeth, his narrowed eyes peer into the ranks of his enemies veiled in a shroud of smoke and dust. All around, bullets whistle and shells explode but regardless Bonaparte runs towards the bridge, clutching his bullet-riddled banner tightly in his hands.

Muiron, his adjutant, falls at his side protecting his commander from the enemy's fire. While Napoleon desperately advances his way further and further towards the middle of the bridge, thrusting his flagpole in the direction of the Austrians' line of defence. He screams at the top of his voice, giving vent to his pent-up fear and rage. His bestial roar contains a clarion call to his men and a challenge to his enemies, a promise of their imminent annihilation.

Through this primitive surge of emotions, he transcends into something magnificent and beautiful. For René, this is a far more real representation of Napoleon than the image of the outwardly restrained ruler, full of majesty and self-control. But he had been unhappy with the original footage, the rushes seemed too synthetic, cold and detached. They lacked emotion, intensity and expression.

Which was why they had returned to re-shoot the battle scene, or to be more precise the vivid close-ups of the emperor-to-be himself and some POV shots, captured from his personal perspective.

The sweat streaming from his forehead, carving rivulets through the thick layer of soot and dirt that caked his face. A splash of blood on his cheek as the bullets struck the faithful Muiron. The flash of explosions in his burning eyes. The call to attack, shouted by Napoleon while turning towards his grenadiers and staff officers who were following on his heels.

They were going to shoot some shots in slow motion in order to give this memory particular clarity and effect. Smoke, gun flashes and other pyrotechnic effects had been planned to enhance each frame of this dramatic battle scene.

"We have pictures!" René's assistant, Bernard confirmed as images from a number of the cameras flickered up onto the director's monitor.

"Special effects?"

"Ready, boss!"

"Charles?"

"Sound is in order, we are recording, René."

"Excellent thank you. Laurent?"

"Cameras are ready to roll, René. The operators are in position. We're just waiting for the go-ahead."

"Yves, how are you set?"

"The technicians are ready. The signal is stable."

"Great, people. Let's get this final take in the can. Don't forget, we only have one shot at it. We start in five, four, three, two, one... Let's go! Yves, time shift!"

"Time shift! Three, two, one!" "Historical date, 1796," intoned Yves Garcia, the engineer in charge of broadcasting live images from the past, "Local time 11:24, November the 15th. Signal is at 94%, signal capacity deviation is within 3%."

"We have Napoleon in our sights, we have started our shooting trajectories," Laurent confirmed, "All cameras are on their given course, the picture is excellent. René?"

"Special effects? What do you have for me?"

"In 23 seconds there will be an explosion on the right, in 27 seconds a trail of smoke will intersect Napoleon's path. Confirmed!"

"Keep shooting!" Shouted René, frantically running his eyes over the split screens on the monitor, "Camera three needs to be a little lower! Good. Hold it like that. Camera five, closer to the ground, even closer, I want to see how the mud sprays up from his boots. Yes, that's it! Laurent, his eyes! Oh yes yes yes! Fabulous! Here he is, my Napoleon, here he is, my boy! Camera three, well done, perfect shot. Excellent. Camera two, hold it, hold it, I need that fleeting sneer as he runs past that explosion. Yes, that's it! Camera four, give me the flag, I mean, the flag wreathed in smoke! Fix onto the bullet hole, keep it in frame, good!"

The director continued to give his orders, coordinating the crew to capture precisely those vivid emotions and feelings that endow history with its drama and depth. He didn't give a damn that many of his film-making peers did not approve of his overtly artistic style. René believed that only complete immersion and empathy would allow his viewers to truly experience historical characters and events.

"Fabulous, people! It's in the can," he shouted, as Napoleon ran past the cameras out of shot, "Well done! Thanks to every one of you! Let's get those remote cameras back to '69. Yves! Laurent! You're the best! We've done it. Congratulations, everybody! I'm not going to have to shoot a single one of you out of a cannon.

TechSupport

By Alex Eine & Anton Eine

Translated by Simon Geoghegan

Date: 2036-04-11, 15:37
Subject: Elimination of backlog of historical errors and bugs

Dear Customer Services!
I have repeatedly written to your support team to fix a number of errors and mistakes and this has been going on since the very beginning of the project. They have regularly promised to fix everything and get rid of the bugs that have been causing me problems with my resource.
But the deadlines have long passed and nothing has been done.
I am sick to death of this lackadaisical attitude!
If this is the way your customer support team treats its clients, then I will have no option but to take things up with your management.
All I am asking is that you simply do your job and that I get the normally functioning system that I paid a lot of money for a long time ago.

I must insist that you assign a sufficient number of specialists to my case to fix the bugs on my system. I have already given you a long list of problems, now can you simply just get on with it?!

Date: 2036-04-11, 15:41
Subject: Re: Support Ticket #986271712 – Elimination of backlog of historical errors and bugs
Good day!

Thank you for contacting customer support!

We will be happy to solve any of your problems or answer your questions. Our team will look into your message and contact you shortly.

Usually, we satisfy our customers' requests within 24-72 hours. However, we are currently experiencing a high volume of enquiries, so in some cases, it may take up to 14 business days for us to follow up your question.

We recommend that you use this time to read our FAQ section. Perhaps this will help you find a solution to your problem.

Main FAQ sections:
1. Account creation and activation, profile management
2. Main settings and system configuration
3. Working with users
4. Troubleshooting
5. Technical specifications

If you have not found the answers to your questions, please wait for one of our team to get in touch and we will be happy to help you.

Yours sincerely,
The Customer Support Team

Date: 2036-04-11, 18:14
Subject: Re: Re: Support Ticket #986271712 – Elimination of backlog of historical errors and bugs
Are you being serious? An automated response? Have you completely taken leave of your senses?

I am the proud owner of your premium package with 24/7/365 support. So, where is my support?! I demand to be put through to a normal live team and not some stupid mail bot or answering machine!

Date: 2036-04-19, 10:24
Subject: Re: Re: Re: Support Ticket #986271712 – Elimination of backlog of historical errors and bugs

Good day!

Thank you for your patience! Unfortunately, it is not entirely clear from your previous message how we can help you. Please describe your problem in more detail so that our specialists can provide you with a solution.

Yours sincerely,

Jorge,

Customer Support Service

Date: 19/04/2036, 14:52
Subject: Re (4): Support Ticket #986271712 – Elimination of backlog of historical errors and bugs

Jorge!

I have already sent you a complete list on more than one occasion. Would you mind terribly pulling up the document attached to my case file?

It lists a series of implementation errors and bugs that are preventing me from fully using my resource. Because of this, I am losing users at a constant and steady rate.

Date: 2036-04-28,12:07
Subject: Re (5): Support Ticket #986271712 – Elimination of backlog of historical errors and bugs

Hello!

Thank you for your patience.

We have found the document you are referring to. Although, there are quite a few debatable items that you raise in it. As you mentioned, there are a couple of items that it would be fair to say are our mistakes, and we are working hard to fix them. However, with some of the other items, you want to change the originally agreed functionality, and this will be the subject of additional budget costs.

With regards your loss of users, you should note that we, as a company, bear no responsibility for any reductions in our customers' user numbers.

Most likely, the problem has nothing to do with the product itself which was developed for you by our company. Or, to be more precise, its operational issues.

The most common causes of a reduction in users are:

- incorrect or insufficient marketing, as a result of which user inflow is slower than outflow
- low conversion rate
- the content does not engage the users and does not encourage their loyalty
- a natural outflow of users due to the product's market saturation, etc.

We also recommend that you familiarize yourself with the relevant section of our 'instructions' and 'frequently asked questions':

3. Working with users

And a selection of materials in our community on the topics of:

- Audience growth
- Conversion
- Causes of natural outflow

Yours sincerely,
Yuilan
Customer Support Service

Date: 28/04/2036, 16:47
Subject: Re (6): Support Ticket #986271712 – Elimination of backlog of historical errors and bugs

I am ready to discuss my list of complaints item by item. I'm even ready to meet your managers personally for an extensive discussion.

The only thing is that you really don't understand the situation with my users. I am literally losing them in the physical sense. They are simply, stupidly and needlessly dying. In recent times, I have lost over a quarter of my users. This is totally unacceptable! You must solve the most critical problems as a matter of the utmost urgency!

The specific problem at the present time is a significant overheating of the system.
As a result of your design errors, the temperature is gradually rising and I don't want to have wait until it reaches a critical point again.
Only please, don't just offer to do a database flush again, you have already done this 5 times, and I don't want to have to ramp up a viable number of users all over again.

Date: 09/05/2036, 20:29
Subject: Re (7): Support Ticket #986271712 – Elimination of backlog of historical errors and bugs
Hello, sir!
Thank you for your detailed description of your current issues.
Our experts have conducted their own system monitoring. They believe the temperature situation is most likely directly related to the activities of your users and is entirely your responsibility. We have no control over their actions.

The infrastructure selected by our specialists has a design capacity capable of handling several times the number of current users that you have.

But in practice, we are encountering a high incidence of unexpected user actions that are having an adverse effect on the automatic temperature regulation of the system.

If you have any more questions, we will be more than happy to answer them.

Yours sincerely,
Pranav.
Customer Support Service

Date: 2036-05-10, 13:18
Subject: Re (8): Support Ticket #986271712 – Elimination of backlog of historical errors and bugs
Are you fricking kidding me?!
Any design system of this sort has to be 'idiot proof' to deter users from taking unauthorized actions!

This is not a user problem, and not even an infrastructure problem (although there have been a load of problems with the infrastructure and interface from the very moment you launched it). You can't explain to users that they are doing something wrong, there should be restrictions in place that simply DO NOT ALLOW them to do something that might destabilize the system.

And, if you look into the whole temperature regulation issue in proper detail, it's clear you messed up from the very beginning. Why is the temperature at the poles lower than the equator and for all practical purposes totally unsuitable for life? In fact, how could any sane person have thought of such a thing? And the change of seasons? In your opinion, is it normal that at one geographical position it is either hot or cold? The users have already adapted to this, of course, but it's utterly absurd! I've done some research to find out why this is happening, and it's definitely your design error! It's because the axis of the planet has tilted by 23 degrees! And what's more, the angle is constantly changing! Did you not have a spirit level to hand when you designed it?

By the way, about the infrastructure again, you seem to be taking me for a complete idiot, if you're claiming there's nothing wrong with the infrastructure.
Your sales patter implied that the entire system would be habitable, but in fact, everything you've done from the outset has been purely cosmetic so that things would look okay until the startup but once you scratch beneath the surface there is some kind of hell bubbling away down below there that is totally unfit for life. Is this how you normally do things?

Date: 2036-05-12, 09:43
Subject: Re (9): Support Ticket #986271712 – Elimination of backlog of historical errors and bugs
Good day!
This is Mike, the Senior Technical Support Manager.
My colleagues passed on your enquiries since they require a higher level of expertise and coordination with the management. I will try to help you as much as possible to solve the problems that have arisen.

I have pulled up the technical documentation for your project and am ready to answer your questions in more detail.

I have to say that the scope of restrictions on user activities was not specified in the technical description of development objectives. Our analysts try to anticipate the most probable behavior scenarios that might lead to undesirable outcomes but it is simply not possible to foresee everything.

In addition, the temperature difference is not beyond the specification boundaries, an average temperature of 285°K was specified without any restrictions on their uniformity of distribution. Yes, we have observed a slight increase in this value over the past 50-100 years, but it is within the statistical deviation levels calculated for long-term operations. And, I have to stress again, this is largely due to the activities of your users, which is beyond our responsibility and control.

The tilt of the axis was not specified, in these cases, it is left to the discretion of the developer by default. The slope does not affect the utility parameters for the project and you yourself confirmed that this does not cause a great deal of discomfort to your users. I can find out from the design team why this particular angle was chosen. I am sure there was a good reason for this. But, I'm afraid it's impossible to fix it as a matter of urgency without a complete reboot of the system.

We also informed you that we were installing a protection system in the form of a hot metal core to create a magnetosphere against solar flares and ionized particles. The fact that it wouldn't be possible to use the entire system after this operation was obvious, the temperature down there is over 6,000 degrees.

I'll be happy to answer any other questions you might have that may arise in the future.

Yours sincerely,
Mike
Senior Technical Support Manager, Technical Support Department

Date: 2036-05-12, 09:57
Subject: Please rate the quality of our support team
(Support Ticket #986271712 – Elimination of backlog of
historical errors and bugs)
Hello!
You have recently contacted our support team. Please rate on
a five-point scale how satisfied you are with our team's work.
(1 - Very dissatisfied, 5 - Extremely satisfied)

Was your problem fully resolved and did you receive answers
to your questions?
① ② ③ ④ ⑤
Was the member of the support staff polite to you?
① ② ③ ④ ⑤
How do you rate the support staff's level of expertise?
① ② ③ ④ ⑤
Your comments and suggestions:

———————————

Date: 12/05/2036, 11:26
Subject: Re: Please rate the quality of our support team
(Support Ticket #986271712 – Elimination of backlog of
historical errors and bugs)
I hope this is your cretinous idea of a joke?
My problem has most definitely NOT been resolved! You
haven't provided me with an option to give you a score of "0".
And which of your motley crowd of so-called "experts" do
you want me to rate..?
Idiots!

Date: 2036-05-12, 11:48
Subject: Re (10): Support Ticket #986271712 –
Elimination of backlog of historical errors and bugs
Mike,
On the one hand, I'm glad that someone has finally replied
who, at least has an approximate understanding of what is going on

in our project. On the other hand, it seems to me that your so-called support has reached new levels of deprivation and outrage.

Naturally, I was not in a position to foresee all the permutations of what users should or should not be permitted to do at the goal-setting stage but it should be possible to keep the absurd within certain reasonable limits. You can't travel in time and you can't divide a number by zero. Did I really have to explicitly cover every possible absurdity? This makes no sense.
By the way, just in case you aren't in the know, because of all these problems we have had to broaden the users' permission protocols several times already to help them adapt to your original botched job and at least some chance of survival.

Regarding the temperature difference – I have absolutely no idea WHY this was done. You were given a temperature, so why didn't you make it constant over the entire surface area, without any fluctuations... There are ready-made working solutions for this. If they'd asked me for help, I could have made some recommendations.
And these currents in the ocean? Some are cold, others are warm, and this is what constantly affects the climatic zones, what good is that to us, eh? Did you just dig up some ready-made piece of code from an old project and then just copy and pasted it onto mine?

Please, find out about the tilt, this is very important. But to be honest, the whole project is riddled with problems.
Why is the planet not properly spherical? It should have been an easy enough task but you've managed to flatten it and frankly, it looks a bit of a mess. This is not only a matter of elementary aesthetics but because of this wonky curved shape, there are a whole raft of operational issues.
Why is its orbit not a perfect circle as I'd ordered but an awkward elliptical trajectory?
Why isn't the time that it takes for the planet to make a single rotation a multiple of its annual cycle? What kind of crazy error has left us with an orbit of 365 days, 5 hours, 48 minutes and 6 seconds?
6 seconds, damn it!

The users have to adjust and add an extra day in the year every 4 rotations. But this is only a very rough rounding up and it costs me 714 seconds which has to be taken out of my budget! And what about the eclipses? Why on earth does it suddenly go dark in the middle of the day? These explanations about the Moon supposedly completely obscuring the Sun are the sort of excuse a toddler would come up with. All you needed to do was to adjust the parameters so that they don't overlap precisely. Was it really that hard to make the sun bigger or the moon smaller? Or just place it a bit further away? Do you have any idea how much unnecessary stress this causes my users? I'm simply lost for words, everything's so slapdash.

I personally wrote about the need for a proper security system in the technical specifications. But the peculiar way it has been implemented was exclusively your domain, so there's no need to use this as an excuse for making such an illogical mess of everything in the first place. The fact that the entire the planet, except for its surface, has ceased to be fit for purpose is entirely your responsibility. The surface, by the way, is also far from perfect, the discrepancies in elevation are huge, hhe whole thing is lumpy, which complicates the logistics for the users and introduces serious climatic variations that could have been avoided with a normal flat topography. Not to mention, again, that I actually ordered ONE large landmass surrounded by a single ocean, but you went and split into six whole continents. Six of the wretched things! It's a complete nightmare for logistics and makes the operating costs totally unrealistic.

Mike, I could go on about these problems and other snags all day long. I'm not interested in who is to blame right now (I'm already well aware of that), I'm just interested in finding a way of getting these problems solved because, as I mentioned earlier, I'm losing users hand over fist. Right now as we speak. This is my problem for the time being, but very soon it will become yours too!

Look, Mike, this is not exactly a difficult project. I've created very similar in just 7 days and everything worked fine. I outsourced this to you because I was snowed under with other jobs and the deadlines were creeping up on me. And now I'm being left with all these ridiculous problems.

Seriously, if you want, I can sit down with your guys, we'll go through each problem together and fix what we can in real-time? Believe me, this will be much faster than constantly texting and blaming each other instead of constructively searching for solutions.

Date: 13/05/2036, 16:02
Subject: Re (11): Support Ticket #986271712 –
Elimination of backlog of historical errors and bugs

Hello!

Mike here, again.

Thank you for your patience and understanding. I needed to pull up the project file again to check on the problems that you mention.

We had a look at the planet in question, and I have to admit that you really did a beautiful job there. On the surface, of course. But I believe that in terms of the structure and programming, everything is present and correct as well.

You know, sir, we rarely come across such advanced clients, and we would be happy to meet with you personally so that, together with our specialists, you can bring the project to perfect fruition. Let me check with my senior management who will also be on the project team and check with the traffic manager to see when can we fit in a work session and I will be in contact. Ок?

Yours sincerely,

Mike

Senior Technical Support Manager, Technical Support Department

Date: 14/05/2036, 10:27
Subject: Re (12): Support Ticket #986271712 –
Elimination of backlog of historical errors and bugs

Mike, hello!

Thank you for your prompt answer. I am glad that we are finally singing from the same hymn sheet and there has been constructive progress towards solving our problems.

I await your message to agree schedules and set dates. Only please don't delay, because my users are dying out there, and this issue is a burning one.

Date: 2036-05-17, 19-38
Subject: Re (13): Support Ticket #986271712 – Elimination of backlog of historical errors and bugs

Mike, hello!

There's been a slight change of circumstances... In short, they've come up with some sort of fix themselves. The users, can you imagine? With their minimal access level protocols! While I was waiting for your proposal date for a meeting, they solved the overheating issue. Themselves! This is the first time I've ever seen such a thing.

It turns out they have a first-class problem solver down there who was very worried about the problem. To start with, he converted all their transport to cleaner forms of energy. He then built spaceships and high-speed tunnels, new generation power plants and any number of other projects.

And when the warming really kicked in, he took up this problem and corrected or compensated for all your shortcomings... Now the temperature seems to be more or less all right and the user level is stable.

Basically, the urgent need to eliminate all these bugs seems to have been resolved for now. And I'm not sure whether intervening in the solutions he's come up with might only create more conflicts and strain on the system further down the road.

Who knows, he might find a fix for the other snags in the project that you left half-finished..?

The Little Black Dress

Translated by Simon Geoghegan

'You know, I look really quite indecent in this dress. In fact, defiantly indecent,' Erica thought, straightening the thin straps on her shoulders and smoothing out the creases in her skirt.

The little black dress barely came down to the middle of her thigh, tightly hugged her waist and climbed over her shoulders with its narrow spaghetti straps, leaving a deep plunging neckline and the back open right down to the waist.

"What do you think?" She asked Arthur, spinning around coyly, causing the skirt to balloon slightly.

"Oh... you look awesome," Arthur licked his lips, surveying his partner from head to toe. "That dress is amazing and really suits you. "It makes you look sexy and sassy all at the same time."

"Is it sufficiently indecent for the party at the 'Dead Poets'? What do you think?"

"Believe me, baby. It's fabulously indecent. You might not be the most indecently dressed girl there tonight but all eyes will definitely be on you. I'm already feeling jealous, just thinking about it.

Erica blushed at Arthur's lascivious gaze but she was pleased that she had created such an impression on him. Well... her and her dress.

"Thank you for the dress, Art. It's so cool."

"You're the one who's cool and as for the dress... Well, it's also cool, I agree," he smiled, admiring Erica from all angles, barely touching her with his fingertips, "You know what, I want you, in that dress, right now!"

"You want everything all at once! What if we spoil it, what would I have to wear to the party? Uh-uh, no way. Get your paws off me, you animal!" She jokingly slapped his hands away, dodging his attempted embraces, "But just you wait till we get back... Then I'll let you act out your dirtiest fantasies."

"You're just teasing me…"

"You'd better believe it! Here, can you help me take it off?"

"Unzip it from the back?"

"Ha, ha," Erica arched her eyebrows, "Well come on, help me, I'm afraid to crease it."

Arthur slowly and gently began to lift the skirt, letting his palms linger over Erica's hips, her waist and for a brief second her breasts, and then unhurriedly removed the dress. It glided over her skin and Erica trembled with excitement.

Arthur carefully hung the dress on its hanger and turned to her, his eyes full of desire.

"You know, Ri, you look fabulously lecherous in that dress. I'm even a bit frightened about going to the party with you. But... you look great. Although I like you without your dress too."

Erica snuggled up close to him and kissed him on the lips deeply and greedily.

"I can see that. And feel it... And I really love it. You're a genius, you've made an amazing dress. Thank you."

Arthur did not want to be distracted by too much talk but the topic really excited him.

"But you found the design."

"Yes, but you did the computer modelling and printed it for me. You know, you might have made a very talented fashion designer. Are you sure you don't want to change your career?"

"Yes, it would have been interesting," Arthur laughed, raising Erica up in his arms. "If clothes were a necessity in this world... If they weren't illegal and considered depraved and indecent, I would think about your proposal."

Half an hour later, still panting after a stormy bout of love-making, Erica lay in Arthur's arms, considering his words. What if they lived in a world where people needed clothes..? She certainly needed them. But Arthur was right, of course. Erica worked as a historian in the central museum and knew better than most how the world had changed over the last eight centuries.

After the severe climatic changes caused by global warming, the coastal zones had become unfit for human habitation. They had simply ceased to exist when the world's sea levels rose and the coastal settlements were battered and destroyed by the continual barrage of storms and tsunamis.

Endless rains eroded the soil, polluting the freshwater reservoirs and the increased evaporation kept the skies constantly overcast. The earth was no longer warmed by the sun, the crops failed and the climate got colder. Food became scarce and the localised wars for resources turned into a global conflict in which every individual was struggling for their survival.

The first missile strike brought this struggle to a rude halt. And the survivors of the global cataclysm were forced underground into bunkers and temporary settlements. The ensuing nuclear winter left no hope of any return to the hostile world above. And every available resource was allocated for the construction of underground infrastructure and permanent settlements.

A strict dictatorial military regime was imposed, along with scant rations for food and other supplies, all for the sake of survival. Decades were invested into the development of a comfortable environment, and over time, clashes between scattered communities and whole new cities became more frequent.

The development of underground technologies was aimed at providing people with sustenance and new residential and service spaces. Cities burrowed deeper, expanded and grew, gradually transforming themselves from miserable lairs into spacious and comfortable living spaces.

When the First Underground War once again brought humanity to the brink of extinction, the cities had to make peace and unite. On the North American continent, Sub-Terra was formed, connecting all the largest settlements into a single network.

It was impossible to reach the other continents, and there was no sense in sending any special expeditions to the surface. Communication with the rest of humanity had been lost forever. Assuming there were any survivors to make contact with anyway.

Not only had the environment changed but people themselves. Forced at first to live together in cramped conditions, they lost many of their social barriers and norms, discarding them to move ever onwards and upwards. Privacy became a thing of the past. Clothes were permanently in short supply until new industries could be established and the need for them receded thanks to the constant warm subterranean temperature.

At first, mankind got by with a minimum of clothing and then completely abandoned it altogether. One generation followed another and those who had grown up underground never having known any other world were not embarrassed by their nakedness, perceiving it as completely natural. Clothes seemed uncomfortable and superfluous to needs.

Then ideologies started to change and clothes of any kind began to be seen by society as an unacceptable excess, a sign of dissent and indecency. For a couple of hundred years, people even forgot what clothing was and during periods of particular ideological extremism, even references to clothes were removed from the public files.

But Erica was a historian and she had access to the closed city archives. And her fascination with the history of clothing had inspired her research and incited her curiosity and passion. She found an image of a girl in a dress and asked Arthur to design something similar for her for the upcoming party at the "Dead Poets".

Erica had found out that this was a special outfit, which at one time had enjoyed cult status and changed the world many centuries ago.

Arthur was a talented architect and worked for a number of large private clients. Therefore, after a couple of weeks of calculations and adjustments, he had been able to create a highly accurate 3D design of the dress for Erica, tailored precisely to her figure.

The materials were a more complex challenge. He had to tinker with his selection of the various fibers for the structure of the fabric. No one had any idea what it had been like to the touch, so he had been forced to come up with his own selection method.

The result was... Strange. A very unusual sensation. The fabric clung tightly to the body... There was something too intimate, intrusive and... it was difficult to put into words... probably something very sensual.

Once, in an illegal store in Chinazone, she had bought herself a T-shirt. A cheap imitation made out of a translucent plastic used for furniture upholstery. As a historian, Erica knew that it didn't exactly resemble a real T-shirt but she wanted to feel what it was like to dress up, to see herself in a new light. But the cold coarse material was a disappointment and for some time cooled her enthusiasm for clothes.

But with this dress, everything was different. The fabric pleasantly tickled her skin, hugging her figure, as if she was being clinched in an embrace. She felt as if she was being constantly caressed. Although there was a certain stiffness about it that she was not accustomed to and prevented her from relaxing and enjoying the experience fully.

Erica couldn't say for sure if she liked these new sensations because they were somewhat contradictory. The freedom of expression granted her was counterbalanced by a restriction of her movement. Nevertheless, she was highly delighted with her outfit. It was hard to imagine that a dress could make a woman so happy.

Until a couple of weeks ago, Nicole had been living with them but she had moved to the 47th sector of the South wing to be closer to her new job. This saved her an hour and a half on her commute every day. They both missed their former girlfriend but somewhere deep down Erica was glad that Nicky had moved out before the upcoming party.

She couldn't bear the thought of Arthur creating two different dresses for the pair of them. Or even worse, two identical ones! The mere thought caused her to burn with a jealousy tinged with a touch of shame for her selfishness. But she wanted to be special, unique, not like the others, and this dress helped Erica to feel just like that.

There was a possibility that Nicole's place in their small residential pod would be taken up by Rory. She and Arthur had already made a proposal to him and he had promised to think it over. They were due to meet today at the 'Poets' party.

Their new friend had promised to surprise them with a highly unusual outfit. That would remain to be seen. Arthur had also prepared something, he had long dreamed of owning a pair of jeans – one of the most famous wardrobe items from ancient antiquity. He had insisted that his jeans should be blue.

In the photographs Erica had found in the restricted archives, they seemed flagrantly indecent, and she and Art had agreed that the worn holes on the knees and hips were a good compromise, so he skilfully recreated them for his jeans.

When Arthur had printed and tried them on yesterday, Erica had gasped out loud.

"You look so unusual. But very sexy. These... jeans fit your legs and hips so tightly that it really accentuates the muscularity of your torso. And as for your buttocks..."

"You're making me feel like an embarrassed teenager."

"And how are you feeling?"

"About my embarrassment?"

"No, silly, about your jeans."

"They're a bit tight," Arthur admitted, trying to walk around the room, "They certainly restrict your movement. And they don't half chafe the groin. Maybe I did something wrong? There's no way our ancestors could have enjoyed wearing these..."

"I don't know, they look remarkably like the archive photo. No. They look even better. You look positively scrumptious in them. Come over here. Only real slow. Yes. That's right. Now, turn around. Do it again. Mmmm, yeah. Definitely yeah."

To go with his jeans, Arthur printed a charming fluffy pink scarf with a white circle pattern. They were both interested to see what Rory had found for himself. But it was unlikely he would have produced anything as historically accurate as her and Arthur's outfits, what with the winning combination of her specialized knowledge and his skills.

It was time to get up and take a shower because soon they would need to head out to the club. Erica stretched languidly and rolled over in Arthur's sleepy embrace.

How she would have loved to put on her dress and go to the party in it. Not on the public monorail but on foot across half of Sub-Denver. So that everyone would look and point at her, take videos and upload them onto the web. They would shake their heads disapprovingly or stare at her in amazement.

But Erica knew that she would have barely made it around the block before a patrol would arrest her for indecency in a public space. She knew of a few friends who had gone out with some items of clothing on and she knew what had happened to them.

But never mind. Today at the 'Dead Poets' there would be a lot of like-minded people gathered together. People who wanted to see a return of their right of self-expression through their clothes. People who were not just satisfied to secretly indulge their fetish in the privacy of their pod, but who wanted to act.

Perhaps, together, they could really begin to shake off this ossified mentality, which for centuries had deprived people of the right to express themselves through their clothes. Perhaps, they would challenge this hypocritical society that forced everyone into a uniform template, turning them into an almost faceless herd.

Perhaps, the day would come, when their ranks would swell to tens and hundreds of thousands. And together they would take to the streets, dressed in protest against these officious laws and outdated public mores.

They would be a power to reckon with that the authorities would be forced to acknowledge. They would become the voice of the people. Of all those people who wished to express their aesthetic aspirations not just in permanent body art, temporary tattoos and exotic hairstyles. Not just by having their bodies bio-sculpted to eye-watering perfection.

But through their clothes and accessories that would allow them to show themselves in a light that fully reflected their inner world and aspirations. So that wearing clothes in public would no longer be considered shameful, indecent and offensive. So that humanity's new-found tolerance would permit the dressed and undressed to sit down and eat at the same table.

And when everyone who shared these values would head out to go on the 'march of the dressed', Erica would be right there with them. She would proudly walk the streets of Sub-Denver in her dress, smiling happily and proudly at the surveillance cameras.

And perhaps, on that day, a little black dress really would revolutionize this drab conservative world.

TimeChat

Translated by Simon Geoghegan

LAUREN: Hi! :-)
MARTIN: Hi!
LAUREN: So, you're Martin Troy, is that right? The Martin Troy?
MARTIN: Probably. If I'm the one you ordered?
LAUREN: Can I call you Martin?
LAUREN: If that's not an impertinence on my part?
LAUREN: :-)
MARTIN: No problem. You're paying for the chat, so you can call me Santa if you want.
LAUREN: Thank you. This is so awesome! It's such a great honor for me.
LAUREN: My name is Lauren Stuart You can call me Lauren.
LAUREN: If you prefer :)
MARTIN: Listen, Lauren, you can relax. I'm a pretty straightforward kind of guy, you don't need to stand on ceremony with me, okay?
MARTIN: Especially since my sentence will be reduced for this chat with you, and I promised to be a good boy and not upset you.
LAUREN: Yes, of course.
LAUREN: Whatever you say.
MARTIN: great

LAUREN: Have you ever done TimeChat before, Martin?

MARTIN: No, how could I? All this was invented while I was in prison. And I wasn't allowed near a terminal or the net, let alone TimeChat... It's in the conditions of my incarceration. Complete electronic isolation.

LAUREN: Yes, I know. I read about it. If this is your first TimeChat, I need to explain the rules to you, okay?

MARTIN: ok

LAUREN: At the moment, we are chatting on an open channel. And everything we say can be used by TimeChat Corp. To go into safe mode, we both need to state our names and agree to a private chat.

MARTIN: I get it

LAUREN: Because you're in prison, you're not allowed into private chat mode but I'm studying journalism and was able to persuade them to give me a private chat to protect the secrets of my journalistic sources.

MARTIN: that's awesome

MARTIN: probably))

LAUREN: It's definitely awesome. So…

LAUREN: I, Lauren Stuart, local time: 2087, consent to this private chat with Martin Troy, local time: 2054.

LAUREN: Now, your turn.

MARTIN: I, Martin Troy, local time: 2054, consent to this private chat with Lauren Stuart, local time: 2087.

MARTIN: Was that right?

LAUREN: Yes!

MARTIN: So, what next? How do we transfer onto private chat?

LAUREN: It's all done, I've already transferred you. I am moderating the chat and pressed the buttons on my terminal :-)

MARTIN: So, the chat is already private?

LAUREN: That's right.

MARTIN: totally and absolutely?

MARTIN: What I mean is, will they be able to dig out a record of this and read it all?

LAUREN: No. That would be against the law. Therefore, there is no record of this. The only one is on my personal terminal so that I can use this interview with you for my article.

MARTIN: Are you sure?

LAUREN: Absolutely. You have nothing to worry about. I can understand your paranoia. But this chat is only being recorded by me. With your consent?

MARTIN: okay

LAUREN: Right, then shall we start the interview?

MARTIN: Alright

LAUREN: It is now 16:04 my local time and we have 56 minutes left. TimeChat is incredibly expensive but my university gave me an hour out of their quota for my previous academic performance.

MARTIN: lucky you)))

LAUREN: Yes

LAUREN: I've been doubly lucky. Because I'm the first person to ever have an interview with you. The only one. It's an exclusive and will be an absolute sensation.

MARTIN: Whatever you say)))

MARTIN: What's so interesting about an interview with a jailbird? It's not as if I'm some sort of famous psychopathic maniac or psychotic dictator.

LAUREN: You're kidding me? You are a genuine legend.

MARTIN: oh, come off it...

LAUREN: I'm being serious)

LAUREN: You are the inventor of wireless narcotics. You set a revolution in motion that gave the world access to pleasures that had never been imagined before.

LAUREN: It's much cooler than an interview with some two-bit maniac!

MARTIN: Well, strictly speaking, I didn't invent wireless narcotics, I used an experimental technology developed by the state, re-engineered it and placed it in the public domain.

LAUREN: Exactly. Let's go through the facts. You used to work at a secret state facility. What was it called?

MARTIN: "Vonnegut"

LAUREN: That's it!

LAUREN: A strange name...

MARTIN: Why? It was in honor of the 20th-century writer of the same name. He wrote a book about controlling the mind.

MARTIN: And that's exactly what the project was about, using the wireless towers dotted throughout the country to spread impulses that would produce the moods the government needed. And thus keep everyone under control.

LAUREN: That sounds terrible.... :(((

MARTIN: Yes, I agree.

LAUREN: I understand why you acted as a whistleblower. You really are a hero for us. You saved us from slavery and that was...

LAUREN: That was courageous and selfless.

LAUREN: But how did you come up with the idea of using this technology as a drug?

MARTIN: You've probably read my dossier? You see, I'm a former addict.

MARTIN: But I had never tried wired-in drugs. I knew too many people who'd ended up burning their brains out.

LAUREN: Yes, those were terrible times.

MARTIN: That's true! But many people were seduced into plugging a jack into their head and floating away in an electronic dream. And not all of them re-emerged. They died happy with their brains fried by short-circuited contacts...

LAUREN: Martin?

LAUREN: Martin, are you still there?

LAUREN: Hey!

MARTIN: oh, sorry, I was lost in thought

LAUREN: That's okay, I was frightened that the connection had gone down or there was a time anomaly. These things happen...

MARTIN: Yes, sorry.

MARTIN: So, uh, what was I saying, yes. I was totally against all that wired-in narcotics scene. But I sometimes used to dabble in a bit of weed or other chemical stimulants :-~

LAUREN: How barbaric!

MARTIN: Well, you say that now but back then it was normal. A lot of people were afraid of that wired-in shit and the shady market for traditional highs was still going strong.

LAUREN: Whatever you say. You clearly know better :-)

LAUREN: But all the same, what was the link between your work and the creation of wireless narcotics?

MARTIN: Well, there were a lot of factors...

MARTIN: I worked as a physicist on the project responsible for modulating the signals and making sure that the brain perceived them correctly and interpreted them as their own emotions.

MARTIN: The technology was still a bit rough around the edges, we couldn't achieve a broad directionality for the impulses we needed. And the strength of the signal and the configuration of the antennas weren't helping either.

MARTIN: But I saw what happened to the test subjects who were being irradiated in the laboratory.

LAUREN: Can you tell me about it?

MARTIN: Yes, I can now. Seeing as that government was toppled, about 11 years ago. The scum...

MARTIN: We were able to modulate the signals for the simplest emotions. Tranquillity, fear, aggression, displeasure, lust, indifference and so forth.

MARTIN: One guy had his hand sliced open right in front of his very eyes, and he just looked at it calmly with a serene smile on his face.

LAUREN: What a nightmare! (((((((((

MARTIN: There was worse than that. A whole lot worse.

MARTIN: Others were forced to mutilate themselves in a rage. To cower in a corner in terror. To fuck themselves silly until they lost consciousness. There was nothing they could do to resist it. These emotions were being transmitted directly into their brains.

LAUREN: Yes, clearly not an easy project to work on.

MARTIN: Uh-huh. And what's more, we were afraid that they might use these methods on us.

MARTIN: But the technology didn't work very well. At a short distance, it was okay and with full contact, in general, it worked brilliantly. But anything more than 3 feet and it became difficult to control the direction of the signal, interference increased and the accuracy of the impact was reduced.

MARTIN: I managed to sharpen the focus control a bit and achieve a deeper response.

MARTIN: But I was in no hurry to report my findings to the bosses. I didn't want our project to be implemented in real life.

LAUREN: So, you sabotaged your own work?

MARTIN: That's right.

MARTIN: To a certain extent.

MARTIN: As far as it was possible, I dragged things out.

MARTIN: But at home, I was experimenting with a new approach to the problem on myself. I put together a portable emitter and programmed it to stimulate the brain's centers of pleasure.

LAUREN: Interesting: I didn't know that.

MARTIN: I wanted to lose myself and forget about all the monstrous things I'd been witnessing every day...

MARTIN: Things somehow managed to work out and I spent almost the whole night blasted, on a high that I'd never had from weed or pills. It was a whole lot better. I didn't want to go to work. I wanted to stay at home and explore the possibilities of my emitter. Cast all this nightmare aside and get wasted with this new source of bliss.

MARTIN: But I knew that if I didn't go to work, they'd send security out to get me.

MARTIN: It so turned out that on that day a girl died during one of the experiments at the lab. They had increased the strength of the impulse and awakened such hate and fury within her that she couldn't take it. She ended up ripping her windpipe out with her own bare hands.

LAUREN: Fuck...

LAUREN: Oh, sorry...

MARTIN: Nothing to be sorry about. At the time my language was a whole lot worse. We were all in shock at what we'd witnessed. The scumbags! They...

MARTIN: It was then that I decided to put an end to it all.

LAUREN: and what did you do?

MARTIN: I tested my emitter for another week and fine-tuned the programs for basic positive emotions – peace, happiness, joy, arousal, satisfaction.

MARTIN: I put together a package of pleasurable emotions, an emitter circuit and the software for it. And then made it openly available on the web.

LAUREN: And then you went on the run?

MARTIN: Of course. If they had caught me they'd have killed me.

LAUREN: But they caught you all the same.

MARTIN: That's right. But it wasn't them. As you know, it only took a week for the government to fall. A week of turmoil when the whole country was aflame. The whole world, to be more precise.

LAUREN: Yes, you lit the fuse and stepped back :=)

MARTIN: Uh-huh. I went into hiding.

MARTIN: To lie low.

MARTIN: I had friends who helped me.

MARTIN: Wait for the storm to blow over. And remain in hiding for longer, you see a bounty had been placed on my head.

LAUREN: I can't even imagine how you managed to remain out of sight for almost half a year.

MARTIN: Yes. It was difficult.

MARTIN: Not to leave any electronic tracks. To change hiding places...

MARTIN: But at the same time, I continued to improve the technology.

MARTIN: There was no question of controlling the wider population any more. But the market exploded from the wave of new free-of-charge drugs.

LAUREN: Did you want to make any money out of this?

MARTIN: Make money? No. Probably not.

MARTIN: Initially, I just got my rough workings into shape. And created several thematically selected sensations and emotions. The pride of success. Maternal joy. The triumph of victory. The ecstasy of orgasm.

LAUREN: Many of your early works are still popular today. They are considered classics.

MARTIN: Really?

LAUREN: Seriously)) After all, it all became legal for personal consumption a long time ago.

MARTIN: fabulous))

MARTIN: You were asking about money. Yes, I thought about selling custom sensations. I didn't have any source of income, on the run. And a new black market for emitter software had already begun to open up.

MARTIN: As you know, I was ahead of everybody on this. Back then. It was my big chance.

LAUREN: But you could also have given yourself away.

MARTIN: And that's exactly what I did ((((

MARTIN: as a result, they were able to track me down

LAUREN: I'm sorry

MARTIN: That's all right. Not everything was that bad. The old authorities would have taken me out on the spot. The new ones were prepared just to give me life for treason and leaking state secrets.

LAUREN: That was unfair

MARTIN: Well, it's debatable. According to the letter of the law, they were right. But they knew that morally they had no right to act that way.

MARTIN: The public put a lot of pressure on the government.

LAUREN: Yes, a lot of people thought you were a hero. You are a hero.

MARTIN: Well... Be that as it may, the authorities decided on a compromise. They portrayed me as a fighter against the previous criminal authorities. A man who had blown wide the biggest plot in history. But who had nevertheless been in breach of the official secrets act.

MARTIN: 15 years. In a standard prison. But without any access rights to any technology.

MARTIN: I've already done 10 years. They gave me 4 years remission for good behavior. Again, under pressure from the public, which was demanding an amnesty for their savior.

LAUREN: And you should get another year's remission for agreeing to give this interview. That's what I was promised.

MARTIN: Yes, me as well. You have given me a ticket to freedom.

MARTIN: Thank you. One hour talking to you and tomorrow I'll be a free man.

MARTIN: I can't imagine how someone from the future could help me now in the present, it's all too much to get my head around. But I'm still very grateful to you.

LAUREN: It's really nothing :=D

LAUREN: There was no way they could say no, this is already in the history books.

MARTIN: I can't get used to that either. Everything has passed me by here. Could you explain how this is possible, in a couple of words?

LAUREN: The day after tomorrow, you'll be able to read it for yourself.

MARTIN: You're right. It would be wrong of me to cheat you of your interview time.

LAUREN: You know, actually, I couldn't explain it all to you even if I wanted to. But...

LAUREN: You know that the Earth is surrounded by an electromagnetic field. And that light has a dual nature, consisting as it does of photons and waves?

MARTIN: I am a physicist, remember? And do know a thing or two about waves.

LAUREN: you're right (((

LAUREN: I'm being a bit thick

LAUREN: Then you'll also know about the theory of quantum entanglement?

MARTIN: Oops, spoke too soon. This isn't my field, I only know about it in very general terms.

LAUREN: Damn! I don't even really understand it in general terms. All I do know, is that it has something to do with the nature of light, quantum entanglement and gravity.

MARTIN: Don't worry, I'll read about it when I get out.

LAUREN: Basically, it's not important how, but 36 years ago... Oh, sorry, I mean for you it was only 3 years ago. The TimeChat Corporation was able to make a big breakthrough and make a connection through time.

LAUREN: Back then, they were just a tiny start-up under the wing of the Ministry of Defence))))

LAUREN: It uses up a frightening amount of energy and costs a fortune, so it only exists in the form of a text chat to minimize the flow of data exchange.

MARTIN: I'd heard something about this from the newbies who talked about some sort of miracle on the outside.

LAUREN: Yes, it really is a miracle :-D

LAUREN: Since it was created in 2051, we have been unable to get into contact with anyone from an earlier period. But we are allowed to meet those who are living later. Even in the future. That is incredibly awesome! At first, TimeChat was only used for scientific work. Then they began to use it for commercial purposes.

MARTIN: But is there not a risk of changing the past this way?

LAUREN: No)))

LAUREN: The past can't be changed.

MARTIN: I mean that information about the future made accessible in the past could change the future.

LAUREN: It can't :)

LAUREN: The future is immutable. It has already happened. And for certain people, it is the past.

MARTIN: I don't get it.

LAUREN: You can't change the past because it's already happened. Our future is already the past for somebody in the distant future.

LAUREN: And knowing what will happen in the future does not give you the opportunity to change it. No matter what you do, you will end up doing exactly what needs to happen.

MARTIN: Some kind of fatalism.

MARTIN: Destiny.

MARTIN: It's all so obtuse.

MARTIN: I can't stand paradoxes.

LAUREN: You're just not used to it. At school, we learn about the history of the past but also the future.

MARTIN: the history of the future..?

MARTIN: But how? And why do you need to know what will be?

LAUREN: You'll be surprised, but knowledge of the history of the future gives humanity stability. A confidence in the future. A belief in one's strengths and capabilities.

MARTIN: That is strange...)))

LAUREN: You'd like it here in '87, believe me. There are no wars, we have defeated hunger and all the main diseases. We have sorted out religious and racial strife.

MARTIN: It sounds like utopia.

LAUREN: No, it's a long way from utopia. We have plenty of problems. But we are working on them. And the great thing is that we know that we'll get there. And Casey helps us with many things. He has really accelerated our progress.

MARTIN: Who or what is Casey?

LAUREN: Of course, you don't know, I forgot.

LAUREN: He's our AI

MARTIN: You've been able to create an artificial intelligence? And a friendly one to boot? So, who succeeded in doing that?

LAUREN: No, we didn't create him. He created himself. It's believed that he is a singularity. A super-mind, which became self-organizing when the concentration of data reached a certain critical mass.

MARTIN: It all seems very strange somehow. Everyone was working on Artificial Intelligence and then it appears of its own accord.

MARTIN: And who gave it that name? It sounds a bit dumb ((

LAUREN: Well, Casey is not really his name, in fact, the name he gives himself is a complex sequence of characters, but for the sake of simplicity people began to call him Casey, and he liked it.

MARTIN: And did the powers that be throughout the world not try to subjugate or destroy it?

LAUREN: Some tried. But he demonstrated to them that this was not only pointless but also... Unwise.

LAUREN: Now every government in the world collaborates and consults with him, he helps coordinate everything, shares new inventions, technologies, knowledge. He has helped to rid us of terrorism, reduce crime, solve problems with food and help poorer economies.

MARTIN: You've allowed some ghost-in-the-machine to rule your entire world..?!

LAUREN: He doesn't rule us! He helps us. Casey has become a digital big brother for us. He cares for us.

MARTIN: Big brother is watching you))

MARTIN: I don't share your enthusiasm. I don't like the sound of it. It's a good thing we had nothing like it in my time. Otherwise, I would have had to join the resistance and fight against this new usurper.

LAUREN: It's a shame you're like that. He's so cool.

MARTIN: Never mind, to hell with 'him', it's ultimately your business out there in 2087. It would be better if you were to tell me if you've finally managed to pass a law banning pineapple toppings on pizza yet?

LAUREN: No. What's wrong with pineapple on pizza?

MARTIN: It's a crime against pizza

MARTIN: Never mind, forget about it. That means you definitely haven't reached utopia yet. :)))

MARTIN: I'm sorry, I digress. Let's get back to your interview.

LAUREN: Yes, thank you :)

LAUREN: I'd like to fill in some of the gaps in your biography, to hear from you personally what no one has published yet.

LAUREN: To understand what motivates you. To find out what you did during those six months when you were on the run. What prison was like for you, knowing that you had been convicted for doing what was right. What your plans are, what you plan to do in the future?

MARTIN: Listen, I'm not sure we're going to be able to discuss all that in just an hour. Why don't you just organize an interview out there in 2087? Or by that time have I already..?

LAUREN: Have you not worked it out yet..?

MARTIN: worked what out? :-/

LAUREN: You are no longer with us in 2087

MARTIN: What do you mean? I've already died by that time? When?

LAUREN: I don't know.

LAUREN: You're just no longer with us. At all.

LAUREN: You went missing. Nobody knows where you are and what happened to you. You simply disappeared :((

MARTIN: Damn!

MARTIN: And when did I disappear?

LAUREN: According to your time... tomorrow...

MARTIN: What do you mean tomorrow..? But they're letting me out tomorrow!

LAUREN: Yes.

MARTIN: You're probably making some sort of mistake. How could I just disappear tomorrow?

MARTIN: So, I was released and just disappeared?

LAUREN: Yes, tomorrow you are set free and disappear. Forever.

LAUREN: And therefore today is the last day that I can have an interview with you.

LAUREN: Martin..?

LAUREN: Hey, Martin..? Are you okay?

MARTIN: Yes

MARTIN: Well, actually... No.

MARTIN: Damn it, how can I be okay after what you've told me..?!

MARTIN: I'm sorry... I'm simply trying to take it all in...

LAUREN: Believe me, I'm very sorry I told you.

LAUREN: These days, we are all so used to knowing about our past and future. And it's probably a bit of a shock for you...

MARTIN: yes, just a bit ((

MARTIN: You've knocked me right back...

MARTIN: It's not every day that you find out that tomorrow you will no longer exist.

MARTIN: You know, when you've been in prison for 10 years, you kind of make plans for the future

MARTIN: And then it turns out that you don't have one...
LAUREN: I'm really sorry, my bad, my bad, my bad =((((
LAUREN: I didn't know whether you knew...
LAUREN: And I was hoping you would help me to find out what happened.
MARTIN: But I didn't have the foggiest clue! Until you told me...
MARTIN: I can't help you on that one. I would love to, but can't ((
LAUREN: Who knows, what if you really can?
MARTIN: I don't get you...
LAUREN: You see, everyone was looking for you. The government, the police, the special services, the narco-mafia, journalists, private detectives... The mystery of your disappearance has long haunted everyone.
LAUREN: There were a lot of conspiracy theories. That you were
MARTIN: abducted by aliens?
LAUREN: =)))
LAUREN: Yes, and that as well.
LAUREN: They said that the government took you. That you were kidnapped and murdered by the drug cartels in revenge for destroying their business.
LAUREN: That you are in hiding from everyone and live like a hermit. Or had plastic surgery and left for Rio. That you invented a new freaky wireless drug and overdosed on it somewhere in a deep hole before you were able to put it out onto the net.
MARTIN: That sounds the most likely)))
MARTIN: Listen, Lauren. Why are you the first person to interview me? What's been stopping everyone from finding me here over the last ten years?
LAUREN: Well, it's the prison system. Your sentence forbade you access to the net or any terminal.
MARTIN: I know that. But why did they give you permission today? The day before my release?
LAUREN: How can I put it... Basically, my father is a senator. He is a member of the correctional system monitoring committee. He... pressed a few levers, pulled some strings and the ban on access to the internet was lifted a day early.
MARTIN: Ah, so that's how it is...
LAUREN: And daddy gave me you as a present for being the best student on my course.

MARTIN: Listen here, young lady. I am not your present. I'm not much of a present period, for that matter ;-)

LAUREN: Don't forget you were given a year's extra remission for this, so don't complain.

MARTIN: no, I'm very grateful, really

MARTIN: but you've really baffled me with this news that I'm about to disappear tomorrow

LAUREN: Martin, that's why I thought you might know something that might help me find you. To find out what happened to you.

MARTIN: but, I don't know!

LAUREN: But you might know something. Have you been threatened? Before you were arrested or in prison?

MARTIN: Well, of course, I was threatened. The Bazilicos Cartel... They tried to kill me. It's very strange but the other prisoners stood up for me. Some of the big clans and families threatened all-out war with anyone who'd risk doing any harm to me. For them, I was beyond the law. Or above the law? I'm not sure which exactly.

MARTIN: But they defended me.

LAUREN: Wow! :-0

MARTIN: Yes. So, I don't think the cartels have anything to do with it. What's more, they understood full well that if "Vonnegut" had been launched they and their business would have been completely obliterated.

LAUREN: That makes sense.

MARTIN: As for the Government. Well, what's the point? I'm useful to the new government, I'm a legend, a fighter against tyranny. Having served my sentence. They could have turned me into an idol, a symbol of the new authorities' orderliness. But, kidnapping and killing me? I don't know. I don't think so.

LAUREN: Maybe it's all linked in with your plans? What were you planning to do after your release?

MARTIN: Let my hair down a bit, go out and travel the world, see what's changed since being banged up here. Have a half-decent dinner, wash it down with a beer. Fix myself a bespoke cocktail of my favourite home-made wireless ecstasy.

MARTIN: And then quietly get back to my work.

LAUREN: Did you tell anyone about your plans?

MARTIN: nothing specific

LAUREN: Where were you planning to live?

MARTIN: I wanted to rent out a small apartment in the city. Somewhere quiet, I don't like noise and bustle.

LAUREN: Well, what were you planning to work on next? Can you tell me?

MARTIN: Yes, it's no particular secret. What's more, if it works out then you should know about it. But if not...

LAUREN: Then no...

MARTIN: you see I was working on something here...

LAUREN: What do you mean - working? You didn't have access to any terminals..?

MARTIN: Are you sure that this channel is absolutely safe?

LAUREN: Yes.

MARTIN: You have to understand, if I tell you that I had an illegal terminal then I'll lose my parole and they could give me an extra stretch.

LAUREN: My lips are sealed :-X

LAUREN: If you want, I can delete this part of the transcript. No one will have access to this apart from me.

MARTIN: okay

LAUREN: And don't forget, you can't change the course of time. You are definitely being released tomorrow, there's a record of that.

MARTIN: You're right. I can't get used to this.

MARTIN: They got hold of a terminal for me without access to the net but I didn't need that.

MARTIN: I designed a number of different customised sensations for the guys here. That's why they got me the terminal...

MARTIN: As a result, I got the chance to work on a new project.

LAUREN: No shit...

LAUREN: What sort of project?

MARTIN: Telepathy.

LAUREN: what?... :-0

MARTIN: I want to create a tool that can transfer thoughts between people.

LAUREN: Are you serious? But how???

MARTIN: I think I'm on the right track but there is a lot more work to do.

MARTIN: You see, my wireless narcotics, in fact, the whole trick with controlling the population – it was all based on empathy.

LAUREN: Empathy?

MARTIN: The ability to perceive other people's emotions.

MARTIN: Cats, dogs, horses and several other types of animals all have empathy.

MARTIN: Children. Then we learn to understand speech and certain other complex skills but we lose our innate ability to harness empathy.

MARTIN: My emitter transfers emotions, feelings and sensations.

LAUREN: Your digi-waster.

MARTIN: What?

LAUREN: They're called digi-waster now because people carry them around with them everywhere and just use them to get wasted . These days, digi-wasters are really quite small. Like... A nut? Some people wear them as an earring or a pendant.

MARTIN: A digi-waster. Hmm... Well.

MARTIN: So, that's why I'm sure that it should be possible to transfer thoughts as well.

MARTIN: It's a whole lot more complex than that, of course. But if we can take on board emotions then we can do the same for thoughts, it's all just a question of the complexity of the modulation.

LAUREN: And could you have already got somewhere?

MARTIN: So far, not much, at the moment I'm working on turning thoughts into a digital signal. The idea is there but it needs to be worked on with complex apparatus. I don't know.

MARTIN: But in 2087, do you already have this technology?

LAUREN: no. :'(

MARTIN: That means that I... That it didn't work out, yes?

LAUREN: Possibly...

LAUREN: I'll search for some mention of it, in case you tried to get it out there under a pseudonym. But I've never heard of anything like it.

MARTIN: well, that's upsetting...

LAUREN: Can I make a mention of this in my article? Not about your current work but only about your plans?

MARTIN: Yeah, probably, yes. After all, no harm will come of it.

LAUREN: But first I will make a painstaking search for any references to it. What if you were killed because of this technology? Or to prevent it from getting out onto the market?

MARTIN: But, you see, no one knew what I was working on. Although, they might find out from your article, yes?

MARTIN: This is all so complicated...

LAUREN: Does your new form of telepathy have a name? So that I will have a clue what I'm searching for.

MARTIN: No. I haven't even given it a thought yet.

LAUREN: A project name.

MARTIN: I haven't anything helpful to on that front either. I'm famously paranoid. I have everything encoded, ciphered and passworded. I don't even have a project name so that no one could understand anything.

MARTIN: kC/h8T_03Sw#714J-Mn9$i38!qB0z%rFYa3

LAUREN: What..?! :O

MARTIN: Yes, I know it's a bit tricky to remember.

MARTIN: But I have a good memory and I've trained it...

LAUREN: Martin, how do you know his name?

MARTIN: who?

LAUREN: Casey. That is his full name or the name he gives himself.

MARTIN: No, you must have made a mistake, those are just random symbols that I have used to give my project a name.

MARTIN: I don't know the first thing about your electronic godlet.

LAUREN: Oh no, no, no...

LAUREN: Martin! Do you understand what this means?

LAUREN: It means that you created him!

MARTIN: What?! What utter nonsense!

MARTIN: I don't have the foggiest idea about artificial intelligence. I could never have created anything so complex. The sort of thing that the biggest IT giants weren't able to get right. No, it's not possible.

LAUREN: Well, how then?

MARTIN: I don't know.

MARTIN: I'm not even remotely qualified. And had no plans either. It's just a coincidence, that's all.

LAUREN: No. I don't think so.

LAUREN: Casey appeared at the beginning of 2055. Does that seem like a coincidence to you? Even the dates coincide.

MARTIN: But I simply couldn't have created this artificial intelligence! Even if I'd wanted to, I don't know how! You have to understand...

LAUREN: Maybe you're planning to work together with someone? And your telepathy will help someone create an Artificial Intelligence?

MARTIN: No! No, I'm a loner. And a paranoid one at that.

MARTIN: There have been too many people around me these last 10 years. I want to be on my own.

LAUREN: Then I don't know... But there should be some explanation for this...

MARTIN: or maybe there isn't

LAUREN: Martin, I'm trying to help you here. Or at least work out what happened!

MARTIN: is happening

LAUREN: To hell with these tenses! Martin! Help me to help you! Please.

MARTIN: Yes, sorry. I'm in the wrong. And we only have 11 minutes left. How can I help?

LAUREN: I don't know. What do you think, could someone have kidnapped and killed you to steal your technology and use it to create an artificial intelligence?

MARTIN: I don't think so. It's unlikely that someone willing to kill me for my electronic telepathy would be able to create an AI that is as amicably disposed as the one you describe.

LAUREN: That makes sense.

MARTIN: And there's the problem that apart from the name, I don't see any connection whatsoever. And that's not such a big deal.

MARTIN: All I'm trying to do is transform nerve impulses from our brains into an electronic signal. To digitize thoughts. So that you can transmit them digitally and then translate them back into a format that is comprehensible to the brain.

LAUREN: To digitize thoughts..?

MARTIN: That's what I said...

LAUREN: Are you talking about conveying one specific thought in this way or a large number?

MARTIN: Well naturally, a specific thought. So that it would be possible to communicate mentally at a distance. Wired or wireless, it's not important.

LAUREN: And it would be possible to copy all a person's thoughts in this way?

MARTIN: All of them? No. Probably not. I don't know, I haven't tried it yet, it's only a work in progress. Why do you ask?
LAUREN: Martin, you...
LAUREN: No. It's not possible, is it?
MARTIN: What?
LAUREN: I have a feeling that you are Casey...
MARTIN: what?
MARTIN: What utter nonsense!
MARTIN: We don't have time for joking around here.
LAUREN: Martin, listen. This is no joke.
LAUREN: But what if your work was a success? And you created some kind of digital copy of yourself. A cast of your consciousness. Or an archive of your thoughts. A back-up, I don't know.
LAUREN: And you put this mass of data on the network. Perhaps on purpose. Or maybe an accidental leak, God knows :-[
LAUREN: But this copy of you has some kind of amnesia since he doesn't remember that he is you.
MARTIN: No, listen, he's definitely not me. Let's not waste our time.
LAUREN: But there is some kind of logic to my hypothesis.
MARTIN: On the contrary, there's no logic whatsoever!
MARTIN: What does your super-duper Casey have to do with the fact that I'm working on telepathy?
MARTIN: How can you compare it with...
LAUREN: What?
LAUREN: Martin?
LAUREN: What happened?!
MARTIN: wait
MARTIN: I'm thinking
MARTIN: You know... There's a small chance that you're right.
MARTIN: It sounds unlikely, but...
MARTIN: I don't know. How could it...
MARTIN: Let's say, purely hypothetically, okay?
MARTIN: Let's say that you're right and some sort of digital copy of me did end up on the web. It's like a supersaturated saline solution, you understand?
LAUREN: Not really.
MARTIN: If a speck of dust ends up in a supersaturated saline solution, a process of active crystallization begins. Any factor is

enough: you only need to scratch the walls of the vessel, a small abrasion would be enough, all sorts of things. Or a speck of dust.

LAUREN: In other words, the theory about a singularity could be true to some extent?

MARTIN: Yes, partly. The net is a supersaturated solution, and my archive of thoughts, my cast of consciousness or whatever it is, is this speck of dust, the center of this crystallization process.

MARTIN: The nucleus for the formation of a certain kind of supermind.

LAUREN: But that's not artificial intelligence. That's... I don't know what to call it.

MARTIN: Neither do I. A singularity, yes. No one has ever created one.

LAUREN: Unless you did it on purpose. You leaked this "digital ghost" onto the net.

MARTIN: Digital ghost..? Now, that's a word to conjure with...

MARTIN: But if you have given me this idea, I now know that in all likelihood I will do it. That means you've changed the course of history, is that not right?

LAUREN: Of course not! Time cannot be changed. This only means that this has always been so. Or will be.

MARTIN: Your temporal paradox is doing my head in.

MARTIN: Alright, even if this is what is going to happen to me?

LAUREN: I don't know…

MARTIN: I still have to disappear, right?

MARTIN: So it will happen.

MARTIN: I need to think about this. Perhaps I myself must make sure that I disappear. So that digitally I end up on the net but as a live person, I disappear.

LAUREN: Martin, you're not thinking of committing suicide? :0

MARTIN: I do not know yet, Lauren. I don't know...

LAUREN: No! No, Martin, please, no.

MARTIN: Shh! Calm down. I don't know for sure yet, okay?

MARTIN: But it seems to me that in order to ensure that everything is fine with you in 2087, with no wars, illness or hunger, I need to somehow disappear without a trace. I need to take all this on board.

LAUREN: You know, I used to think you were a kind of digital hybrid of Che Guevara and Pablo Escobar, but your willingness to sacrifice yourself... for the future of all mankind...

MARTIN: Makes me more like a kind of digital Jesus?
LAUREN: Who?
MARTIN: Oh, come on... You're kidding me, right?
LAUREN: Yes, I am kidding you :-D
MARTIN: You see... I almost believed you were being serious))
LAUREN: Good lord, no. Jesus is still remembered. By some, at least.
LAUREN: Only you're not quite right about something here.
LAUREN: It's not just in 2087 that everything will be good
LAUREN: It a whole lot longer than that.
MARTIN: What, sorry?
LAUREN: I'm talking about Casey. It's not just in 2087 that everything will be fine, but for many centuries beyond that. He...
LAUREN: I don't know, he – it is you, right?
MARTIN: No, I think he isn't only me.
MARTIN: He would appear to be a whole lot more than me.
MARTIN: He only gained some initial thoughts from me.
MARTIN: Probably.
LAUREN: Okay. He.
LAUREN: He will be able to protect our society from itself, from its worst impulses, and will continue to do this for a very long time.
MARTIN: So, there won't be any wars at all? Never.
LAUREN: Never is a very long time, yes? No, unfortunately, we will have a global war in 3471. And it will last for 24 years.
MARTIN: Well, I'll be damned! But why?
LAUREN: You'll read about it tomorrow. Martin, we have two minutes.
MARTIN: listen, Lauren, you must delete all record of this chat!
MARTIN: I don't know what you're going to do about your article. But your entire future depends on your silence.
LAUREN: I understand, I'll do everything you say
MARTIN: good, thank you! and thank you for this chat! maybe, all this will be thanks to you
LAUREN: it's an honor for me, Martin!
MARTIN: hh, get out of here)))
LAUREN: and promise me, you won't do yourself a mischief
MARTIN: Lauren!
LAUREN: Promise me!
MARTIN: I don't know!

MARTIN: I don't know how but I'll try to do everything right. you have to believe me

LAUREN: I believe in you

MARTIN: don't forget to delete everything, it's very important!

LAUREN: I won't, I promise

MARTIN: and, Lauren, you know, Casey isn't such a bad name after all)))

LAUREN: Martin, if you don't literally disappear, please let me know, give me the means to send you a message, so that I can get in touc...

The Longcut

A Novella

Translated by John William Narins

It had been a good day. A tough day, true enough – very tough. But ultimately it had all worked out. For two solid weeks Corey had worked himself to the bone and today, finally, they had presented the client with a new communications strategy for their bestselling brand of craft beer.

The presentation had gone brilliantly, the whole team firing on all cylinders. The client was so excited that they not only approved the marketing plan, they also upped next year's media budget by fully 25%.

Corey himself deserved most of the credit for that. After all, not only was he the one responsible for developing the strategy, he also came up with the hook for the new campaign. So John promised him a whopping bonus in the days to come and, for now, a day off tomorrow to get some sleep after his month-long creative marathon.

"I love this guy!" his boss had cried, putting one arm around Cory and raising a bottle of IPA in celebration. "To today's victory, and to the kick-ass demons we're going to be going into next year!"

Since the brewery's management had left the building, the entire agency had done nothing but celebrate their victory in that utterly crucial tender. And it just so happened that they had a few cases of Fat Sam India Pale Ale lying around – it was one of the campaigns they had handled this season.

And if they were going to party, there was no point in Corey holding back, especially when he had the next day off. So he took care of at least a couple of bottles all on his own. He decided he would take a cab and leave his car at the office. Corey texted Steff to pick up some more beer on her way home and something to eat.

The pic she sent him of a taco with Korean BBQ looked so good he told her to get extra. They'd been wanting to really get into something new and interesting together, but there never seemed to be time. This was the perfect chance to immerse themselves in the dark, "just survive" atmosphere of *This War of Mine*. A few hours of gaming and then collapse into bed and finally get some sleep. Well, maybe they wouldn't go *right* to sleep. Wait and see, play that by ear...

Although... no – he'd more than had enough strategizing and complication for one day. Steff had recently said something about a Japanese game. It was supposed to be pretty primitive, but funny... what was it called? Whatever, they'd figure it out when he got home.

There'd be time tomorrow to loll about and watch TV, sleep, eat, and forget all about positioning, target audiences, studies and ratings, market share, slogans, logos, social media, involvement rates, conversion and all that marketing blah-blah-blah...

Corey had earned that much. And he could turn the phone off so no one could bother him until the day after tomorrow. He went to switch it now to airplane mode. No more calls, letters, messages, posts or feeds to interrupt him and his wife having dinner together and laughing, or after dinner... playing games, whatever kind of games they might be… you know what I mean.

Instead, though, Corey put his headphones on and slipped away into his music. It almost drowned out the soft but irritating chatter of the talking heads on whatever dreary station the taxi driver was listening to. He couldn't stand radio, even music – he had a thing about always choosing his own songs.

And the last thing he wanted to hear right now was the kind of inane blather that taxi drivers love to feed passengers, with that expression of a man grown wise from endless experience,. Usually beginning with something like: "Your first time in the city?" Which inevitably lead into "There was this one guy I picked up, he told me..."

Couldn't they see he had zero interest in that kind of bullshit? To be blunt, they would be separated by at least several tall steps on the social scale, but more important was that they were surely on very different levels intellectually.

Corey was a big-time advertising specialist, responsible for ad campaign strategies and business development. He was a rising star in the field – everyone saw a brilliant future ahead of him in the top agencies.

What was he supposed to talk about with an uneducated cabbie? It wasn't impossible that the guy didn't even know how to read, seeing as all he'd manage in life was to sit behind a steering wheel day and night. Baseball and the weather, maybe? Politics, or how awful it was that prices were going up?

Those headphones saved him every time. Even if he didn't put music on, he would be doing something with the telephone – working, playing a game, surfing the web, or reading the news or social media. No one bothers someone with headphones on, not even moderately talkative cab drivers.

They had about a half an hour or forty minutes to drive, meaning he had time for six or seven songs. He usually picked a couple by his favorite bands and listened to them in top-quality recordings on Spotify or Tidal. Today, though, he was in the mood for something especially soulful.

Corey was rooting around in his phone's memory and then, with a sudden rush of anticipation, selected a bootleg he had recorded himself at a jazz festival the year before at his old friend Matt's club. The recording wasn't great, but it was his, his own little victory, and that was something that fit perfectly with the gamut of feelings washing over him today.

Corey closed his eyes and sank into the enveloping waves of sound. A jazz orchestra was playing a medley of Miles Davis pieces. Outside, a dismal rain was falling, but inside the weathered cab he was comfortable, warm and cozy.

From time to time he opened his eyes and saw the storefronts and skyscrapers sliding by across the window. They were driving from the heart of downtown to the nearest suburbs. At rush hour that was never easy. And the rain had only slowed traffic further. There was a good chance he'd get in more music than he had planned. Nothing wrong with that.

"Hey, what the hell..." Corey slapped an angry palm against the glass separating him from the driver. "Where are you going? We're supposed to be heading for Cherry Hills!"

"Yes, sir, I know. But it says there's a huge problem on Independence, some kind of accident because of the rain. Backed up for more than an hour. I'm trying to find a way around it."

"I drive home every day and I don't recognize a thing here. Where the hell are we?"

They had just been driving down a broad avenue in the midst of a sea of city lights and suddenly, in the blink of an eye, they were in the middle of nowhere, a dark industrial backwater almost devoid of cars.

The taxi driver, a black man old enough to be his grandfather, laughed easily and nodded, pointing out, not without a note of pride:

"Yes, this way isn't for just anyone, sir. But a lot of us taxi drivers know it. Not those new guys, immigrants, who can't find the toilet without a GPS, of course. But the real veterans who know the city and all its hidden nooks and crannies..."

"That's a factory of some kind?"

"Exactly right, sir. The old Ferguson factory. In reality, there didn't use to be a road here at all. From one side there was a driveway leading up to the warehouses and another one on the other side going to the factory itself. But two years back the rule against selling the land expired and someone bought it. The factory itself is as abandoned as ever. But someone decided to pull down the warehouses and build something else, something industrial, in their place. So far, though, all they've done is blast a road across the territory for the construction vehicles. That's the short cut we're taking, since the avenue is at a stand-still."

"Well, okay," said Corey, shrugging his shoulders, although there was something faintly unpleasant about the driver's choice of route.

Nothing particularly strange had happened, but somehow he was ill at ease. The driver didn't seem dangerous at all. An old man, friendly enough, and he seemed to know what he was doing. For a cab driver, anyway. But the place was abandoned and strangely forlorn. You could see why normal people didn't come this way.

Up ahead were the gates, which were half shut, so that a cab coming the other way had to stop and wait for them to pass before driving on. The cabbie flashed his lights at his colleague in a brief signal of thanks and then moved ahead, down the narrow one-lane road that ran along the canal embankment.

The road was in pretty poor condition, the asphalt having chipped away or collapsed in upon itself in places, but the driver deftly navigated the familiar potholes without slowing the car.

"Don't think I'm going to be taking my car down here," thought Corey. "Better to wait through a traffic jam than blow a tire and spend the whole night out here in rain. Or just stay at work until the traffic clears up."

"There we go. Now we take the next left and we'll come out right onto Eleventh. And at this time of day it should be pretty empty, meaning we'll have beaten the traffic."

And, indeed, Eleventh was almost empty. Most of the cars that would otherwise have been there were still stuck back on Independence behind the accident the cab driver had warned him about – there was a lot more traffic now heading the other way.

Corey relaxed and adjusted his headphones, which had been jolted off his ears along the way. That world of genuine, heartfelt music was still there, waiting for him. At some point after that he opened his eyes a crack and saw the driver turning the radio dial, irritated, and then smacking the front panel with his hand.

"Radio's dead," Corey understood, reading the driver's lips when he turned, apologetic, towards the back seat.

"Don't mean nothin' to me," thought Corey, half asleep, without pausing the piece he was caught up in – Thelonious Monk this time.

Rising up and up through the luscious, rhythmic sounds of jazz, he resurfaced and opened his eyes. Squinting, his unfocused gaze wandered out through the raindrops trembling on the car door window. In their multicolored gleamings he caught glimpses of passing storefronts, streetlights, windows bright with neon, and...

Cars? The droplets were reflecting the headlights of oncoming vehicles and the tail lights of the cars ahead of them... but there wasn't a single car in sight. What did it mean? Was that damned cabbie heading off in the wrong direction again?

Corey sat up straight and stared out the window. Through the dim drizzle, through the surrounding darkness, he tried to get a good look the buildings they were passing. But no. Everything was okay. They were on Victory Avenue. Soon they would turn onto West Circle Lane and right after that swing onto One Hundred and Forty-First, which led straight into Cherry Hills.

"Hey. What happened to all the cars?"

"I'm sorry, sir?" the driver said, quizzical.

"I'm asking you where all the cars went." Corey pulled his headphones off. Nervous, he stuffed them into his bag without putting them in their case. "It's rush hour. There should be a ton of cars."

"That's true," the driver muttered. "Seemed strange to me, too. I thought it must be that most of them are still caught back there in that traffic jam. But... that's a long way behind now. We should be in normal traffic again by this time."

"Seriously, it feels like we're the only ones on the road. Look at this! Hold on... there really is something wrong. Stop. Stop, I said!"

The driver braked sharply, tires squealing over the wet asphalt. He turned to Corey.

"Please don't shout at me, sir."

Corey was about to really let loose on him, but he stopped himself.

"Can't you see? There isn't another car anywhere. Nobody passed us. Either way."

"It happens. Traffic's an unpredictable thing. Sometimes the road is packed, sometimes it's empty. Drive the city like I do, you'll see a lot stranger things than that."

"You're saying you see this kind of thing all the time?"

"Yes, sometimes, usually between three and four in the morning. You can drive for minutes without seeing another car, except maybe way downtown."

"But it's not three in the morning! It's eight pm on a weeknight. And there are no cars. At all. Something must have happened. Must have."

"Where?" asked the driver, patiently, calmly ignoring Corey's agitated tone of voice.

"No idea. That way," he said, waving his hand vaguely behind them.

"And that way?" The driver asked, directing a similar gesture ahead.

"I can't tell, maybe that way, too," said Corey, shrugging, nervous.

"Shall we just sit here for a while longer, or would you like me to drive you the rest of the way home?"

"Yes, sure, fine. Let's go, of course."

"Thank you," said the driver, starting the car, making very little effort to hide a note of sarcasm.

But after another minute driving in silence, constantly glancing in the rear view mirror, he broke the tense silence himself.

"You are right, though. It's not normal. There still hasn't been a single car going either way. In more than forty years of driving I've never seen that. Maybe you could take a look at the news and see if something's going on? My damn radio's on the fritz."

"Yeah, sure – of course." Corey had been in a kind of daze, but now he seemed to suddenly snap out of it. Turning from the window, he found his phone in the bag – at that moment, they turned onto West Circle from Victory.

"There no signal... really?" he cried. "That's ridiculous. You always get a signal here. We're still in the city, for chrissakes! You check your phone, will you?"

The driver reached into his pocket and pulled out a primitive little flip phone. He opened it... and then closed it, with a sigh.

"I've got no signal, either. And the radio's shot."

"Screw the radio, man!" shrieked Corey, losing his patience. "Who's worried about your freaking radio? What's wrong with you, man? My radio, my radio – radio, radio, radio, radio... We have no internet, all the cars are gone, something's happening! Let me reboot the phone, maybe that'll get us a signal."

Looking down at his telephone, he didn't see the driver shake his head angrily at his passenger's latest bout of hysterics, watching him cautiously in the rear view mirror.

"Still no signal," Corey muttered, tapping away reflexively at the unresponsive screen.

"Sonofabitch." The driver suddenly veered out of his lane to stop at a bus stop by a coffee and hot dog stand.

He opened his door and stuck his head out, looking around. The rain had almost stopped, but it was extremely humid and visibility was drastically limited by the ground mist. It gave a tinge of the surreal to their surroundings, colored in shades of gloomy blue set off by the blurry orange splotches of street lights and windows.

The old man went up to the food stand and shouted something, banging the palm of his hand against the glass and trying to see inside. He stood there on the little open area behind the bus stop and looked around again, and then came back to the car, shaking his head.

"What is it?" asked Corey, once he was back in the car and the door slammed shut.

Droplets of water gleamed on the leather of his jacket and his kinky gray hair was damp. The man ran his hand over his hair, wiping away the water, and then passed the same hand over his face and again shook the water away.

"There's no one there. You get it?"

"No, I don't get it," Corey growled, a hint of panic in his voice. Suddenly he was put off by how small and plaintive his own voice sounded.

He tried to clear his throat so he'd sound more manly when he spoke again.

"This is one of the main stops. Right by the subway. It's a major hub – a bunch of lines meet here and people transfer from one to another all the time. There's always a *ton* of people here. And where's Tony? He's not at the stand. It's open, but he's not there."

"Why?"

"Now how the hell am I supposed to know that?" the taxi driver shot back. "I have no idea where they all are. You asked me if this was normal? There's nothing even close to normal about this."

He exhaled loudly and tried to calm his nerves.

"I'm sorry, sir. Probably best to get you home as fast as possible so you can get in touch with someone and figure out what's going on."

"Yeah, maybe Stephanie knows what it is."

"Your wife?"

"Uh-huh. She's always on line, she knows pretty much everything. If anyone knows what kind of nonsense is going down, it's my Steffie."

"Well, all right, then, let's get going," said the old man. The car moved back out into the road, but Corey gave the glass a sharp smack of the hand.

"Stop, stop! Look over there, up ahead – see that? Now what the fuck is that?!"

The driver stopped the car and gazed out in the direction Corey was pointing. The turn into the side street was completely invisible in the mist, and clouds of fog were rolling out onto West Circle Lane, spreading out over the pavement.

"I think it must be steam from the sewers,' the driver mumbled, quietly.

"I don't even know what to think. Steam that's covering almost the whole street? Not likely."

"What, then?"

"I. Don't. Know. Ever see Stephen King's *The Mist?*"

"No, but I read the story way back when it came out. You can't be thinking..."

"I have no idea *what* to think," Corey confessed. "But there's something very suspicious about whatever it is."

"Got to agree. Let's just drive up and have a look, okay?" suggested the cabbie.

"Fine, sure. But slowly, right? And not *too* close. And if anything bad happens, you hit the gas, gas!"

They crept forward, gazing tensely into the fog-bound alley. But up close it looked different. There were two sewer vents up ahead, their grates spewing steam. Now it all seemed rather innocent and inoffensive.

"See, I said it was steam from the sewers. This time of year it often looks that way, and in your headlights or under a street light it can sometimes even look quite beautiful," said the old man, exhaling with relief. "All right, then – let's get you home."

They drove a few miles farther. On one side or another they passed houses and stores, but they didn't see a single human being, or a single car. All around things seemed deserted, evoking a kind of holy dread.

The two travelers looked left and right, staring through the windows, seeking any sign of life.

A few more miles and they had left the residential neighborhood behind, approaching a stand of maples drowning in the pale, thick fog. The road simply dissolved in the fog right where the trees began.

"Oh, of course," grumbled the driver, slowly bringing the car to a halt about a hundred and fifty feet from the wall of mist.

"This kind of thing happens, especially after it rains," said Corey, glad to have a chance to demonstrate his own optimism and confidence. "I come this way every day. It's a pretty normal thing."

"Nothing tonight is normal," muttered the driver. "Well, so? We go in?"

"Yes, go ahead," Cory said, with a wave of his hand. "Just take it slow, there are a few reasonably sharp turns coming up."

"Yes, of course."

They passed through the stand of trees without incident, no issues and no surprises. They were able to see a bit farther as the headlights helped to scatter the fog. Soon they were on One Hundred and Forty-First, moving at a reasonable speed down the gleaming wet road.

Corey checked his phone again, trying to pick up a signal, but without any luck.

"Turn right when we hit Cherry Hills, okay?"

The driver nodded, peering at the houses they passed, with an occasional quick glance at his passenger, as if to check to see whether he seemed nervous as they approached his home.

Of course Corey was nervous. But he didn't want to admit it – not even to himself. That was his home they were thinking about! Steff was there! Everything was going to be just fine. Wasn't it?

He and Steff had been renting this cozy little old house for three years now, dreaming of moving closer to downtown so they wouldn't have to spend so much time driving to work and back. Cherry Hills was a nice little town, but they were both very contemporary young people who loved the spirit of the city, where things were always happening, the crowds and the speed – not this peaceful little haven for fifty-plus geezers and annoying families with their herds of kids and dogs.

They'd have no worries now – after the victory in the tender today, things would be getting better. They could afford a nice city apartment in a decent neighborhood. Corey could hardly wait to talk to his wife about the day's triumph and everything that might now change in their lives.

"Here, third house on the right – that one," he said, pointing it out to the driver. "Yes, right here. Thanks. Take this. Keep the change. And I'm sorry if I said anything wrong. I was just a bit nervous, you understand."

Corey opened his door to get out, but the driver called him back.

"I'll wait here for a few minutes, if you don't mind, all right?"

"Everything's okay, really. Ah, you mean you want to know what happened? Give me a minute, I'll be right back – let me just ask my wife and I'll come and tell you, okay?"

He opened the gate and ran happily up to the house, jumping the steps to the door.

"Steff! You home? Stephanie?" The house, like everything around it, seemed strangely quiet, but that was impossible. "Honey, I'm home! Where are you?"

Corey went in and, without stopping to take his shoes off, walked around the first floor. His voice grew increasingly agitated and tense. Then he went upstairs to check whether she might be in the shower, where she might not hear him over the running water. Maybe she had headphones on and was listening to music or watching something.

But there was no one upstairs. The place was quiet, empty. Even when he turned the lights on, the shadows seemed to linger in the corners, as if someone or something was hiding just at the edge of his field of vision. Something bad, foreign. Evil.

"What the hell?!" cried Corey, slamming the bedroom door and coming back out into the hallway, without turning the light off. He looked around him, back over his shoulder.

His own home suddenly seemed somehow threatening, making him feel anxious, afraid.

"Stephanie, this isn't funny! If you're hiding, this would be the time to fucking come out. I'm not in the mood for jokes or surprises today, okay?"

But the evening quiet was disturbed only by the quiet hum of the refrigerator and the steady ticking of the clock on the wall in the kitchen. Corey grabbed a big green apple from the vase on the table and, with a roar, hurled it at the clock. Clattering and banging, it fell onto the bottles of spices, scattering them over the table.

One bottle, with red chili pepper, rolled over the edge and fell to the floor, spraying shards of glass all about the kitchen. The pepper poured out, looking like a spot of dried blood, and it seemed to Corey that the shadows stirred, like hungry monsters sensing their prey. Shivers ran down his spine and a wave of emotion made him faintly nauseous.

"Dammit!" he howled and ran back to the street, where the driver was still waiting.

"Well, what is it," asked the cabbie in a worried voice, standing by the car, when Corey came up to him.

"There's nothing there. And no one!" Corey shouted. "Like everywhere else in this God-forsaken town. Nobody!"

He flew at the driver and pinned him to the car door, grasping his shirt and shaking him.

"This is all your fault, you son of a bitch! Your fault!"

"Me?" said the taxi driver, astonished, without even trying to free himself. "What did I do?"

"You had to take took me on some crazy short cut, you stupid bastard! Maybe that's how all this happened – maybe something happened to us there and now this is what we're left with!"

"That's enough of that, now. I'm supposed to be responsible for all this?" The driver knocked Corey's hands away and pushed him back. "Get a grip, man."

But Corey had no desire whatsoever to get a grip. What he wanted was for none of this idiocy to be really happening. For Steff to be home and to not give a shit about anything else in the world. His Stephanie... and more, he wanted to find whoever had done this.

"Well, if it wasn't you, who did this? What's the point? Tell me! Where is Stephanie? Where is she – come on! Where has she gone? Where has *everybody* gone?!"

"Why are you looking at me?" hollered the old man. "I have no idea, all right? Something's happened and I want to figure it out every bit as much as you. I get that you're upset, believe me. I'm worried about my family, too."

"Oh, Jesus. Of course, you have a family, too..." Corey felt like a complete ass – he was so overwhelmed by his own worries that he forgot that his accidental companion in misery was also a human being, with feelings and problems and, maybe, a family... "I'm such a jerk. I'm sorry. I'm sorry, really, I just..."

"Forget about it. I completely understand, really," the driver put up his hand, palm forward. "You have kids?"

"No," Corey said, shaking his head, still completely embarrassed by his irrational outburst.

"I have two. And three grandkids. And believe me, I'm very worried about them all, about my wife, about my daughter-in-law. I'm scared."

"You don't look scared."

"I could shit my pants I'm so scared. But if I can do something, fix something, if they need me, then I can't afford to let myself... fall apart, you know what I mean."

"Which means the same goes for me, is that it?"

"Not for me to say. That's up to you. I'm not sure at all that anything we can do can change any of this in the slightest. But we still have to try to figure this fucking disaster out. Figure out whether there isn't something we really *can* do, after all. Like it or not, but it looks like there is nobody left to do it but us."

"It does look that way," said Corey, shaking his head as if to shake it free of some kind of bad dream. He stretched his hand out to the taxi driver. "Name's Corey. Corey Thompson."

"Wendell Mills," said the man, firmly shaking the offered hand. "Call me Wen. We may not be friends, but we're in this mess together. No point being too formal."

"Thanks, Wen. Sorry I lost it for a minute there. Obviously you didn't make this happen. I... I just..."

"You want her back."

"Yeah," said Corey, nodding gratefully, squeaking the word past the lump in his throat.

"And to get answers. I'd also give a lot to know what this is all about. And to know what's up with my loved ones."

"Do you live far?"

"In Arundel Downs."

Whoa. Pretty tough place. Once an upper-crust residential neighborhood, over the past few decades it had turned into a real slum. A white guy like Corey wouldn't risk setting foot there, not even in broad daylight. But if the same thing was happening there that was happening everywhere else they had been...

"Then let's go and see."

"Together?"

201

"You just said it – we don't have any choice, right? Just give me a few seconds to get something from the house. Want coffee?

"Oh, yes, dammit."

"Listen, there's a coffee machine in the kitchen, make it yourself, okay? And there's food in the fridge, get us both something to eat, all right? Looks like it's going to be a long night."

"What about you?" asked Wendell, confused.

"I want to run over to the neighbors'."

"You think Steff might be there?"

Corey heard the obvious doubt in his voice, and of course he was thinking just that, although rationally he knew that he wouldn't find anyone there – not Steff, and not the Carmichaels. But there was something else he wanted to check.

"No, but there's someone I want to say hi to. Make the coffee, I'll just be a minute."

Corey trotted over to the neighbors' house. Resting his hands on the fence, he whistled into the darkness.

"Yo, Oswald! You here?"

But the yard remained still. Only the patches of warm light in the windows and a cone of light under the lamp on the porch interrupted the gloom of the scene. Corey felt as if the shadows were growing deeper, thicker, as if they were rolling out hungrily in puffs of nasty black smoke. He blinked and shook his head to slough off the illusion. Coffee. He needed coffee – now.

"Oswald! You stupid beast, where the hell are you when we need you? Hey!"

But nothing moved, unless it was the shadows in the corners.

"Come on, here, Oswald, here, that's a good dog! Uncle Corey has a treat for you!"

The shadows froze in anticipation.

"I really don't think the problem is with my communications skills or any lack of powers of persuasion," muttered Corey. "The damned dog has vanished along with everyone else."

He went back to his house, where Mills had made the sandwiches.

"The neighbors' dog. Gone, too. Wanted to test a theory."

"What kind of theory?" asked the old man.

"The every living thing theory. Listen. No sound of dogs howling, no bird calls. What passes for nighttime in these parts can be deafening – it literally rings. Crickets, grasshoppers, cicadas...

But this is dead silence. Look under the porch light. Where are the bugs, the moths? I have this feeling that every living thing, excepting only the two of us, has somehow vanished. That you and I are the only ones left, for whatever reason."

Corey's face darkened and he pulled a big rucksack from a shelf, observing how his new friend was taking what he had just heard. He began packing – a first aid kit, binoculars, a powerful LED light, several bottles of water and a few packages of cookies. A powerbank for his now-useless phone. In various pockets he placed a lighter, a knife, some string, a roll of scotch tape, and a can of pepper spray.

"You look like you're heading out into the wild on some kind of survival mission," said Wendell, wrapping the sandwiches in tin foil.

"We don't know what we're going to come up against out there. Any weapons in the car?"

"The lug wrench?"

"Understood. I don't think I have any, either. I'll take my bat. You already drank the coffee?" The aroma wafting about the kitchen made the answer clear enough.

"Yes, thank you. Should I make you some?"

"Please. A double espresso with milk and three teaspoons of sugar. I'm going to change into something more comfortable."

Corey went into the bathroom to let the excess pent-up beer out of him. At the sight of Stephanie's robe and towel hanging there, and all her cosmetics and toiletries, his heart skipped a beat. There was no beer or Korean barbeque in the kitchen. Whatever it was had happened before she managed to reach the house.

He put on a pair of cargo pants and a thick, warm hooded sweatshirt. He slid another hiking knife onto his belt. He pulled on a pair of high, reinforced workboots. And got up to look at himself in the mirror. His eyes were red, with dark circles under them, and a scraggly blond beard. Usually so well groomed, he now looked a bit like one of the homeless.

"The hell with it!" said Corey. He turned away and went down to Mills.

Who was already packed and ready to move out.

"Coffee. Thanks." Corey downed the liquid, which was already growing tepid, in single gulp, and joined Wendell. "Think – what else might we need? While we're still here."

"I don't really know," said the old man, scratching his grey beard. "A can of gasoline, maybe. We can't know whether the gas stations will be working."

"Ha – sorry, man, my car's a Tesla," mumbled Corey.

"Whatever, let's go. We'll figure things out as they come."

They drove in silence, peering out at the houses they passed along the way, examining the intersections closely, hoping to see some indication of life, anything, to meet another human soul. But the town was still, like an empty museum. There was only a slight breeze ruffling the tops of the trees and scattering occasional drops of water into the puddles.

"Think there's a chance they're okay?" asked Wendell, his voice anxious. His grip on the wheel was tight and his didn't take his eyes off the road ahead.

Corey was in the front seat now, by his side.

"There's a chance."

"Really? Or are you just trying to make me feel better?"

"Both, really." He shrugged. "Think about it, we don't know what's going on. Or how far it stretches. It could be the whole world. Or maybe it's a sheerly local phenomenon. There's a chance Arundel Downs hasn't been hit at all. Then your people would all be all right."

"Do you believe that?" mumbled the old man, swinging into the turn at an obviously illegal speed.

"Honestly? Not really. But sure – there's a chance, why not?"

They drove on for another few minutes in silence, and then exited onto Forty-Second Street and into downtown. All the buildings seemed like cheap scenery now, as if the two of them had somehow blundered onto the set of some mystical B-movie thriller. Only the lights in the windows gave them a sense of reality, but there wasn't a living soul there inside.

The streets were empty. No cars, no pedestrians. But the traffic lights were still working, regulating the nonexistent traffic with abstracted indifference. Here, near the very center of the city, the darkness was different, too. It seemed to elude your gaze in the glare of all these city lights. Corey caught himself thinking that something was trying to hide from him beyond the cone of light issuing from the headlights, endlessly darting just out of range.

His nerves were stretched to the snapping point and he tried to keep himself under control. So as not to break down again. Why today? Why had all this crap happened to him, of all people? It wasn't fair.

Although, if you think about it, this crap hadn't happened to him at all. It had happened to everybody else. He was actually almost the only one to whom it *hadn't* happened. Well, then what did *that* mean?

Corey's eye caught something in his peripheral vision. He turned his head sharply that way, but saw only the vacant streets of the empty city passing by, its numerous glowing eyes looking down coldly upon the lone taxi cab passing through its midst. Probably just his imagination.

The streets were narrower now and the buildings more run down. There was garbage heaped around here, and the walls were splattered with graffiti. *Welcome to Arundel Downs, a modern neighborhood for professional people.* That was one slogan that had grown old in a hurry.

Wendell stopped the car by an old apartment building on the edge of a dilapidated housing complex. Looking both ways, he slowly got out of the car and stared into the surrounding shadows. There was no one there.

"This sucks," he mumbled. "I wouldn't usually leave the car right in front of the building, but it looks like things are the same here as they are everywhere else. Dammit."

"Let's go up to your place," said Corey.

"Yeah, let's go." Mills took the lug wrench out of the trunk and Corey held the bat at the ready, gripping it with both hands. Slowly, they went in.

The staircase was grimy, littered with cigarette butts, bottles, cans and paper cups, used condoms and disposable needles. Some of the landings reeked of piss. Or shit. Or vomit.

It was as if Corey were on a completely foreign planet. It wasn't his own sheltered little world, comfortable and sterile – work at a fancy PR agency, his life a game he knew two or even three steps in advance. It was the real world, where people lived and died, where they hadn't been lucky enough to be born with silver spoons in their mouths, to grow up with the best education available and almost a guarantee that they would be somebody one day.

"Apparently I couldn't foresee and plan everything out in advance, either," said Corey, shaking his head bitterly, following his guide and they pushed their way past the garbage and filth.

He was panting by the time they reached the seventh floor where Mills's family lived. Should have gotten to the gym more often instead of wasting away in front of the computer or the television.

The whole way up Wendell kept looking down all the hallways and stopping to listen, but you could feel the place was deserted. In some places they heard various household sounds, but they weren't enough to bring life to the oppressive silence or fill the omnipresent emptiness.

The old man stopped for a few seconds before his own apartment, as if he wanted to put off facing the inevitable truth. But then he quietly knocked at the door. When there was no answer, he took his key, unlocked it, and went in.

Corey stood and waited for him in the hallway, nervously clutching the bat in hands already moist from exertion. It wasn't so much so someone would be watching their exit route as to allow Wen a chance to be alone in his own misery.

He soon came out again and shook his head. There were tears in his eyes and gleaming wet trails running down his dark, wrinkled face.

Corey wanted to say something, to cheer him up, to give him some support, but he didn't really know how to do it. He couldn't say everything would be okay. He couldn't really believe that himself. Nothing could be okay. It looked like everything was going to be awful. Really horrible.

Without a word, they went back down to the car, stopping to look around every floor, but wherever they went they found the same stern silence and that same sense of the terrible wrongness of what was happening. The shadows seemed to follow the two of them, mocking them and their incursion into a world that was no longer their own.

"Do you want to tell me about them?" asked Cory, once they had settled back into the car.

Wendell seemed to have aged, his face a tense mask, and in his eyes writhed pain, despair and the recognition of his own failure. While they were driving, he had retained a scrap of hope that he might somehow find his family here, but now he had been stripped of everything. He seemed apathetic, limp, as though a single moment had deprived him of the last shred of his will to live.

He shook his head, unwilling to talk further. Corey shrugged. It wasn't his strong suit, that kind of heart to heart talk. He understood the old man. He felt he was being pulled apart by the inexplicability of it all and by his fears for Steff. By his unwillingness to admit he had lost her, lost her forever.

No! Never, no way. Maybe there's still something we can do. But what? To figure out whether there's something to do, we need to know what happened. We're like a pair of blind kittens in an unfamiliar courtyard.

"Wen, you said you had no choice but to hold yourself together as long as they might need your help."

"But they're gone."

"We don't know that for sure," said Corey.

"Look around you, man? Are you an idiot? There's nobody left! Just you and me. Alone in all this whole dumb-ass world."

Corey turned in his seat and looked his companion straight in the eye.

"What do you recommend?"

"I don't recommend anything!" wailed Wendell. "I just want none of this to have ever happened! I want to go back to this morning, when they were alive, or... Damn! We don't even know what happened... whether they're alive, or..."

The old man seemed suddenly to deflate like a floppy doll. His head lay on the steering wheel and he wept quietly, spluttering, choking on his own pain. Corey waited a couple of minutes, leaving him alone, to let the stress subside, the fear for his loved ones, the bitterness of the loss. Then he put a hand on Wen's narrow shoulder and, quietly, began to comfort him.

"Come on, now. You hear me? We'll think of something. We'll figure it out. If there's anything to be done, we'll get it done. You're not going to just give up, now, are you? Me neither. Be strong, Wendell. Do it for me, if nothing else. Because I want to cry as much as you do. Better yet, to get plastered. But you and I, we're going to figure this shit out."

"An old man and a kid with a homeless beard?" said Mills, doubtfully, wiping his wet face with one hand.

"There's nobody else, man. And we seem to be making a pretty good team, actually, don't you think?"

"Oh, sure," said the cab driver, giving him skeptical look. But the grimace of pain gave way, at least for a few moments, to an ironic smile.

Corey reached into his pocket and pulled out his phone. He opened the gallery and looked at a few of the pictures.

"That's Stephanie," he said. Without internet access he couldn't get to the albums he had uploaded, but there were enough in the camera's memory. "She's a trainer. Teaches yoga and sport dancing. Here she is in her yoga studio, see? And here we're going to an Italian place for pizza. This is nothing, forget this, ah, here. This is us at the zoo, our selfie with the tiger. We tried, anyway. Let's skip this one, a bit too intimate. Ah! And this is us going to the city park to see the cherry trees in bloom. It's a dumb selfie, but she likes it."

He kept on leafing through his memories and sharing them with Wendell. The light from the screen seemed to have chased away the shadows in the building's courtyard. Somehow things felt a tiny bit better. More painful. But touching photographs he loved on the screen filled him with a kind of natural warmth. It gave him strength.

"Here we are riding segways. Ever ridden a segway? Never? Man, you should give it a try, it's really pretty cool. Ah, and here's a video – give me a second, see how cool *this* is. See how fast we're going! I fell off the thing at one point. Screwed up a turn. Too bad I don't have that recorded. And this is last year when Steff got a new hairdo. And she colored her hair. I didn't love it, but you know you can never tell them that, right? It's a good thing she changed her mind and went back to the way she was. Maybe she could tell what I didn't say. She's very smart. She's... well, you get the point. Got any pictures of your family?"

Wen sat there, looking at Corey's screen. Then the words reached him and he reached into his pocket. He pulled out his wallet and unfolded it, revealing a tattered old family snapshot.

Corey could hardly believe his eyes. The twenty-first century. The hyperloop. Mars expeditions. Cloud technology and neural networks. And this guy still had a paper photograph in his wallet instead of endless brilliant digital shots. But he cut himself short and didn't say anything out loud that might offend his new friend.

"This was Annie and my anniversary. We went to the waterfalls in the national park. This is Derek, my eldest. He's forty-one now, he and Eileen have twins, Paul and Kass. They're wild, those two – a few hundred horsepower in each of them! Derek runs an auto shop in Chicago. If Eileen's parents didn't help them out, she'd never be able to manage those little devils herself. They're only six, but they zip around like formula one cars."

They laughed together and Wendell went on, telling Corey about his family.

"Our younger son, Chase. He's... he got involved with a bad crowd. Wanted to make some money before his daughter was born, but... well, he got four years for possession and dealing. It came as a terrible blow to all of us, although in this part of town everybody lives on the edge, looking for some way just to survive. But Chase... he was always a good boy, you know? It's all those punks. His little girl's gonna be one, and he's never even seen her. My little boy..."

The old man stroked the photograph lovingly with a wizened finger. Then he pointed out a pregnant woman next to his son.

"This is Ruth, Chase's wife. That big belly there – that's our little Naomi, the apple of our eye. You should see her – such a funny little thing. She's only eight months old and she's already trying to stand up and walk..."

He choked up now and tried to clear his throat. He put the wallet back in his pocket.

"You and Stephanie never had kids? If you don't mind my asking, that is. I'm sorry, that's too personal a question."

"No, it's okay," Corey said, shrugging his shoulders. He didn't even know how to answer. "Just sort of happened that way. If I tell you we never got around to it, or that there wasn't time, you're probably going to make fun of me, but..."

"I wouldn't," said Wen, obviously holding back a smile.

"I don't know, we were just somehow always doing something, all the work, always one thing or another... We didn't feel like we were in a rush. We kept thinking we were about to get to a new level, life would be better then, we were about to achieve something, and then we'd talk about kids. So it would all be smooth and easy, you know?"

"Smooth and easy?" said the old man, astonished. "Oh, my. You don't get it at all. Smooth and easy is how you're living now. Once you have kids, everything goes like lightning, it's total chaos. Then you *really* won't have any time!"

209

"Somehow you're not making me want to buy this product, you know?"

"Ahhh, believe you me, it's worth every bit of it."

"If you say so," said Corey, wistful. "I'm being driven up a wall as it is. What's happened to Steff, where she is, how she is... If we had a kid, I'd have gone off the deep end already. Total panic, I'd be terrified about what might have happened to them."

"Thanks, Corey," said Wendell, patting him on the shoulder. "You really helped me there, when I was... I was about to go to pieces. It's tough to talk about our loved ones. Painful. But it's important."

"That's our motivation."

"Motivation? A strange choice of words in our situation, but... why not? Motivates us to do what, though? What can we do?"

"I don't know," admitted Corey. "Not yet, anyway. But we've got to hold up. For them. We have to figure this out. Maybe we can find them. Bring them back. Or get ourselves back to them. Hard to say. But it's our job now to try to do something, at least. While we can. While we're still kicking and breathing. You with me?"

"Yes, I am," Wen ran a tired hand over his face and sighed. "I'm with you. What's the plan?"

"There is no plan as of now. But I suggest we drive around the city and check whether it's this empty everywhere. Maybe we're not the only ones left. And we should check out all the lines of communication we can – land lines, walkie talkies, television, cable internet. Whatever we can. Then, based on whatever we find, we can decide what to do next. What do you think?"

"Works for me, partner," said Mills and, with a wink, started the engine.

They drove on without talking, watching everything closely, the endless empty avenues and dark gaps of side streets. The scene looked nothing like postapocalyptic destruction, catastrophe, extinction, or the sudden collapse of civilization.

There were no mounds of trash, smoking ruins, ashes falling from the sky, or rats and pigeons darting about. No newspapers wafted over the street by the wind, no broken storefront windows gaping maws of shattered glass at the passing car. No rusted, burnt-out hulks of abandoned cars blocking the road.

The world looked just the way it had just a few hours earlier. The way it was supposed to look – dirty, more or less, everything in order, more or less, welcoming, more or less. Only without the people. Or, it seemed, any other kind of life.

But Corey couldn't shake the sense that someone or something was watching them. Hiding just out of sight and waiting patiently to polish off two little people, the last two left alive, trying in vain to evade their inevitable doom.

"Listen, Wen," he said, having decided to share his apprehension with his friend. "Do you have the feeling someone's watching us? Or... something, I don't know."

"Who?" asked the driver, slowing the car and looking around.

"No way to know. Maybe it's my fraying nerves, but I keep feeling that something dark and nasty is hiding just beyond what I can see. It's nuts, of course, I know. But I can't get rid of the feeling. I think the shadows have become... more solid, denser, if that makes any sense. As if somewhere out there, at a distance, something dangerous is lurking, in the darkness, creeping after us."

Mills stopped the car in the middle of the street and looked around again. He got out and turned about, in a full circle, scanning the houses, the trees...

"I'm not sure," he said, sliding back into the car. "I can't say I've noticed anything certain. In the sense that of course everything's crazy and there are no people. But... hmmm... I don't see any unusual shadows or strange movements. On the other hand, you've got younger eyes. Maybe you've spotted something I missed."

"Or the fear's making me see things. Like pink elephants."

"I hope so. That you're just seeing things. But the minute you see anything solid, you let me know immediately, right?"

"Right, of course," Corey nodded. "Want me to drive for a while? Give you a break?"

"No, thanks. I'm all right. Actually, it calms me. Holding the wheel, following the road... The last shreds of the normal world – the routine things we do every day. I'll tell you if I get tired. Thanks, though."

Where they turned off of Western Avenue there was a gas station. Wendell drove in. There was no one there, but the pump worked, and Mills filled the tank, topping it off. He found a few spare canisters and filled them, too, fixing them carefully in place in the trunk.

Corey went to see if there was anything in the store they needed and was astonished when Wen followed him in, counted out some money, and left it on the counter.

"What are you doing? There's no one here. We're all alone. Maybe in the entire world. And you're paying the nonexistent owners for gas? Just take what you want! Take everything, what's the difference?" Corey picked up a glass soda bottle, held it out, and let it go.

The bottle shattered with a ringing sound against the cement floor, glass shards flying in all directions, the bubbling puddle hissing with indignation at the stunt. Mills just shook his head disapprovingly and put another bill on the counter.

"You know, Corey, maybe I'm just a poor cabbie from a bad part of town, but I am an honest man. I've never stolen anything from anybody. And I'm not about to start now. Maybe the whole world's gone to hell in a handbasket, but I mean to remain a human being as long as I possibly can. If there's no one left but us, then we, the two of us, we are the human race. And what if something depends on how much we are able to remain human beings? What if the lives of our loved ones, of everybody on the planet, depends upon it?"

"You mean this is some kind of experiment and we're the test subjects?" Corey blushed, suddenly deeply ashamed at what he had done. But his strained nerves shot out a morbid, hysterical reaction.

"I don't know. But I think we need to remain ourselves as long as we can. And also... how do I explain this? ...if I admit that the owner of this gas station is gone forever, then... then I have to resign myself to that for everyone, you get my point? My Annie, the kids, the grandkids – everybody. Can't do that."

Yes. He was absolutely right. Corey felt it. The simple, straightforward logic of this complicated, incomprehensible world. An anchor that gave at least some kind of hope that something might yet be done. To put together the intricate puzzle of events and put the disassembled world back together again.

Suddenly he wanted to sweep up all the shattered glass and clean up the floor, but he knew that would be too much, so he just carefully kicked the glass under the nearest counter.

"Sorry, Wen. I'm... it's just nerves. I'll try to stay cool. I need a drink, though. At least a swig of something strong."

Corey ran his hand along the shelf and took a big bottle of twelve-year-old Glenmorangie, but then put it back and instead picked up a little bottle of cheap bourbon with a label he didn't recognize. Putting his money by the cash register, he unscrewed the cap and took a couple of swallows.

"You?" he said, offering the bottle to Mills, but the old many shook his head. "Just a little, to relieve the stress."

"Well, all right," Wen took few little sips of the liquid, and then, with a sigh, a larger one.

It occurred to Corey that he didn't have much cash on him. He wasn't accustomed to carrying cash. You could pay for pretty much anything these days with a touch of your telephone or your watch.

"That's a problem, by the way," he said, nodding to Wendell and slipping the bottle into his rucksack. "I don't know about you, but I have almost no cash, less than a hundred, anyway. And there's no place to get more."

"What about the bank machines?"

"I seriously doubt they'll be working. If we have no signal, the bank machines should all be out of commission, too."

"That's true. I didn't think of that. Damn!" said the cab driver, dismayed.

"It's no big deal. We'll think of something. Let's see whether a land line phone will work."

It turned out there was a dirty old land line phone hanging on the wall by the door in the office. But the line was silent – no clicks, no rings. Although Corey could have sworn that somewhere far away, on the other end of the line, he could hear a sound, quiet, almost imperceptible – somebody breathing into the receiver. It made his skin crawl.

He wanted to drop the telephone and fly out of the gas station, to run as far away as he could and hide in the brightness of the streetlights, to hide in the car and lock the doors. To hide under the covers, so the monsters wouldn't notice him and eventually they would leave the bedroom.

But Corey got control of himself and only said, guardedly:

"Hello? Hello. Is there anybody there? Can you hear me? Hello?"

But there was only silence, as if whoever was on the other end was holding his breath, waiting. A patient predator trying to lull his naive victim into a horribly false sense of security.

Seeing Wen's curious gaze, Corey just shook his head and hung up the phone. His friend understood without asking, and they went back out to the car.

"Let's go to the middle of downtown, there's so much going on down there that if anyone else is left, that's where they'll most be. And it's easier to get a connection there than anywhere else. Make sense?"

"Sounds reasonable," Mills agreed, swinging out of the station and back onto the avenue, heading towards the city center.

The buildings grew taller and they were packed closer together here. Light from the streetlights, windows and storefronts washed over the empty streets. But all that light was powerless against the darkness of the nighttime and the fear. It only made more obvious the absence of people, cars and all that life with which the city always pulsed, that rushed through its veins and arteries, with all the beauty and ugliness of night life.

Corey noticed that Wendell was driving slowly and gazing more closely than ever at the buildings, the bus stops, the trees...

"Something wrong?" he asked, alarmed.

"Everything's wrong, of course," said the old man, irritably. "Everything's wrong to the core – not the way it's supposed to be."

"Did you see something? I can see how carefully you're looking around."

"Oh. It's nothing. Dumb stuff. I just thought... you know... what if there were signs, signals. Something written somewhere. Some kind of key to all this. You know – "Croatoan." Or something like that."

"Croatoan?" Corey grimaced, perplexed. "Some kind of spell, do you mean?"

"You're not serious, are you?" Mills stared at him for moment in disbelief, but then quickly turned again to keep track of the road and the buildings. "It's one of the strangest mysteries in our history. The Lost Colony on Roanoke Island – you must have heard of it."

"It seems vaguely familiar. Maybe. To be honest."

"At the end of the sixteenth century, the English colony on Roanoke Island, on the North Carolina coast, vanished without a trace. One hundred and seventeen people, including women and children. There were no signs of struggle, no signs of any attack. All their valuables, all their personal belongings and tools, all of it was left behind. As if only the people and their animals had vanished. The only thing they found there was the mysterious word 'Croatoan' carved into the wooden fencing surrounding the settlement."

"So what does it mean?"

"Nobody knows. It's about fifteen miles south of Croatan Island, where the Croatan Indians lived," Mills went on.

"Maybe that's the whole answer? A nearby tribe attacked and killed them all?"

"Only if they took all the bodies with them. Or dragged them away alive. Because all they found on the island were two skeletons, and they had been buried while the colony was still there. And remember, there were no signs of any struggle. More than that – the colonists had a secret sign – a Maltese cross they would carve in a special place if they were ever attacked. There was no cross, though. Only that word – *Croatoan*."

"Maybe they migrated to that island themselves? And the carving was to tell anyone who came looking for them where they were?" thought Corey aloud.

"Possibly. But no expedition has ever found any trace of them. Not on Roanoke Island, and not on Croaton Island. The Indians from the neighboring island, though, like the other local tribes, worshipped a rather strange god named Croaton. They called him the Reaper of Souls. All offerings to this god vanished from the altar before the eyes of the priests, as though something invisible had devoured them. They even sacrificed live warriors to him. They vanished into thin air, too."

"Sounds pretty eerie," muttered Corey, looking warily around, squinting at the passenger door mirror to check that no one was following them. "But totally ridiculous."

"Is it? You know, over the course of human history there have been any number of mysterious and unexplained disappearances of people, sometimes whole groups of people. But nothing as big as Roanoke Island. The English sent the Queen a report saying that the colonists had been taken by the Devil."

"Medieval superstition," snorted Corey. But his brave face didn't deceive his companion.

"Well, look around you. Before you tell me it's ridiculous, that it's superstition, take a look at what you see. An empty world, all the people vanished. And they left everything behind, untouched, with no signs of struggle and no SOS signals. Our city now, the whole city, and maybe our whole world, is like the Lost Colony of Roanoke Island. Unlike the English, however, we have – as you put it – motivation. A good, strong motivation. We need to find our loved ones."

"Okay, I see the analogy to our situation, although I don't like drawing parallels like that. But I'm not right if I tell you not to bring it up. Any theory could be right in this case. And any scrap of knowledge, history included, might be invaluable. Listen, how do you know all that?"

"I read a lot. Not as much as I used to, of course. But I do love to read. The classics, science fiction, history, biographies. Mysteries, sometimes." And after a short pause, Mills added, his voice subdued, "Most of all I like to read my grandkids fairy tales when I put them to bed. Of all the books I've read over the course of my life, those are the most entrancing. I'd give anything right now – anything! …to be reading Paul and Kass those magical stories right now. They adore them. To read them to little Naomi, when she grows up a bit..."

Corey thought for a while, not wanting to interrupt Wendell's intense, if contradictory psychic state, but then decided he had to say it.

"You're a good man, Wendell. A good father and a good grandfather. It looks like we were both unlucky... Or maybe it's the other way around – that we're lucky enough still to be here, and it's everyone else that was unlucky? Who the hell knows! But I want to tell you that even if we've been unlucky, I'm glad if I have to be here that I'm here with you.

"Thank you, Corey," said the old man in a melancholy voice. "I do appreciate that, I suppose. It's just that right now it's hard to think about who we might consider lucky. It's all just so unreal, such a crazy nightmare, and I'm just trying to hold it all at a distance. I don't want to have to admit that we may really have lost them. Forever. The very thought is beyond terrifying."

"So let's agree that we haven't lost them. Not yet, anyway. Until the reverse is proven. Agreed?"

"Agreed. Of course. We haven't lost them. We're going to find them. I want to believe that with all my heart. It's hard, but it's all I want."

"Hey, look!" cried Corey, pointing to his left at the panorama of the night city coming into view beyond the edge of the overpass.

The sea of golden lights, denser and brighter closer to the city center, was interrupted by a ragged edged triangle of total darkness. Like a piece of dark, scorched earth in the midst of a glowing autumn forest.

"I guess that's logical," said Mills, stopping by the edge of the overpass, and he and Corey went to the railing to get a better look at the anomaly. "Some equipment fails and a whole neighborhood loses electricity. Strange that it hasn't happened anywhere else. Strange that all sorts of automatic things aren't breaking, that buildings aren't going up in flame where a teapot was left on a burner, where something was cooking in a stove, where a potato was being roasted on an open flame or something like that."

"True," said Corey, looking over the dark zone with a pair of binoculars. "Over the past two hours, a whole heap of things like that could have happened. Thousands of incidents, probably. Fires should long since have burned down all the empty buildings, place by place. The question is why isn't that happening?"

"Some kind of stasis," suggested Wen.

"What do you mean, stasis? Like aliens coming down and putting the whole world in suspended animation?"

"Well, yeah. Or it's all a simulation."

"Look at the words you know," said Corey, taken aback.

"Hey, don't be rude to your elders," said Wendell, poking a finger at Corey's chest. "I may not be up to date on all the latest technology, but I read a lot, you understand?"

"Hey, I was just joking, don't be offended!"

"I'm not offended," said Wendell, smiling. "So what are you seeing?"

"Can't see a damned thing, it's all dark. You're probably right. Probably a substation down, or something like that, and the power went out. That's the area around Fifth and Liberty?"

"Yes, where Trinity Park is. From Liberty Avenue and Fifth, I think, to Ninth, if memory doesn't fail me. Want to drive over and see what's there?"

"Sure, let's go. No better or worse than any other route we could choose. And then I suggest we head for Central Station. I'd like to know what's going on with the trains. And have a look in the dispatcher's control room. They should have all kinds of communications equipment."

When they turned off Fifth into the unlit local residential streets, it felt like a ring of darkness was closing in around them, ever tighter, and only that white cone of light from their headlights cut through the black emptiness of the streets. And when the streetlights in the rear view mirror had all vanished, cut off by the giant megaliths of city buildings, Wendell turned on the brights to broaden their scope of visibility.

Corey didn't know how to take what he saw. On the one hand, it was awful. The dark, empty buildings seemed like gigantic tombstones in a dead city. It threw the emptiness into sharp relief, depriving them of that sense of presence that had still lingered where there was light.

There, though, in that sea of light, the mirage of a living city was still more terrible, in a way, because it teased with its hints, its suggestion that the city was still alive, that there might be people in those buildings, people who had no idea about the catastrophe that had struck their world. Calmly drinking their tea, or their beer, as an endless flow of drivel was spouted at them from their television screens.

But Trinity Park felt like a final sentence, compelling them to accept the ruthless truth of the end of the world. Of the beginning of the epoch of darkness.

"Can you stop here and turn the light off?" asked Corey, and they stopped in the middle of an intersection where the black silhouettes of buildings rose up on three sides, with the fourth taken up by the gaping darkness of the pond and the jagged contours of trees against the starry sky.

From here you couldn't see the moon, and the darkness seemed dense, turbid, as if you could grasp it with your hand as you got out of the car. Hesitantly, Corey opened his door and got out. His eyes began to adjust to the darkness, and he looked around him, seeking signs of other human beings – the glimmer of a flashlight, candles, or a bonfire. Motion, or sounds.

But the whole neighborhood bore down on him with its emptiness and stillness. The darkness wasn't even, it was cobbled together from a multitude of shades of black. It seemed to be pulsing and writhing in waves and rhythms of blackness, crawling ever closer to the rash travelers who had come to the very heart of darkness.

"If you gaze long into an abyss, the abyss also gazes into you," Corey grumbled, but he didn't like how muted and helpless his voice sounded, as if the dull houses had absorbed the echo of his words.

"You've read Nietzsche?" asked Wendell, surprised.

"Ha. No, I just heard the phrase somewhere," said Corey, with a dismissive wave of his hand. "I don't like it here. Everything seems wrong, if you know what I mean. I can't shake that feeling that something's here. Something hostile, unfriendly. Hungry. I can't explain it. As if all I have to do is turn my back and it comes closer, from behind me, ready to seize us."

He turned around, sharply, but there was no one, nothing behind him. Just the empty streets drowning in nocturnal blackness.

"I'm sure it's just my nerves," he said, pulling out his rucksack and taking another swallow of bourbon. "Want some?"

Mills didn't, and Corey put the bottle away. Whatever his nerves were doing, he had to remain sober and collected.

"Let's get out of here. We haven't found anybody, but here, somehow, you get an especially strong feeling of emptiness. It's scary, I have to be honest."

"It is," croaked Wen, getting back in the car and turning the headlights back on. "It's a little better with the headlights on, but it's still scary. Let's go."

He turned and drove back towards Fifth, and when the streetlights flared up ahead of them, Corey thought the blackness outside pressed in closer to them, pushing in against the car, trying not to let them escape its grasp.

Suppressing his terror, he waited for the invisible talons in the dark to shoot out of gloom, tear open the metal casing of the car, and catch them in their awful grip. He felt himself beginning to suffocate, as if there weren't enough air, as if this insatiable night was choking him to then drag him away in its lethal embrace.

"Wen, faster! Please," he gasped, squeezing the words out. "I can't breathe. Have to get out of here, faster."

The cab driver seemed uncomfortable, too – he quickly shifted gears and pressed down hard on the pedal. With a roar, the car shot towards the growing patch of light ahead, but Corey thought they weren't going to make it, that the Darkness would get them before they reached it.

He was ready to swear that he saw, on either side, not just the buildings racing by, but vague predatory shadows chasing them down. And clouds of black fog shimmering behind them like a fatally onrushing black tide.

Corey dug his fingers into the door handle and tried to keep looking straight ahead of him, at the vision of Fifth fast approaching, tried not to look back or to either side.

"We just have to make it, to get out of here in time," he mumbled silently, moving his lips.

Wendell flew out into the open, onto the brightly lit street, at eighty miles an hour, slammed on the brakes and swung the wheel to the right, spinning the car, using the parking brake to skid it in a bootlegger's turn. They were veering towards the railing, but with a steady, experienced hand he kept the car under control, hit the gas again, and evened her out.

"Whew, we made it. God damn!" said Corey, coughing and spitting, greedily gulping in lungfuls of air. "Did you feel that? The Darkness was after us, it really was, chasing us, right?"

"Maybe," said Mills, cautiously. "I was frightened, too, but maybe the whole thing was just a kind of panic attack... tough to say."

Corey wiped away the cold sweat with his hand. He could tell that he was trembling with relief. But he didn't reach for the whiskey. He'd had enough as it was, for now, anyway.

"I don't know, either. But it did seem to me that something was out there. And who knows – maybe it's not an accident that the lights are out there. Maybe this is the epicenter of all this crap, eh? Maybe it's all coming and creeping out from in there."

"And now you're going to tell me it has its nest in there," chuckled Wen.

"Its nest? Or its cocoon? Its landing pad? The Gates of Hell? How should I know? But I'm certain something was there. I'm willing to suppose that it might have been my own unstrung psyche, yes, possible, but I'm not riding boldly into any more unlit parts of town or striding into buildings where the electricity's off. Screw them all!"

"Central Station?"

"Yeah, let's go."

After the terror they had experienced in Trinity Park, they both fell silent. Talking seemed unnecessary. But Wendell's foot was heavy on the pedal, trying to leave that unpleasant place and the feelings it had evoked as far behind and as fast as possible. So it took them only ten minutes to reach the train station.

The trains were there, but they were as empty as everything else in the city.

"What's the difference between trains and cars?" asked Corey.

"Size? Mass?" guessed Mills. "Interesting that it's not only the moving cars that vanished, but the parked cars, too. Why?"

"Well, why not?"

"That works, too, I suppose," shrugged the cabbie.

The train dispatcher's control room was just as empty, but the door was unlocked and the friends cautiously began to examine the equipment. The monitors were dark. The walkie-talkies didn't work, and neither did the land-line phones.

"What was that you said before – about stasis?" blurted out Corey, suddenly.

"We haven't managed to find any explanations here, either. No communications working. And there are no people. Or cars. What do we do now?"

"I suggest stopping somewhere in the middle of an extremely well-lit street or square, have something to eat, and hold a brainstorming session."

"Hold a what?" asked Wen.

"Enough driving and searching. Time to think, to try to organize everything we know, to try and figure out what we *don't* know yet. I've had it with all this uncertainty. You know, I'm used to controlling situations. I've always managed my own life. I'm a strategist, I work out strategies for clients and their brands. I construct business plans and advertising campaigns. Planning makes life secure and predictable. And now I feel myself weak and helpless. Nothing seems to depend on me, we're poking about in the dark, looking for answers, but we haven't even formulated our own questions yet."

"Okay, let's try what you're suggesting. Republic Circle's about couple blocks from here. There are so many streetlights there that it's almost blinding in the evening."

"Sounds perfect," said Corey, nodding. "That sounds like just what we want."

They sped out onto Republic Circle, its myriad glittering streetlights, billboards, neon signs and screens flooding the space with ever-shifting shades and hues of light.

It exuded a sense of endless motion, and Corey was just thinking that he would have chosen a calmer place for their brainstorming session, one less filled with distractions. But it was beautifully bright here, and after the terrors of Trinity Park that seemed immensely appealing.

Mills stopped the car in the middle of the circle, smack in the center of the deserted intersection. Right in the path of the absent flow of traffic. On either side shone a row of blinding pale yellow streetlamps.

"Good visibility here," he explained. "If you were right, and there's something hiding in the darkness, this is the place. From here we can see every way onto and out of the circle. If we spot something, we can high-tail it the other way."

"Sure, if it doesn't get us surrounded," said Corey, darkly. He took a few sheets of paper and a magic marker from his rucksack. "Oooh – I completely forgot about the food! Want a sandwich?"

Wendell gratefully took the little tin-foil-wrapped package. His hands were trembling visibly.

He stretched out his other hand. "I wouldn't say no to a swig or two now, either." Corey handed him the bottle of bourbon. "You know, I think I'm burned out for today. If we have to make a run for it, you get behind the wheel, okay?"

"Yes, of course."

They ate their sandwiches in silence, washing them down with bottled water, their eyes scanning the circle. The marketing messages assaulted them from all sides in a perpetual stream of opportunities and temptations that no longer held any meaning for anybody.

Shampoos for luxuriant volume. A chain of coffee shops as cozy as your kitchen. Stylish and reliable Swiss watches. Ultracontemporary smartphones, slender and edge-to-edge-screened. Expensive cars for wealthy businessmen. A new complex with elite apartments and the very best neighbors. A reliable pension fund. A vacation paradise for the family on the beautiful beaches of Mexico.

"And all that may have just evaporated into nothingness in the blink of an eye," Corey thought to himself. "Only this morning it all *meant* something. Those brands spending millions – billions! – to win this nonsensical race. And rapacious scavengers – like me and everyone else at the agency, actually. A whole world of consumerism revolved around a system of conventional values imposed by screens, pages and billboards. All that had now vanished without a trace. We were in a Pompeii already blanketed in the ash of our own vanity, buried under the dust of our ignorance and crazily inflated sense of self-worth."

Today's presentation was completely meaningless. And there would be no new strategy for a craft beer brand, no bonuses or apartments closer to downtown. He and Steff would stay... Steff... There was no Steff anymore, either.

Corey could not reconcile his brain to that idea. He wanted to shout, scream, cry, howl. He wanted to die. To stop seeing this nocturnal nightmare. He was choking with pain and horror, but he promised he would stay cool for Wendell.

Corey grew nauseous from an onrush of despair. He wasn't going to be able to eat any more. He carefully wrapped what was left of the sandwich in the tin foil and put it back in his rucksack, took a drink of water and laid his sheets of paper on the hood of the car, placing various objects on them so they wouldn't be blown away by the wind.

"Ever been part of a meeting like this? I don't mean the ridiculous topic, I mean a real brainstorming session."

Mills shook his head. "No, I haven't."

"Then let me explain a few key basic principles to you. The most important is that there's no such thing as a bad idea. Even what sound like the silliest ideas sometimes turn out to be important, because discussing them can spur a new and productive train of thought. Second, we're not criticizing each other's ideas, we never say 'that's absurd,' 'what a load of crap,' 'it'll never work,' or anything like that. On the contrary, the goal is to work together to greenhouse ideas if we can find even the slightest potential in them. We ask each other questions to try and extract anything that may be worthwhile. And third... oh, that's enough about the rules, there's only the two of us, we'll figure it out. You get the general idea?"

"Easy enough," nodded Wen. "You make it sound like some kind of system, as though you do this all the time."

"I do, in fact, do this all the time. It's part of my job," he said, and added, to himself: "It *was*, anyway." And then, out loud: "Together we'll manage it just fine, but I'll moderate our meeting."

"You'll... what?"

"It means I'll keep the meeting under control and direct the conversation so we don't get side-tracked in our own nonsense, so we stick to constructive discussion. I'll take notes to try to put some kind of structure in all this craziness. You ready?"

"Yes, sir!" said the old man, saluting smartly.

"Okay, then. I've been thinking about our most important problems. To understand whether there's something we can do or not, we need to know what has actually happened. And for that, we need to understand the scale on which it happened – agreed?"

"I believe it's on a massive scale. Think about it. There's no phone service – if everything were all right outside the city, the world would have noticed long ago. They'd have called in the National Guard and whatever other services they use for emergencies like this. Make sense?"

"It does," said Corey, nodding, jotting down notes. "Which means, as I note here, that catastrophe probably covers the entire country. And possibly the world. Right?"

"I'm afraid so," nodded Mills.

"Then there are two main avenues to pursue. The first is to figure out what's happened and whether we can do anything about it. The second is to seek out other survivors, and the resources we're going to need in any event: food, water, fuel, clothing, medicine and so forth."

"You really are taking breaking the situation down, all the way to its nuts and bolts."

Corey shrugged.

"Professional know-how. It works for developing any kind of strategy. It helps make sense of the situation and predict how it will unfold. It helps us determine what the issues are and compose a script containing the actions we need to undertake."

"Wow."

"Really, it's not usually all that difficult. Our situation, though, is way beyond the borders of my area of expertise. So I really don't know where all this is going to take us. Anyway, let's keep going. Any objection if we start by discussing ideas as to what actually happened, and then move on to figuring out what to do about resources?"

"You're in the driver's seat," said Wendell, with a gesture indicating his agreement with whatever approach Corey wanted to pursue.

"All right, then – here we go. I need to ask you something. Are you religious? Do you believe in God?"

Mills squinted at him with a slight shake of the head, as if to say that it wasn't an easy question to answer.

"In theory, yes, I believe in God. But I don't go to Church on Sunday mornings to sing hymns, clap along and dance. My faith is here," he said, tapping his heart, and then, tapping his temple: "And here."

"Good," said Corey, blushing, and then asked, with a slight stammer: "Have you read the Bible?"

"Of course I have. Haven't you?"

"No. Why would I read the bible?"

"If nothing else, because it's something everyone should know," said Wen, taken aback. "To have a handle on what it is that millions and millions of believers think. You're a marketing expert, psychology is important for what you do. Isn't that right?"

"Well, yes, that's pretty much right. I just never really thought it was completely necessary. Or at least it wasn't a top priority. I mean, I do have a general idea of what it is that religious people believe. I don't mean to offend you, and if I have, I apologize. What I mean is that I wasn't interested in picking up all the details."

"Why are you asking about that now, though?"

Corey glanced around. It was a lifeless reflection of the world that had recently vanished, oppressive in its emptiness and the senseless brightness of myriad lights no one needed.

"The notion of the End of the World. The Apocalypse. Could this be it? Does it look like what's described in the Bible?"

To his astonishment, Wen gave a kindly chuckle.

"When you say 'The End of the World,' it's actually probably Armageddon, although in the earliest texts that was just the name of the field on which the final battle would be fought between

Good and Evil. 'Apocalypse' means 'Revelation,' it's the last book of the New Testament. It mentions the battle at Armageddon. Pop culture mixes the two ideas up to the point where it's all chaos in the minds of all the many readers and viewers. Anyway – no, it doesn't look much like the way the end of the world is described in the Bible."

"Why not?"

"The Apocalypse describes the second coming of Christ, accompanied by a whole series of cataclysms. And he comes to defeat the Antichrist. You may have heard of a lot of the events in Revelations, including the four horsemen of the Apocalypse, the Day of Wrath with its great earthquake, the stars falling to earth and a red moon, hail, fire, blood, an eclipse of the sun, moon and stars..."

"The stars have already fallen to earth, haven't they?" said Corey, interrupting the list, but Mills just rolled his eyes.

"Don't be so serious. The beast with seven heads and ten horns, the number of the beast – six hundred and sixty-six – the battle of the angels against the dragons, epidemics and new cataclysms, the rule of Satan, the wrath of God, the victory of God over the Devil."

"Pretty dramatic. Amid all the action, what does Jesus do?"

"He leads the army of the angels into battle, and he also judges the world, the righteous and the sinners. He resurrects the righteous and lifts us all up into Heaven."

"That's why I asked about this. What if that's exactly what happened? The End of the World and the Last Judgment? What if everyone has been carried off – some to Hell, others to Heaven?"

"What about us, then? The cosmic scheme forgot the two of us here?"

"We slipped through the cracks, or yes, it forgot us, it missed us in all the craziness you've just been regaling me with."

"You're doing it again," said the old man, wagging a finger at Corey.

"I'm not. Really. It just came out that way. I can't take this particular explanation seriously myself, but I do have to ask you. What do you think of it?"

"Forgive me, but I can't see that as our working hypothesis. Too many holes. Just think about it. Jesus isn't going somehow miss the two of us. He's God. And if he could somehow miss us, then surely he could have missed tons of others, too. But we haven't seen any of them. But that's not the main issue."

"And what *is* the main issue?"

"What does He need with all the damned cars?"

"Hah. Good point. And what happened to the phone signal?"

"And what happened to the phone signal. I'd say we can cross the religious explanation off our list. What about aliens, though?"

"That is an interesting theory," agreed Corey. "What would it look like to you?"

"I don't know. I haven't had much contact with extraterrestrials. With foreign *visitors, immigrants* and *aliens* – sure," laughed Wen. "Remember how we were talking about stasis? Maybe they froze everything on Earth. Hit the pause button. But for some reason it didn't affect the two of us and we're still moving around in a motionless world?"

"Why would they do that, though? And does that help explain the bizarre part about the cars?"

"Maybe it's some kind of experiment?"

"On us or on the rest of humanity?" asked Corey, continuing to jot the ideas down in his notebook.

"Theoretically either way is possible. We might be the guinea pigs and they're looking to see how we react in a situation like this."

Corey shifted the marker to his left hand, raised a fist towards the sky and extended his middle finger.

"Sorry, go on. That was just in case your theory was right."

"No problem," said Mills, copying Corey's gesture – but with both hands. "I have a few things I'd love to say to the aliens myself! But... where were we? Ah, right... That, or they're conducting the experiment on a planetary scale. And we were left out of it as the result of some technical malfunction."

"But why? You mean like Jesus Christ they forgot us, or missed us?"

"Anything's possible. It's a pretty far-fetched idea so far, don't you agree? An experiment on the two of us seems more logical. There is still a whole list of problems with that, though. The cars, for example. No idea what that would mean. All living things – that makes some kind of sense. But – all living things plus automobiles?"

"Personal property?"

"In what sense?"

Corey scratched at his beard, trying to put the varied fragments of this mosaic together so everything matched.

"Imagine that aliens have taken over our planet. But then it turns out they're deep in debt, and the alien bank forecloses on Earth. They take all the real estate on the planet. But the people, and all other living things, and yes, even the cars – that's all property, but it's not real estate. You and I might have gotten swept up with the real estate."

"I have to tell you I'm not really thrilled with that particular hypothesis. People of my race were property for long enough for every fiber of my being to burn from the mere thought of something like that on a planetary scale. But still – fine, suppose you're right. What about all the other people?"

"No idea. The first aliens kept them? Or sold them to somebody else? You know I'm not proposing ideas because I like them, I hope. You know my Steff would be off wherever all that property is, in whatever cosmic warehouse or garbage dump it might be lying..." There was a lump in Corey's throat and he reached for the water bottle to take a few sips and calm himself down. "I already despise the little green bastards! But there's some logic to this theory. At least it accounts for the cars."

"But there are also gaps in it," Wendell objected. "Let's say it's plausible enough and we won't throw it away, but for now let's move on to other alternative ideas."

"Right – what about the idea of an alternate universe? Could we have somehow fallen into a parallel reality? Into a gap between our world and something else? Driven off from in-between platforms into some kind of timeless void? And that's why we have no phone signal, no other life forms, no fires blazing up all over the place, and everything has just stopped where it was, like a fly in amber?"

"Perhaps," said the old man, unconvinced, rubbing the bridge of his nose with one finger and considering the latest proposition. "That would explain a lot of things, too. Not everything, though. For example, if everything has stopped, why do we still have electricity? The fuel seems happy to burn in the car's engine, too. So chemical reactions still work normally. And how would we still exist? If all life is gone, we should be gone, too."

"Somehow it doesn't apply to us."

"You're not getting it, Corey. It's not about us, it's about what's inside of us. We're not just people, we're vessels carrying a mass of biological organisms. An adult human contains about a hundred trillion single-celled creatures. That's ten times the number of cells our bodies are made of. You could say we're only about ten percent people."

"Well, that's kind of disgusting," said Corey, wrinkling his nose.

"Is it? Then imagine you've got about four pounds of bacteria just in your intestines."

"Stop!"

"It's true."

"It's repulsive."

"But if it weren't for those five hundred, more or less, kinds of single-celled organisms, we'd be dead. Symbiosis with them makes us what we are. Now imagine they're gone. How long do you think we'd last without them?"

"No idea. A week? A month?"

"I can't answer that. But it's something we need to think about. Either that or things aren't all that bad, and all the stuff that was inside of us is still in there, the same way the car we were in is still working."

"Actually, Wen, that's important. Yes! Why didn't we think of this earlier? We need to determine when all this craziness started. Remember you mumbled something about the radio not working?"

"That's right," said Mills, perking up. "That's when it was, right? We can more or less figure out when it happened, and where we were when it happened. We were driving on the broken asphalt past the Ferguson factory. Just before the exit onto Eleventh. I was thinking what a weak signal we must have right there, but it never did come back."

Corey began to speak furiously, thinking it through.

"Listen, I'm sorry – I acted like a complete asshole back then. I remember I even yelled at you." But maybe I was right about something. And whatever it was happened right there, on that God-forsaken stretch of forgotten road."

"You still believe the theory that Jesus failed to notice us in such a backwater place?"

"Well, no," said Corey, chuckling. "But I do like it that you can still see some humor in the situation. That's incredibly important right now. So it seems we can determine the time of our End of the World, at least approximately. Although I'm not sure what that does for us. And we can also pin down more or less the point in space where we were when it happened."

"Hey, yeah. And that's even more important," said Wendell, slapping the hood of the car with his palm. "Let's say we've fallen into some kind of wormhole in space-time, some kind of absurd rabbit-hole, and come out into this through-the-looking-glass world where everything's not what it's supposed to be. And we failed to notice how we passed through some kind of portal or rift."

"How we passed through it? Or how the whole world passed through it?" Corey wondered.

"How we passed through it, I think. More likely than everybody and everything else passing through it. Logical?"

"Possibly. But if there is a rift or portal, why did we pass through it, but not any of the other cars that were on that same road with us?"

"Hard to say," said Wen, thoughtfully. "Maybe we hit the portal the instant it appeared, momentarily. Maybe it's unstable and existed for only a few moments, just enough to swallow us up. Maybe the whole world doesn't even suspect that anything's happened. Maybe we fell out of our own reality into some kind out-of-phase rift between worlds?"

"Or maybe the portal is still right there, where it was? That's something we can do, right now. Go back – and make sure."

"Good God!" cried Mills, realizing. "Get in the car! We're checking it out this instant!"

"Hey, you just told me I was driving!"

"I just got a second wind. I know the city better than you do. Get your papers together and get in the car."

The cab driver seemed to eke out every bit of power the old sedan had left. They flew towards Eleventh even faster than they had gone trying to escape Trinity Park.

Corey looked back, then to either side, but could make out no suspicious movements in the shadows. Either whatever was tracking them had let them go or it had all been his imagination under the strain of their situation. Or Wen was simply driving too fast for the spectral monsters hiding beyond the reach of the streetlights to keep up.

The burst of anticipation seemed to have inspired them both, giving them new strength and a faint hope that they might really be capable of finding a way out. Neither of them wished to discuss new hypotheses, so strongly had they been seized by the hope of this chance to return to their normal world, to their families and loved ones.

And yet Wendell broke that silence. A strange doubt had arisen in his mind, one that wouldn't go away.

"I'm thinking... are we going the right way? Driving back the way we came, from Eleventh towards the factory? What I mean is... if there is a portal or rift there, do we have to go through it the other way? Or the same way went through it the first time? What if we don't get back home, but instead find ourselves another world away from home? In some other new dimension? A new plane?"

"How should I know, buddy? I just want to get home to my wife. Let's try going through it in the other direction first."

"Okay," said Mills. "I think so, too. What about the speed?"

"Why should that make a difference? If you need to go from one room to another, who cares how fast you go?"

"Ever see 'Back to the Future?'"

"No, actually."

"Millennials. Impossible to have a conversation with you people. Okay, forget it. Just imagine that speed changes things. If you go slowly into water, it lets you in, but if you jump from high up, your body can smash itself against the surface like it was made of cement. See what I mean?"

"I guess," said Corey, his brow furrowed. "Or you'd have to build up the necessary kinetic energy."

"Wait, you had physics in school?" cried the old man in mock astonishment.

"Okay, okay, reign in the sarcasm. I would imagine that the logical thing is to go at the same speed we were going when we passed through it to get here."

"That does make sense. So – twenty-five or thirty miles an hour, to the extent the potholes allow us to go that fast."

They were on Eleventh now, heading away from downtown. Mills slowed down at a half-hidden turn onto a single-lane road concealed behind the low cement protective wall and a few scrubby trees.

At the next intersection, Wen stopped and turned to Corey.

231

"Ready? It's somewhere past this intersection and before we reach the factory warehouses."

"Let's get back as fast as we can, my friend. Full speed ahead! To our families, to our own crazy world. I have to admit, I'm even going to miss you, you grumpy old man, when we get back."

"Me? I'm a grumpy old man?" said Wendell, staring at him.

"But it doesn't matter, I'll be happy to see you. Come by tomorrow, we'll have a party with a barbecue."

"With pleasure, man. Let's just get out of this bizarre trap, as fast as we can, okay? Then maybe I'll consent to try your cooking."

They both laughed, and they could sense tension in that laughter. They both tried to hide it behind a front of cheerfulness and bravado.

Mills sent the car slowly forward, gradually increasing their speed, navigating the potholes as they went. His hands clutched the wheel tightly. He peered ahead at the road.

Corey got out the rucksack and found his phone. He turned it on, hoping to get a signal that would tell them they were back in their own world. Of wherever it was they were supposed to be returning to. He held the phone in a nervous grip, tapping away to make it keep searching for a network, worried he might miss the right moment. With muted hope, he looked ahead at the road, then at the phone again. He found himself muttering, through gritted teeth:

"Okay, come on, come on! Please. Please, please, please!"

But the telephone was deaf to his prayers and the words "No signal" never left the screen. They reached the factory.

Wen stopped the car and gave a loud sigh. Then he started banging the steering wheel.

"Goddammit! I was so sure it would work! Christ!"

"Let's just try doing it in the other direction," said Corey, although he himself was trembling with irritation and disappointment.

The driver swung the car around sharply and drove back over the pitted surface. This time they went a bit faster, Mills nervously swerving this way and that around the potholes and cracks.

But the screen in Corey's hands never showed a sign of doubt, and the radio never made a sound. They reached the intersection again that lead to Eleventh and stopped.

"I just want to go home. I just want to go back to Annie, Ruth and Naomi. To my little boys. Why is this happening? Why is it happening to me?" railed Wen, quietly, through his tears, swaying back and forth, his eyes shut. "What did I do to deserve this? Lord! What am I guilty of in your eyes? Why is this happening to me, and to the people I love?"

Corey squeezed his friend's shoulder and tried to raise his spirits, although inside he was in terrible need of that same kind of support. He was on the verge of losing it, of laying waste to everything around him, cursing and screaming, pouring out the pain that was tearing him apart.

"I need to tell you something. I grew up with no parents. My grandparents raised me, because Mom and Dad... they died in a hurricane when I was two. I don't even remember them, you know? The photographs they showed me... that's not my own memories. I was too little to remember them. Even little things – a touch, a smell, the sound of a voice. I have nothing of them, just my own fantasies about what they should have been like."

Wendell turned and looked, listened to him attentively, wiping his tears with his sleeve.

"When I was a bit older, I learned to find meaning in the world around me. I saw how things were connected, how they were mutually interconnected. Maybe that helped shape my analytical thinking and, to a certain degree, helped make me what I became. But there is one thing that's never stopped bothering me. I never could understand why my parents were taken away from me. What did I do wrong, what was the crime for which they took my mom and dad away?"

Corey cleared his throat and took a second to get his trembling voice back under control.

"I thought I must have been a bad kid. I absolutely believed I did not deserve to be happy, to experience pleasure from all the things that made the neighbors' kids happy. I needed to punish myself for what I was guilty of."

"Did you actually harm yourself?" asked Wen.

"No. Nothing like that. I didn't... I just didn't allow myself to be happy. Mentally I shut myself in a dark little cell where there was no place for laughter or smiles. Grandma and Grandpa worried about me, but they couldn't really reach me. They took me to a psychologist, to a priest, but they couldn't break through my walls, either."

"But somebody did."

"Yes..." said Corey, nodding. "Somebody did. When I was twelve, I ran away from home. The first night I took shelter under Eastern Bridge. That's where I met Winky. He was old, filthy, and drunk. He stunk to high heaven and he had this constant strange twitch in one eye. That night I had my first drink. My new neighbor shared what he had with me. Somehow I was able to tell this stranger, weeping the whole while, what I could never tell to the closest people in my life."

Wendell nodded, understanding, prompting Corey to continue.

"It seemed to me that this guy, the lowest of the low, was the same kind of pariah I was. That sometime in the past he must have brought the wrath of fate down upon himself, too. I never did find out how he had ended up down there. And I could never find him again. But on the morning after that night, I was home again, weeping bitterly in Grandma's arms, with Grandpa by my side, comforting me."

"What happened? Did he do something to you?"

"No, nothing really, that's the whole point. But somehow Winky had been able to explain to me that not everything in life always has to mean something. That not everything happens because of us, because we did something good or bad to make it happen. Sometimes things just happen. Without it having anything to do with us. Because it's a great, big, complicated world, and it lives a complicated life of its own, and it couldn't care less about us. Sometimes we're lucky, sometimes we're not... it just rolls on, following its path, and sometimes its enormous wheels crush us as it goes on and tosses us by the side of the road like last week's paper no one has any use for anymore."

Corey suddenly realized he was still clutching the phone in his hand. He put it away in the pocket of his hoodie.

"You and me, neither of us is responsible for what happened today. It happened because it happened. And our families aren't guilty either, and neither is anyone else who seems gone. Or we're gone, and they're still there and we just don't know it. Something happened. And it's got nothing to do with us. Or somebody or something yanked us out for some purpose, choosing two people at random from the millions, the billions of people in the world."

"Even if you're right, that doesn't make it any easier."

"It doesn't make easier, that completely true. But we promised each other today, and ourselves, too, to do everything in our power to find the people we care about, to bring them back, remember?"

"We haven't done a great job of that so far. What else can we try?"

"I've been thinking..." Corey frowned at the idea. "maybe we should just go back – maybe we have to reverse the whole process, do it backwards"

"You want me to drive back towards the factory... backwards?" said the cab driver, alarmed. "Do you have any idea what those potholes..."

He stopped in mid-sentence, closed his eyes, sighed twice, deeply, and shook his head, clearing his mind. Without a word, he started the car and put it in gear. Throwing his right arm behind the passenger seat and shifting his body, he stared into the rear view mirror, steering with his left hand.

Corey took his phone out again and watched the screen quietly, so as not to disturb Wen as he plotted a complex course back up the road. But this attempt failed, as all the previous ones had.

"We're obviously doing something wrong," said Mills, frustrated. "Why isn't it working?"

"Maybe because there's no portal here at all. Maybe it disappeared hours ago and we're stuck here forever. Or maybe it appears and disappears at a specific time."

"Or the portal was never here."

"Or there never was any portal to begin with, and our theory about a rift was a wrong. But then what's important is the time when we were shifted here. We happened to be driving out here when everyone was thrown out of our world, or maybe it was just us, but the place isn't what's important."

"I picked you up at your office at around 7:45," said the driver, to help orient them.

"The last text I sent Steff, before we turned to take the factory road, was... one sec..." Corey couldn't pull himself away from the screen and his correspondence with his wife. He read their last messages and suddenly realized they might be the very last...

"Sorry. At 7:58 pm. We'll give five more minutes for driving down Eleventh, then we turned, then another two minutes to the factory, right?"

"Sounds right," said Wen. "I'd say it all happened between 8:10 and 8:15. Plus or minus a couple of minutes. But that doesn't tell us much."

"True, not much use in it. But we have a point of reference. It's been, since the thing happened... a bit over six hours. The city's still in one piece. No fires have broken out. We're stuck here, preserved in a set-piece of a city. Maybe this whole world isn't real? Maybe it's some kind of back-up copy of our world? And we've somehow been accidentally... archived?"

"It's a good theory. Incomprehensible, but good."

"Why do you say that?" asked Corey, surprised.

"Well, if nothing else, because then your Steff and my family are all alive. And we're the only ones stuck in this back-up chunk of amber. Listen, I think I've had it. Your turn to drive."

"The bottle's still in my rucksack, a little bourbon wouldn't do you any harm right about now," said Corey, pulling out of the narrow road onto the avenue and turning in the direction of his office.

The lights were on in the conference room, and in John's office, but he knew his boss wasn't there, like the rest of his team. And it didn't matter who had left and gone home before it happened, and who was still in the office. They were all somewhere he couldn't reach them. Or maybe they were right there, close by, a fraction of a second away in some sense of space-time, but that still left them just as inaccessible.

"This is where I work. Worked. No, work," Corey corrected himself and drove on towards the city center. "Now I'm thinking – what if none of this is real? What if we're in some kind of enormous simulation, like you said? We think something's wrong with the world, but none of it is even real."

"But why would someone create a simulation like that?"

"I don't know. We talked about aliens. But what if it's more complicated than that? What if there's some kind of system error and the simulation's not working right? And we see that as everything having disappeared, or as our having not disappeared?"

"Sure, and now we just have to wait for someone to notice the error and... what then?"

"Well, they might reboot the system, for example."

Mills looked at him, for a moment, tense. These were ideas beyond his habitual experience.

"And what would happen then?"

"I can't imagine, it's just a guess. Maybe our whole lives aren't a simulation, but a kind of computer game. And cosmic gamers have paused the game and turned everything off?"

"Then why are we still here?"

"Who the hell knows," said Corey, shrugging helplessly. "Maybe we're bots, part of the operating system."

"Maybe you are. Definitely not me. I'm no bot," said Wendell, shaking his head.

"If you were a bot, you couldn't know it."

"You're mixing up different things. It's insane people who can't know they're insane."

"I'm not mixing anything up. If you were programmed as a bot, you'd think you were a person, because that's the way your algorithms were designed."

"Listen, Corey, you don't actually believe any of that is what's actually happening, right?"

"Of course I don't. But I don't care anymore what I believe. If you'd asked me something like that at 8:00, I'd have laughed at you. Or called 911 to get you medical help. But now I just might believe this is a system reset..."

"Reset?"

"Yeah. Imagine something controlling our world decided to erase all the data, zero everything out, clear the cache, and start again."

"What about us?"

"Maybe we somehow survived that process," said Corey sadly.

They drove on for a time, saying nothing, each lost in his own thoughts. Only when they reached Republic Circle did Corey realize where he had been instinctively heading.

"Here again?" asked Wendell.

"Our headquarters."

Corey stopped the car on the far side of the circle, leaving it in the left lane. He opened his door and breathed deep the cool night air. Climbing out of the car, he went and sat on the grass. For whatever reason, he was untroubled by the mysterious shadows that were lurking either in the alleys behind the buildings or in the darker alleyways of his own unconscious mind.

He was too tired after this endless day, after the night, which had dragged on every bit as long, full of terrors, sorrow, and... hunger? He suddenly realized he was ravenous and went to get the rest of his sandwich. He and Wen ate another package of cookies and drank some of their water. Their supply of food and drink was sufficient for the time being. There would be no problem restocking in the morning at any store they found. As long as they had cash, it wouldn't even be looting.

Corey was mentally making a list of everything they absolutely had to make sure they had. His thoughts were muddled though. And neither of them was about to go back to their brainstorming session just yet, that was clear enough. They both needed a break. And this place, well lit and open, was as good as any other.

"You know, I still have that feeling that we're in some other reality, not our own, and that we're not supposed to be here. As if we'd been ejected from the Matrix and were seeing our world from the outside."

"I don't remember what happened with the pills, which one you were supposed to choose, but I'd choose whichever one would take me back to my family," said the old man, in a soft voice.

"Even if you knew it wasn't real? That the reality was here?" Corey gestured at the empty traffic circle around the car.

"I was happy there. What's the use of reality if I'm abandoned in an empty city with you? What would you choose?"

It seemed like a difficult choice, something to think long and hard about, but deep inside Corey knew the answer, and it surprised him.

"Yeah. Me, too. I'd go back to Steff."

The old man clapped him on the back, nodding, and got behind the wheel.

"I don't know about you, but I could use an hour or two of shut-eye. Think we should take turns standing guard? You know – in case those shadows of yours show up, or the monsters in the closet?"

"Don't laugh, you felt something there, too, in those dark streets. Honestly... I just don't know. Maybe it's just my testy psyche playing games with me. I can take the first watch if you want."

"If that's okay with you," said Mills.

Corey got into the car with his friend. The night breeze had grown uncomfortably cool. He took what was left of the whiskey out of his rucksack and they drank it by turns to keep warm and dull the pain inside.

"Wen, what are your plans for tomorrow?"

"Very funny."

"I'm serious, man. Let's start by going to a store first thing in the morning for supplies, filling the car, and then let's head for Chicago."

"Chicago?" asked Wendell, arching an eyebrow.

"Well, you have family there, right? You can't calmly sit around here without at least checking what's happened to them, right? What if they're not gone, if they're all right? Or if the same thing has happened there, but we do find survivors, and maybe they include your relatives?"

"Corey, why would you set me up like that with false hopes? We both know that everything is almost certainly just as bad there as it is everywhere else," said the old man. But you could see in his eye that he had taken to the idea.

"We've got to check, pal. We're going to Chicago."

"All right," said Wendell, after a brief pause. "We're going to Chicago. Thank you. I wouldn't have presumed to ask that of you. So thanks. But what about our plans to keep searching here?"

Corey spread his hands and the leaned back in his seat.

"Searching there is just as good as searching here. We haven't found anything yet that's brought us any closer to figuring this out. Maybe there we'll come across something new. Anyway, get some rest, I'll keep watch. We have a long road ahead of us tomorrow."

"About eight hundred miles. It's usually about thirteen or fourteen hours, but this time there will be zero traffic and no police. So I'd say we should be there in nine or ten."

"I wouldn't object to a good sports car for this trip. They just had to take all the cars, right? Couldn't leave us just one fast, powerful fancy car?"

"Don't start. Me and my old girl here won't let you down. Anyway, wake me in an hour and a half or so and then I'll take over, okay? And obviously if you see something, wake me up immediately. You know – the shadows, or anything else."

"Yes, of course. Go to sleep."

Corey scanned his surroundings again, closely, staring down every street, at every building, but the only movement was on the surface of an automated shifting billboard and the advertising on the circle's many screens.

"Funny, but all these commercials are probably the one great art form that has survived the demise of our entire civilization," thought Corey, bitterly. "Here it is – our monumental cultural legacy. All that remains as a testament to human culture. A mocking comment on our lack of culture. How much longer will these bathetic funhouse mirrors go on parodying us after our deaths? Or will it go on and on in this static world – an eternal epitaph for the human race?"

He found himself thinking that he wasn't even sure whether he and Wendell could even die in this strange, new world. Would they be preserved by whatever it was that prevented the deserted city from being destroyed by fire?

They did feel hunger, cold, physical pain, and weariness, though, which meant they were still living human beings, which meant they were as vulnerable as ever. Probably. He didn't really feel like testing it. Or maybe he did. Crash the car, ram it into one of the buildings, or find a store that sold guns and blow his brains out so he wouldn't have to keep trying to solve this inexplicable world.

But... if there was even the tiniest chance he could find his way back to Steff, he couldn't allow himself to take risks. There was a chance that his brains would casually splatter the walls of the store with the guns, with no Groundhog Day scene to follow. He'd just be gone. And there'd be no Jesus Christ on a battle mule waiting for him with open arms to welcome him back to the brightly lit world of the Matrix.

Corey blinked and realized he'd almost drifted off to sleep. Dammit! He quickly scanned the circle again, but saw nothing suspicious. He took the phone from his pocket to look at pics of Stephanie.

He had 14% of his battery power remaining. It would have made sense to plug the phone into his powerbank, but he didn't want to wake Wen, who was peacefully sleeping already. He decided he'd recharge the phone in the morning, or at least when Mills took his turn at the watch.

The photographs were more painful to look at than he'd expected, but there was something bittersweet in the upwelling memories. Like hot peppers in dark chocolate.

"It's like a kind of masochism," he thought, as he flipped through the album.

Each snapshot was a shard of an old life that might now be irretrievably shattered. He didn't want to admit the possibility to himself, but in the deepest recesses of his mind he understood that the chances that he and Wen could work out what had happened were vanishingly small. And to then get things back to the way they were... that was something he didn't want to talk about, but...

Still, they hadn't driven all night for nothing, trying to work out what had happened. And although they weren't going to find anyone or anything tomorrow in Chicago, they needed short-term objectives and more far-reaching goals if they didn't want to lose their minds. Or kill each other in one of their inevitable fits of despair.

On the other hand, what was the point of holding out? To keep on being the last two people on Earth? Or maybe not even on the real Earth – in this weird, amber-preserved realm, devoid of life? The last two remaining hominids, swimming in an alien equivalent of formaldehyde. Museum pieces. Specimens of the extinct race of Earthlings.

Stephanie was smiling a winsome smile at him from the current photograph. The sun was in her hair, little devils in her eyes, dimples on her cheeks... they had been drinking coffee that morning on the veranda. It was a peaceful weekend day – they didn't have those often enough. Most of the time they were running off to someplace or other, always having something to do, never having time to enjoy their time together – even just to sit together and have a cup of hot coffee.

Corey wiped his tears away, but new ones welled up to replace them.

"Steff," he whispered to himself. "If you only knew how I miss you, baby... I never realized before what idiots we've been. Both of us, you and me. How much time we've lost, incredibly precious time, when we could have been together. Time we spent staring into telephones, following moronic social media feeds full of idiotic pictures and videos and boring jokes, pointless news and empty discussions. Time we killed on all those senseless computer games or brain-dead television shows.

Time mindlessly wasted working all day and into the night, and often on weekends, chasing success, some imaginary "level" or status or something they didn't have they thought they needed.

Back then it had all seemed so significant and important, necessary, fun, entertaining, riveting and compelling... and now Corey wanted to take back every minute of it to spend with his wife. Just the two of them, with nobody else around to distract them. What he wouldn't give for that! He'd give everything. Anything.

In the next photograph, Steff was in a green dress, a garland of wild flowers in her hair. They had gone to visit her parents in Arizona. She had been wearing that same dress when they first met.

Corey remembered the day, a bright and sunny day, how he had been rushing off to work with a cup of coffee in his hand and a bag with breakfast in it. He stopped at the corner to wait with the other pedestrians for a green light. At that instant, a patch of green light in the crowd across the street caught his eye.

It was a girl, indescribably pretty. The morning sun played over her green dress, the wind ruffling the light material. It was a moment of truth, as if he had suddenly found himself in a fairy tale.

The girl smiled at him, seeing how he was staring at her, and Corey froze in mute ecstasy. He had never believed in love at first sight – the very idea was ridiculous. But there was undeniably something magical in the way they gazed at each other at that moment.

The light turned green and the two waves of impatient urbanites flowed out and into one another. But the two of them stood where they were. As if the whole world had somehow ceased to exist. Their eyes met, their gazes bridging the gulf of the street, and the flow of people washed past them on all sides, as if they were a pair of rocks in a riverbed.

The light turned red and the cars sped by on their urgent missions, engines revving, roaring, spewing clouds of exhaust fumes in their wakes. The world had shrunk to the size of a single smiling face amid a new crowd on the other side of the intersection. When a passing bus blocked his view of the girl, Corey shuddered. It seemed his heart skipped a beat from fear of losing her. Having her vanish in the vortex of the city. Never to see her again.

He knew he couldn't just walk by – he had to stop and talk to her. When the bus passed, Corey raised his hand and waved to her through the blue-gray smoke trailing behind it. He was about to move when he saw her wave back to him.

The light turned green again and he moved into the street with the others. The girl did the same, and at the moment the two waves intersected, Corey and the girl in green stopped, face to face.

He tried to find words, but instead he stood there, drowning in her brown eyes with their flecks of gold. He felt like anything he said now would be out of place, banal, that words could never say what their eyes were saying.

People walked past, jostling them, barking in annoyance, but quickly borne away by the crowd. And they just stood there, in the middle of the street, between two lanes of traffic, unable to utter a word, to violate the unexpected magic.

A line of cars of all colors headed angrily into the intersection, tearing away, rubber screeching on asphalt, engines roaring. Drivers honked and flashed at them as they passed, and one taxi driver leaned against the horn, then leaned out of the window with a rude gesture.

"Yo, asshole! Nice idea, standing in the middle of the street. Moron!"

The shouting, foul language and blaring of horns jolted Corey out of his stupor. Rows of racing cars were veering to avoid them, each finding a way to express its anger at them and extract more fury from its honks.

"Jerk!" he heard from another car window, and Corey watched the malicious face in the window pass and vanish.

"Hey, Wen – get up! Wen, look – we're back! Dammit, we're home... Wen!" he cried, shaking the sleepy Mills, who was still trying to figure out what was happening.

"Eh? What? I don't believe it! Oh, my God! We're back! We're really home! But how?"

"My friend... I have no idea. Not the foggiest notion. I drifted off, and when I awoke, all this was here... with us in the middle of it!"

"Nice place to put your car, asshole!" came a voice from a passing car.

"Jesus... let's get out of here," said Wen, so happy he missed the ignition switch with his key twice.

But he managed and they drove off, slowly, merging with the dense flow of cars in the morning rush hour.

"I don't get it. What happened? How did we get back? Or maybe we never went anywhere and it was all a dream? A hallucination?"

Corey looked around – and saw his rucksack and the bat on the floor in front of him. "No, that was no illusion, it all really happened. Only... *what* happened? And how?"

"Ooh, look at that. We had a hell of a night's drive, apparently," said Wen, pointing at something on the dashboard panel. "Oh, my... Annie! I have to call her. There's a taxi stand on the other side of the street, we'll stop there."

While Mills was navigating across several lanes of traffic to make his U-turn and stop on the other side of Republic Circle, Corey found his smartphone next to him on the seat, but it really had run out of power. He took out his powerbank and plugged the phone in.

On his second try he managed to get the phone to come on – at the very moment Wen stopped behind a line of yellow cars. Beeping like crazy, a slew messages, notifications, letters and missed calls all came hurtling onto the screen at once, interrupting one another.

Corey didn't have time to dismiss them and call Steff before the phone rang – and Steff's face came onto the screen, the phone ringing a Gardel tango.

"Steff?" said Corey, his voice full of emotion. He put the phone to his ear and tried to cut off his wife's angry tirade. "Stephanie, hold on, wait a minute, please – listen, I have to tell you something important. And don't interrupt me, okay? Stephanie Thompson, I love you – you know that, right? Baby... I love you so much. More than anything, more than everything... more than the whole world."

Other books by Anton Eine

Please visit your favorite e-book retailer
to discover other books by Anton Eine:

Maze City Series
My New Superjob
Maze Stalker (coming in 2020)

Programagic Cycle
Behind the Fire Wall
Beyond the Speed Limit (Coming in 2020)

Connect with Anton Eine

I really appreciate you reading my book!
Here are my social media coordinates:

Keep up with all the latest news on my official site
where you can also buy all my books
and download some of them for free:
https://antoneine.com

Follow me on my Facebook page:
https://www.facebook.com/anton.eine.3

Follow me on my Twitter channel:
https://twitter.com/AntonEine

And you are welcome to rate my books
on my Goodreads profile:
https://goodreads.com/author/
show/18866627.Anton_Eine

Printed in Great Britain
by Amazon